CAPASHEEA'S LEADMINE

a novel

by
Foster Mullenax

The title of this book is, in part, derived from the Brazilian-Portuguese word Capabaxia, pronounced Cap-a-shee-a. The other half of the title is for the village Leadmine, in the northern mountains of West Virginia. It was derived from a legendary lead mine believed to be used by the Indians, who were hunting and fishing in the area when the White Men arrived.

mpc
McClain Printing Company
Parsons, West Virginia

1989

International Standard Book Number 0-87012-484-6
Library of Congress Catalog Card Number 89-91807
Printed in the United States of America
Copyright © 1989 by Foster Mullenax
Parsons, West Virginia
All Rights Reserved

ACKNOWLEDGMENT

The author wishes to thank professional forester Harry Mahoney, consultant on the big-eared bat.

ONE

The Daylight Savings Time sun crossed the mountain, and shot finger rays into Leadmine, sixty seconds later than yesterday. August clipped each day two minutes, hardly noticed by anyone but Cloy, for he cherished daylight with a gusto, as native brook trout relish the cold drinkable water of Horseshoe Run.

The old man pulled the chain on the thin gold timepiece and flipped open the crystal cover to see that morning arrived at 5:25. Today would be thirteen hours and eighteen minutes. He and Stripe just stood there two steps off the porch, Cloy inspecting the day—the sun, a few high clouds, the aroma of hay curing in the field across the road, and the rich fragrance of smoke from the sassafras wood he'd burned in the cookstove to fix breakfast and boil the coffee.

He went straight to the well house, Stripe at his heels, to crank up a bucket of water to fill the World War I canteen. The callused 74-year-old fingers fumbled uncapping the lid and maneuvering the tiny hole of the canvas-covered water bottle to catch the gush from the battered well bucket. Overflow rolled off the weathered boards and fell through the cracks sounding like rain when it hit forty feet down into the well. True, there was other water besides the well, such as the sparkling Horseshoe running all the way through the small farm, but the field-rock-lined well was the extent of pipes or plumbing at this humble widower's home.

Cloy put the canteen into the shoulder bag, on top of the six-cell flashlight, beside the paper bag of lunch—still warm, sugar cured fried ham, four biscuits, and three miniatures of raisins. He ducked his small bald head under the strap, groaning from the pain in his shoulder joint, and let the packed bag fall to rest on his left side. Back to the porch, Stripe eyeing every move, he picked up the sang hoe and grabbed the pinstripe railroader's cap off a nail on the wall. Now they were ready for another leisure-paced day, just the two of them, up the Horseshoe and along its branches of the headwaters.

It was easy walking along the creek, for August was dry, the water was low, and the trout hid in little pools below the foot-high falls; falls that functioned like stairsteps to Hogback Mountain. There was no trace of water up there, not even dew on the leaves this morning.

Yes, it was daybreak and at least an hour before other residents of the heavenly Horseshoe Run valley stirred on their pillows or set foot on their bedroom floors. At 5:39, Cloy Clay and his knee-high brown dog, a mixed breed with white stripe down his face, walked as inseparable partners beneath the hemlocks and around the clumps of rhododendron. A fervor forced the root hunter's quickened step as he reared back his thin shoulders and moved briskly on skinny legs, propelling his 129-pound body upstream, rattling the loose, smooth creek rocks.

In a short while they stopped. Cloy sweated through the blue chambray shirt and Stripe got hot enough to pant hard and lap water from the trout haven. They halted not because Cloy was tired, for he was accustomed to the long hikes. He used the stop to survey the area and to listen to the birds, for it would be another mile before they headed up Thunderstruck. Today they would be in big-root country, rich coves of sky-high maples and oaks and poplars. Ginseng roots there were as big as your hand with branches looking for the world like his gnarled fingers. They would fill the bag by noon, he figured.

Each year the old "residenters" were left as seed stock and only mature sang was dug. At least up till now that was the case. Other ginseng diggers never quite made it up to Thunderstruck, for there was so much other fine territory in the Monongahela. Besides, only a few sangers were left in the area, nothing like it was back in the thirties, when the ginseng, and ramps too, were nearly wiped out. Then, whole families searched through the woods and dug every root they could find to sell. And ginseng did sell, even during the depression, and ramps they dug to eat to live.

A hint of a smile formed on Cloy's thin wrinkled face, sporting four days of gray beard, when he thought of how the ginseng diggers, way back here in these isolated mountains, provide so much pleasure for sex partners, all the way around the world, and even in China. "Does it really work?" he mused, "or is it just imagined?" Regardless, to the poor mountain man, dried ginseng roots were "worth their weight in gold" people used to say, and even now, they were worth more per ounce than anything else a person could sell, yes, including gold, if you had it or could get it back up one of these creeks.

An hour later they were so far back up Thunderstruck Creek that Cloy felt he need not fear intruders, for that's the way it always had been, until today. This, as he viewed the world, was about as near heaven, as he understood it to be, as one could find—crystal clear pure water, lush growth on the forest floor, occasional solar openings to the sky, and the lightning-fast native brook trout flitting freely in the shaded waters, that begin here and run all the way to New Orleans, passing Pittsburgh and Cincinnati on the way.

"Funny thing," Cloy said aloud to Stripe, the first time today he had talked to the dog like another Homo sapiens, "for some strange reason I feel like something really special is going to happen to us today." It was not unusual for him to talk to Stripe, as he had done to other "best friends," his only close companions during these past fifty-five years that he had spent alone. Of course there were the neighbors, and the period when he worked on the WPA, but when night came he was alone. It was pretty much the way he wanted it to be after Betty, his one and only love, had died with the flu.

Now that the day's dig was done, the determined loner felt compelled to once again experience the most exciting adventure that he and his dog did together. "Okay, Stripe, let's go in there one more time," Cloy said, as he dumped the full bag's contents on to the smooth flat rock by the water. He did it gently, exposing the naked human forms of ginseng roots, the lunch bag, the raisins and the light. "Whatta ya think, Stripe, better eat before we go in there? How about it?" Cloy figured it was about noon without looking at his watch.

Like all the times before, at least once a year since that long winter after Betty suffered so and died, when he found it, Cloy Clay had gone inside and marveled, again and again, how such a splendid cavern had remained only the legendary Leadmine.

TWO

The first sign of trouble was when nephew Ralph couldn't get an answer to his phone calls at Uncle Cloy's. For years now he had called from his home in Thomas or driven the eight miles to the farm to visit, often taking grocery items and home-baked goodies. Three times he got through on the party line, and at nine and dark, Cloy did not answer.

A call to Cloy's across-the-road neighbor, Amos Sell, gave further evidence that something had gone wrong. "Yeah, I went over there about seven and he wasn't there," Amos told Ralph. "Fact is, I looked over there while ago and didn't see a light yet; figured he might be up at your place or such or somethin'."

Definitely concerned, Ralph asked Amos to go over and check again and call him back. Twenty minutes and Amos was back telling his Ruby that Cloy just wasn't over there. He called Ralph with the report. "The doors are locked and he's not there. I shined the light in on his bed and it's still made up, just like he left it."

"Well, is Stripe there?" Ralph inquired.

"No, no, he's not there neither."

"Whatta you think I oughta do?"

"I figure you better come on down here and see if we can't find the old boy."

"Yeah, course it's plenty warm out tonight, so he won't get cold, but you know, he's never stayed out overnight. Somethin's wrong."

"I'll be down right away. See you in a little bit."

When Ralph came he and Amos drove out the lane to the yard fence. It puzzled them, what to do. Ten-fifteen at night, no good idea where Cloy and Stripe had gone. They could be up the creek or down the creek, there were at least a dozen tributaries to Horseshoe they could have followed.

With the motor running and the headlights shining on the porch through the paling fence, the worried men just sat there chewing and spitting tobacco juice out into the grass. Pondering their next move, Amos suggested they should drive up the run toward Shaffertown, for if Cloy was headed home after dark he would likely take the county road for easier walking. They drove along the blacktop, in the new '64 Ford pickup, when Amos spotted what he thought was Stripe running toward them. Ralph quickly determined that it was not Cloy's dog.

"You're right, it's not Stripe," said Amos, "that's a strange dog I've never seen around here."

"Could be someone brought him in the last few days, maybe campers. Just might be some people campin' up here, brung him in, and he's a runnin' loose," Ralph reasoned.

At Shaffertown, they parked at the forks of the road and sat in the dark to listen. But the cracking and snapping under the hood from the cooling motor overpowered the familiar night sounds. Outside, they stood under the stars amid the cricket poems, katydid songs and frog yelps, and tried to focus on distant sounds, just in case Cloy might be calling for help. All they heard was a faint dog's bark, high up on Hogback, and that was not the direction where they expected to find poor old Cloy.

At midnight Ralph and Amos were back at Cloy's house. Ralph unlocked the front door padlock with the key he'd had for years. He found the ceiling bulb string and switched on the light. A call to his wife in Thomas was the first order for Ralph, reporting that he'd be coming right home. "May's well leave it alone till morning and we'll go find him," he told Amos. So they closed up and cleared out with Ralph telling Amos, "I'll be down about seven and we'll go get him. Somethin' bad wrong, I figure, or they'd a come on back. Least ways Stripe woulda' come. I can't figure what the matter might be."

Friday morning Ralph, the 53-year-old nephew, bald and graying and somewhat overweight from years in the store munching on potato chips and an occasional beer, and Amos the 68-year-old neighbor, a short slim fellow who kept his weight down following bouts with cholesterol, set out to find the old man Cloy. It was pure instinct that told them the direction in which the old gentleman had embarked upon one of his customary outings, yet this one caused those who knew him best to fear for his welfare. Soon, they saw clues that the two had been this way, for there were shoe and dog tracks in the scattered soft silt spots, along the right side of the creek.

At Thunderstruck branch of Horseshoe, Amos and Ralph, sweaty and tired, rested before parting to search two of the major streams. Ralph chose Thunderstruck, feeling for certain this would be the territory most appealing to Cloy. They agreed to meet back at this same spot by 2:00 p.m.

Up the narrow token of a stream, Ralph deliberately trampled the loose rocks, hoping cloy would hear. He'd walked more than an hour, panting and sweating and occasionally taking time to slip up to the little pools to get a glimpse of the native brookies. Zero wind speed up this valley rendered the air conditioning effects of the dense foliage to be almost nil. The tulip poplar leaves hung limp and still, like mural figures on a canvas, screening this spot from the clear August sky. All the way up to here, there was not a detectable clue that Cloy or the dog had been there.

Finally, after another forty minutes of slow-paced upstream walking and listening, Ralph decided to leave the creek and get up against the hill on the cheek of Thunderstruck, up away from the water running over rocks sound and where he might hear Cloy answer his calls. It was time to start hollering, Ralph thought, and his first "Hey-y-y-y Cloy" fell on the ground, muffled by the dense big-tree leaf cover. Yet, he strained to listen for the old man's voice to answer. Nothing came back, not even an echo made it back through the hardwood forest. Several more attempts failed to get a response from Cloy or the dog. Ralph had no way of knowing exactly where they were, or why they could not hear his calls to them. In fact, he had no way of knowing that the obscure opening into the "Leadmine" was within sight of the main Thunderstruck, tucked away along a small side branch. Finally, he gave up yelling and gave in to time, for it was now past noon. He decided to ease back down the run, to join up with Amos, hoping that Cloy would be with him there at the forks of Horseshoe and Thunderstruck.

By 2:00 p.m., Ralph was back at the rendezvous point, exhausted and weary. Amos caused further concern when at 2:30 he was still up the creek. Five minutes later he arrived, lathered white beneath the arms and across the shoulders of the olive long-sleeve shirt.

"See anything?" Ralph inquired hopefully.

"Not a sign of nothin' up that way." Amos shook his head and continued, "Didn't even see a track up that way."

"I never saw a track nor a trace of 'em up this way either," Ralph pointed, "I swear, I don't know what to think."

"Me neither, but somethin's bound to happened to 'em."

"Course, they may be back at the house by now."

"Could be, knowin' Cloy, he'd make her back if there's any way of doin' it."

"Then again, I doubt they'd be there cause we'd a run into 'em up in here sommers this mornin'."

"Right, likely as not, he'd a come down this way, so much easier walkin'."

A long, refreshing drink from the creek, and a good face washing, including several splashes to the back of the neck, and Ralph was ready for a fresh chew in his right cheek. Amos repeated what Ralph did and then set course for home.

At Cloy's meager farmhouse, built from rough lumber when the railroad took the virgin timber out, only the few chickens moved about, the only livestock Cloy kept these days. For years now Amos had mowed the hay and baled it, the extent of Cloy's farming.

Both hunters were so tired when they reached the porch that they sunk into the shaded seats, Ralph in the split-bottom rocker and Amos in the oak-slat swing. Five minutes or so of silence, except for the grasshopper sounds and the occasional cicada songs, made their concern for Cloy intensify, until Amos offered, "You know we better line up some help for tomorrow if we're gonna find him."

"Yeah, I figure we better call the sheriff and tell him about it, see what he can line up," Ralph said, letting the words out slowly as he thought.

"Gotta get the word around and see how many we can get right around here."

"Yeah, let's see, tomorrow's Saturday, yeah, we oughta get several who'd help."

"I still think I'd better call Sheriff Woodruff and see what he suggests," Ralph concluded, stirring from the rocker.

The call set in motion the makings of a major search party. Not only was Cloy well liked but Ralph had clout. The sheriff pulled out all the stops, calling the adjutant general of the

West Virginia National Guard. That produced a pledge to send the Green Beret unit, on summer training assignment at Camp Dawson. In addition, there would be the volunteer fire departments from Parsons, Thomas and Davis, and Company C of the Department of Public Safety at Elkins. The sheriff also called the *Inter-Mountain*, the Elkins daily newspaper. By Saturday morning, Cloy Clay's disappearance was big news.

THREE

At 6:00 Saturday morning the Guard convoy crossed the single-lane Cheat River Bridge into St. George, following the narrow blacktop road which meandered along the river and seven miles up Horseshoe Run, past the YMCA camp, through Leadmine village and on to where Ralph directed the lead jeep into Cloy's lane. He told the lieutenant colonel to go on into the long open meadow in the bottom bordering the creek. "By th' way," he asked the officer, "can you put one of your men here on the road to direct people to the field as they come?"

"Of course, sir, just a moment," Colonel Apolla responded, calling on the CB to Corporal Aspinall and instructing him to take the post at the road, directing all parties taking part in the search to headquarters in the bottom.

The colonel was the only one of the special forces battalion having combat experience, both in Korea and Vietnam. All of his men had extensive training and most had been on searches such as this. They knew well how to launch and conduct a professional exercise, whether for real or practice.

A steady flow of vehicles followed the military convoy, including fire trucks, police cruisers, pickup trucks, and cars which moved into the twenty-acre meadow.

Ralph and Amos spent the first several minutes telling the colonel every detail they could think of about Cloy, his habits, the territory and the mystery. In the meantime, interest groups clustered. The uniformed military gathered close in, ready to hear the instructions; police officers, including the sheriff, three state troopers, the conservation officer and the county forester formed another cluster; then there was a large group of firemen in their black-billed caps; some fifty to seventy-five men and a dozen women, including Mary Martha Cosner.

Ms. Cosner was a native of the valley, recently returned from eighteen years on the Baltimore City Police department.

She and three younger women formed their own party, waiting while the colonel studied the huge map provided by the forester. Ralph, Amos and forester Jim Hill helped to orient the commander to the big sheet spread on the jeep hood.

Shortly, Colonel Apolla was ready to instruct the noisy crowd, which now numbered well over a hundred. He looked toward his charges, the guardsmen, and began speaking into the battery-powered megaphone. "Now listen up everybody, let me have your attention! Your attention please!" he yelled, bringing some order. "Listen carefully, for here's the way we're going to deploy all those who want to help in this organized search. We've determined the most logical procedure to find the subject is to concentrate on the area west of Horseshoe Run and upstream to Thunderstruck branch."

At that, the women with Mary Martha huddled as she asked, "Do we want to go with them, or should we just strike out on our own, and cover some territory they're not going in today?" The others agreed that the latter sounded better to them, yet they waited, watching the counting off of the Green Berets who stepped ten paces from the next. Then the colonel called for volunteers to fill in, five between each of his twenty men. This was not all of his men, for there were the drivers, the mess crew, the base station radio operators and mechanics.

The colonel's crew lined out across the creek and disappeared into the hemlocks. They would climb straight up the mountainside to the top, making a human chain, each man in sight of the next, before they proceeded north toward the Thunderstruck. If Cloy was against the mountain, they would find him.

The women turned left from Cloy's lane onto the county road, familiar territory to all four of them. They headed toward the dead end at Shaffertown. Well, it was the dead end of the county road of one-lane blacktop but there were private and orphan roads leading three ways. At the Shaffertown triangle, a wide spot at the end of the paved road just over a mile from Mr. Clay's farm, they stopped to plan their separate search for the kindly old man who they were convinced had not an enemy in the world. At least they could not think of a reason why anyone would want to harm the old boy.

Interrupting their collective thoughts, Alice Long offered from the back seat, "I still think we'll find him, had a heart attack or something."

"Yeah, but what about the dog, you'd think he'd come back after this long," Mary Martha replied.

"You're right," Rena said, moving forward, talking to Mary Martha. "Remember now, they've been lost since Thursday."

"Been out two nights all ready," Alice followed up.

Rachel, hesitating to light a cigarette, attempting to say something meaningful, was puzzling over the dog when she chipped in with, "That dog is close to old Cloy, goes with him everywhere. He'd stay with him, no way he'd leave Cloy out there in the woods."

Mary Martha, several years older than the others, asked impatiently, "Well which way we go, girls? Whatta ya say?" Yet they all remained silent, afraid to commit themselves, for once they left this spot they had little idea what lay ahead, and where the old man might be was anybody's guess. So, after a minute or so of silence except for the flick of Rachel's lighter, the driver took charge and headed the jeep into the narrow lane along the weathered and ragged board fence.

On the left, you could get occasional glimpses of Horseshoe Run. The dry dirt road showed signs of use even though weeds and grass reached above the hood and brush scraped the sides of the slow-moving vehicle. Car tracks marked their way, indicating that fishermen or others had been using this hideaway.

"No one lives out here, do they?" Mary Martha asked.

"No," Rena told her, but Alice made a slight correction. "No one lives up here regularly, but all summer people come and go and they do stay up here on weekends."

"You mean they stay in the old Weidimeyer house?" Mary Martha asked.

"That's what I've heard," Alice confirmed. "Well, I know they stay up here because there's a phone in that old house."

Almost in one voice the others questioned, "How'd you know?"

"Only place it could be is up here. They call it the field house."

"Field house," Mary Martha yelled, stopping the jeep and looking straight into Alice's eyes. "How in the name of heavens do you know that?"

Shaking her head at the sudden grilling, Alice said, "You won't believe this one, but one evening back in the spring was the first time it happened."

"For God's sake, Alice, what happened? Come on, tell us!" begged Mary Martha.

"Well, for God's sake, give me a chance to tell you. As I said, one evening, must have been along about Easter, I was there at home, just Mom and I, and this phone call puzzled us. I answered the phone, and this foreign guy asked if this was the field house."

"That doesn't mean it's this place up here," Mary Martha pounced upon this new information in doubt.

"Th' phone kept ringing in and this same guy with the funny accent kept on insisting that he was calling the field house. Then he asked if the number was 478-2282 and I told him it wasn't."

Her companions hanging on every word, Alice struggled to convince them that people were living in the old abandoned house. "It's the only place it could be, the movie people's old place, and the phone number, it's right next to my mom's, it's 2282 and my mom's is 2281."

"Ah, come on Alice, you gotta do better than that," Mary Martha pushed. "You know that phone number could be other places up in here, even one of those godforsaken worn-out potato chip trucks parked in along the creek."

"Listen," Alice pleaded, hesitating, and then coming out with it. "Well, if you must know, we listened in on some of their phone calls."

She looked at each of her friends as if to say "What's wrong with that? Everybody does it." Then she continued, "That first time, when the phone rang in on ours, was after a big thunderstorm, maybe that had something to do with it. But listen, every time there's a call on our line, you know, it's a four-party line, you can hear the ring anyway. Well, you can't hear the ring, exactly, but you can hear a sound clear across the room."

"I know, I've heard it on these phones," Rachel confirmed. It's just a faint hum-like, you can hear, not the ring, but it's sort of a faint ring."

"So you see you can tell when the phone is ringing even when it is not ringing in on yours," Alice went on. "So we listened in at times and we heard them talking about the old house and even giving directions on how to get there. There was someone up there, talking to this foreign guy, and other times we heard a woman talking to another woman and they were talking about D.C. I just know this is it, there's people staying up here."

The ancient board fence, showing faint lines of white paint, formed a ragged border to the bushy land and field cluttered with elderberry bushes and blackberry briers. Huge umbrella-shaped pods of glistening purple berries connected to tiny red stems were destined for bird feed instead of Smucker's jelly jars. Whole panels of fence had fallen into the weeds, the brush, and the briers following thirty years of neglect. The once elegant half mile of land leading to the Weidimeyer estate was a shambles.

They drove on slowly, approaching the tree-lined driveway which looped in a half-circle to the front of the remains of the once spacious summer home of the prominent Hollywood movie mogul. You could imagine how striking the baroque architectural details had been, lavished upon the once stately structure built in 1914. There were numerous trees, strange to the area, accenting the house and bordering the driveway. A profusion of omnipotent larch struck neat green symmetrical patterns against the turquoise sky. In fifty years the larches had shot straight up a good thirty feet above the two-story mansion.

This was the first time any of the women had been up the road, but each had heard of the old Weidimeyer place. Mary Martha, awed at what they saw, exclaimed, "Would you just look!" She slowed the jeep to a stop. "What a place!"

"What a place is right," Alice, the youngest of the group, whispered as though she might be heard by inhabitants of the house.

"Dad told us about this place," Rachel said. "He used to work up here when he was a boy."

"My mom said her mother worked for them too," Rena told them.

Rena and Rachel were the two coal miners of the party, working almost a year at the Beaver Creek mine. Alice was a secretary at the charcoal plant out on Route 219 and Mary Martha only a month before had landed a job as chief security officer at Canaan Valley Resorts. And it was only during the past month that the four, two divorced and two single, had rented the old Bohon house at the edge of Leadmine.

It was obvious that cars that used the lane also used the

Weidimeyer place driveway. No vehicle tracks showed beyond there.

"Wonder if there's anyone up here now?" ventured Mary Martha before suggesting, "Let's see how far we can go on up along the creek."

They were able to drive through the mass of weeds and grass and tree limbs. Just out of sight of the neglected old home, a fallen sycamore tree formed a barricade across the also neglected road.

Colonel Apolla steered the hunt for the old man and dog with a walkie-talkie. It was slow going around the steep, heavily forested mountainside. Over a hundred men combed each foot of the territory known to be a favorite habitat for timber rattlesnakes. It was 2:50 p.m. when the chain of sweat-wet military and civilian scouts escaped the woods and relaxed by the cool waters of Thunderstruck Creek.

There were reports of rattlers jangling up on the big buzzard cliffs near the top of the mountain but no one admitted to being in eye-shot range of one. Obviously, they had failed to find Cloy. No doubt, the most difficult part of the expedition lay behind them, but where to next? Three days was a long time for a 74-year-old man to be lost in this rugged terrain—even in the peak of summer in Appalachia.

It was nearing 4:00 when the colonel ordered a retreat to headquarters. They followed the creek until it paralleled the county road, then they climbed the bank and walked wearily along the left side of the blacktop.

Down in Cloy's meadow the guardsmen devoured a hot meal and cold drinks before erecting tents for the night.

FOUR

Up on Backbone Mountain seven spelunkers in a four-seater utility station wagon bearing Virginia license plates headed for the field house. They towed a Land Rover piled full of hiking and climbing gear and soft satchels stuffed with clean underclothes and toilet kits. It was a fruitless day for them, too, hunting for an endangered species of mammiferous quadrupeds. En route they had explored the old Morris Mine on Route 42, near Elk Garden, their only stop since leaving Fairfax, except for breakfast at Winchester.

Dr. Roberto Vieira Drews dos Santos, the self-appointed leader of the Allegheny expedition, occupied the right front seat of the van. He and the others were on a quest for the rare Virginia big-eared bat (*Plecotus townsendii virginianus*)—a search, to them, as urgent as the one in progress for old man Cloy Clay. Yet the party in the van knew nothing of the manhunt and the Leadmine locals were ignorant of the mephistophiles' mission in their midst.

Dr. Roberto broke the silence to speculate about their approaching arrival at the field house. He turned to Carlos, the driver and long-time manservant to the dos Santos family. "We're going to make it by nine-thirty," he spoke in English with a distinct Brazilian-Portuguese accent.

"Another fifteen minutes and we'll be there, sir," Carlos assured him, unable to speak English as clearly as the man with degrees from the Federal University of Espirito Santo and D.C.'s American University.

Dr. Roberto's wife Felecia, seated directly behind her husband, yelled, "I'm starving. I sure hope Jorge has a feast prepared for dinner." She spoke in cultured middle Atlantic English, very much the Hampton Roads influence of her upbringing.

"Said he would have drinks and food a-plenty for our arrival," Dr. Roberto responded. "I talked to him on the fono last night and he assured me that he and Irenea are living well. He said they have a surprise for us."

All the way from the backseat another explorer yelled, "Maybe he has found the hiding place of the little brown creature."

"Ah, I don't think so," Roberto replied looking straight ahead but oblivious to the crooked road. "I think if it was that he would have been more excited. Yes, I think he would have told me, if that was it."

"They've been up here long enough, maybe Irenea is pregnant and they're going to get married, or something like that," Dr. Roberto's American wife wondered aloud.

No one responded to that suggestion. Apparently, they were too tired and hungry to care. The long day of squatting, bending and crawling had overwhelmed the bat searchers, who on workdays filled important office jobs in the capitol city.

It was dark when they passed Cloy Clay's farm. During the three years some of them had been coming to the field house, they had not met any of the neighbors.

Carlos stopped the wagon and its tow behind the trees and tangle of kudzu vines and overgrown shrubs, next to Jorge's Peugeot station wagon with District of Columbia plates.

Jorge greeted them with a kerosene lantern which dimly lit the wide cutstone walk and the patio leading to the baroque double front doors.

"Come on, leave everything in the Rover for now, we have dinner ready the waiting," Jorge urged, his subtle accent merely hinting of his Brazilian heritage.

Jorge's parents were Brazilian but he was born in Washington where his father was agricultural attache with the Brazilian Embassy. When not searching for bats, Jorge was a graduate student in zoological sciences at Georgetown University.

Inside, after big hugs among everyone, Dr. Roberto came out with, "Okay, Jorge, what is the big surprise?"

"No, no, just wait a bit, sir, till you relax with a drink and then Irenea and I will show you," Jorge insisted, hustling the new arrivals toward the huge barren kitchen and the Teachers Scotch. Two cubes of ice per glass, ice from one of the few modern conveniences in the old house, a bottled gas refrigerator. Scotch and water all the way around, Jorge poured into each hand-held glass the amount permitted by the holder.

They formed a loose circle standing to one side of the kitchen while Dr. Roberto attempted to assist the drinks in reviving spirits within hungry, tired bodies. The leader was not tall, yet he commanded attention through his erect presence, his voice and his hair—graying temples joining a heavy head of black wavy hair that curled upward at the shirt collar.

C. Baxter Bennington stood a foot taller than his 16-year-old daughter Kitty. Harry and Peggy Sue Asserman rounded out the circle. Dr. Roberto lifted his tumbler of Teachers, "to the most successful expedition yet. May we find that elusive little creature with the long ears during these next two weeks."

The circle's response was noisy but short-lived, each person taking a drink in excited agreement with the leader's optimism. Moments later, at Irenea's urging, they moved toward the improvised table to sit on the benches. Three sawhorses made table legs and two-inch rough poplar lumber made the twelve-foot-long top.

Jorge and Irenea, not as tired as the new arrivals, seemed anxious, standing at the end of the table while the others ate salad. Jorge was disappointed at the lack of interest in his surprise. Then, he thought the better to wait for the proper moment, following dinner.

The aroma of steaming rolls of manicotti, thick sauce bubbling, became the center of attraction, manicotti that Jorge had bought frozen from Joe's Italian Supper Club in Thomas. Suddenly, Kitty, the youth of the group, remembered and began flagging her arms for attention. "Jorge," she yelled, "how about the surprise?"

They all followed, urging the revelation from Jorge.

"You know, I think it would be best if we wait, I want to show you. I know you're starving, so let's eat first."

Kitty was still impatient, but she had to agree to the delay. Since not one of them had a good handle on what Jorge and Irenea would reveal as the surprise, they were content to indulge in the pasta feast. They had no idea that what they would learn following dinner would profoundly affect their lives.

Finally, stuffed with pasta and sedated by scotch, Dr. Roberto got up and poured another drink. All the others except Kitty sucked cigarettes and blew smoke at each other across the table. They laughed and small-talked, reveling in reunion, excited at what lay ahead. But when Dr. Roberto slid back on the bench, they stopped to listen, for his cleared-throat signal was the clue.

"My friend, Jorge, it's time to confess. You have a surprise, it's time to be out with it, don't you think so? You have been too long mysterious, old boy, so we need to hear what it is."

Kitty fanned smoke away to better see Jorge. "Yeah, so if you've got a secret it's time to share it. If you think we'll be surprised you better try us, Okay?" Her youthful ponytail swished across her smooth neck with the animated demand.

Normally Jorge would have teased, making them wait, but not this time. "Okay! No problem, we'll do it now."

Both Jorge and Irenea led them, lighting the way with grip-handled battery-powered lights. They went into the hall, back to the rear foyer and up that stairway into a long roomy chamber that might well have been a gameroom from its size.

Jorge stopped just as soon as they were all inside. "Here's where you are going to have the surprise of your life. You're going to wonder why we never made this discovery before now."

They let him talk, attending to every word, but not fully prepared for what Jorge was about to unveil.

"What we found just has to be something people around here know nothing about."

Not daring to delay any longer, Jorge opened what looked like a closet door, entered a small room, then turned right to the solid pine board wall. There were wooden pegs at intervals head-high on the wall. He pulled the broom handle peg from its hole nearest the right corner, then moved to the left corner and pulled the last peg in a row of about a dozen look-alike wall plugs on which to hang coats. To expose the surprise Jorge went back to the first corner, stuck his index finger in the now open hole. As Irenea pushed with one hand, he pulled with one finger and the wall slid open, rusty wheels squeaking, like a barn door on a track.

Here was another room, dark and damp, directly above the spring house. Jorge turned to face the astonished followers.

The two lights, Jorge's and Irenea's together, showed a long ramp sloping into more darkness. They could hear water running down beyond the end of the light. Jorge and Irenea led, and the others, too awestruck to talk, inched along on the heavy wide boards preserved by the cavern atmosphere.

Jorge waited until they reached the bottom before he announced, "Well, my friends, this is the surprise."

Irenea moved close to Jorge, placing her free arm around his waist. Jorge held the light in his right hand and gestured with his left. "This is a cavern that apparently no one knows about, or if they do, no one has been in here since way back when the movie people lived here."

Dr. Roberto interrupted his long dry spell of not talking, not being in charge, "How much have you seen? Is it an extensive cavern? What are the conditions?"

Jorge stopped him to answer all three questions in one. "Well, Irenea and I, we found this only three days ago and since it was only the two of us here we went just into the one large room here," he pointed. "We must go there for a moment so you can see."

Another fifty feet along the stream—the water that flowed through the springhouse—they reached a most revealing sight. Here were fourteen 55-gallon whiskey barrels standing on end and a row of eight smaller barrels lying on their sides on a foot-high platform. Several of the big barrels had one end removed.

"Well, well, well," Harry Asserman spoke up, "there it is, just like it was when they quit using it, the old still. Gosh, that looks like a good one."

Apparently Harry was the only one having seen a still in the wild, outside museums. This one was larger and more sophisticated than any he had ever seen.

"How do you suppose they fired it?" Dr. Roberto asked. "Seems to me smoke would run them out."

"Not only that," Harry added, "the smoke going outside would be a dead giveaway."

"Remember that was during Prohibition," Mr. Bennington reminded. "Of course, you still today can't legally make the stuff."

"But back then they went out and smashed up the stills like the moonshine makers were plotting to overthrow the government." Harry looked more closely to discover that a gas burner was used to boil the stuff off. A small copper tube ran out through the springhouse to a buried tank in the yard. That supplied heat for the still and light for the house and the cave, using carbide activated by water. It was a good system for those who could afford the installation and the big metal cans of carbide.

Dr. Roberto pondered why this cavern, if it was a cavern, was not on the maps as one to be explored in their study of the

19

habitat for the nearly extinct big-eared bat. "Seems unusual that over these past years this cave was not included."

"And it's right here under our noses," said Jorge, also puzzled. "But Irenea and I looked and looked on every map and it's not identified, even though the Greenbrier seam of limestone goes right through here."

"You see what they did here, sometime way back there, was cut into it. Since the water flows out in such a strong stream they must have felt sure that there was a cavern back in here." Harry kept surveying the big room with little of the ornate formations of stalactites hanging from the ceiling as one might expect.

On the floor was an occasional mound of calcified buildup, but again no beauties of stalagmites. It was a rather dull hall, nearly as wide as it was long. In all it would measure 100 feet by 80 feet by some 20 feet high in the center and dome-shaped. Following the small, running stream to its origin, there was a hole the size of an igloo entrance leading to the mysterious interior.

Excitement was building in Dr. Roberto and he in turn was about to convert the others to a big change in their mission plans.

"I say, partners, let's go back and think about this. Maybe we should consider revising our plans, now that we have this secret place to search. After we give it a good try we can go to those caves up in the Sugarlands. We know for sure the capibaxias frequent them, but this one it looks like no person knows where it is."

The scientific mind held hope that a colony of the *Plecotus townsendii virginianus* could be found in this undisturbed sanctuary.

FIVE

Monday morning, the third day of the manhunt, Stripe lay exhausted on his master's porch. Ralph fed him from the big paper sack of dry dog food. He poured well water over the bite-sized morsels and Stripe ate them with noisy gulps like any hungry dog. It was obvious to Ralph and Amos that Cloy's dog had been holed somewhere. Dry dirt clung to his sides and legs as if he had been digging in a groundhog hole. At least that's what it looked like to them, for they had seen Stripe and other dogs look that way before from such activity.

This gave a new dimension to the search for old man Cloy, for they figured Stripe, following food and rest, would lead them straight to the spot where the injured or dead man lay. Now that they had found the dog, Colonel Apolla delayed Monday's planned deployment until Stripe recovered. Amos suggested that an hour or so would do it, and then Stripe would be ready.

While Stripe recovered, the lady searchers were up and busy, for this was a workday for them. Alice had to be at work at the charcoal plant at 8:00 a.m. The others worked the evening shift. Rachel and Rena had to be at work at 5:00 p.m. and Mary Martha began her shift at 6:00 p.m. So, three of them had the day to continue to look for the kindly old man, Cloy Clay.

Alice, standing by the sink, ate her energy food—a chunk of chocolate cake and a cola on ice. While Mary Martha fried bacon, Rachel and Rena sat at the dinette sipping orange juice.

"Alice, by the time you get back this evening we may have a good fix on what's going on up at the old ghost house," Mary Martha commented.

Alice replied impatiently, "Well, don't wait till evening if you find out something—call me."

"Don't worry, we will," Rena offered sleepily, "we'll call for sure."

"And if we don't find anything too exciting, we'll leave you a note, that be okay?" Mary Martha asked, sounding a bit motherly. "No question, we've gotta go up there after what we saw yesterday."

"Yeah, that Land Rover and all. They're up to something, have to be," Alice declared, pressing her fork on the plate to capture the cake crumbs.

By 7:30 Stripe revived enough to wag his tail and Ralph signaled Colonel Apolla that it was time to move out. Today they planned to go straight up Horseshoe beyond the Thunderstruck on both sides to the top of the ridges. Yesterday, they came within twenty yards of the small secret entrance to the cave, the one which Cloy for half a century had been entering to engage in his private seance.

However, Ralph and Amos pointed out to the colonel, if Stripe should take them on a different route than the one planned for today, they certainly should follow him. "No doubt," Ralph said, "Stripe'll take us to 'im."

"Not a bit of a doubt to me neither," Amos agreed. "Stripe'll take us to 'im, we'll find him today for sure."

There were still plenty of searchers, only a few less than when they began Saturday. Today marked the fifth day since the disappearance of the aged old gentleman.

When they reached the junction of Horseshoe and Thunderstruck, Stripe would be their Ouija board. Ralph petted the dirty dog, coaxing him to lead the way, as the army of hunters watched. This would not be simple. The tired dog, bewildered by his days in the cave with his master, now seemed overwhelmed by all the strange people gathered around. Ralph and Amos were the only two in the crowd he knew by sight, scent and sound.

The tired and disheveled Stripe, friend and companion of Cloy, lay listlessly sprawled on the creek rocks, panting. Amos coaxed, "Come on boy, take us where we'll find Cloy. Come on now, you lead the way. Come on, come on, let's go help Cloy." But the encouraging words were lost on Stripe, the changed Stripe.

It was time for action. Time was wasting. The army must get at it. They had to cover the area all the way to the Preston County line. So, taking charge for the moment, Amos hooked a finger under Stripe's collar and led him out away from the crowd. Then he turned him loose, hissing "Go get him" just like he would have urged on a coon hunting night. But Stripe didn't go. He just stood there and turned his sad eyes up to Amos, wagged, panted and laid down. His rose pink tongue air conditioner slid out rapidly and back as if on a track between teeth that were white as a church.

By now they had used a half hour hoping to follow Stripe's nose to Cloy. Stripe wasn't about to budge. Amos and Ralph grew disgusted. Colonel Apolla finally gave up on the Ouija message indicator and barked out orders to the Green Berets and the other sincere, dedicated, concerned citizens of Tucker County. They embarked upon a full day's combing of the headwaters of Horseshoe.

How long the massive manhunt would continue no one had predicted. It could end today, possibly tomorrow, certainly not longer than Wednesday. Beyond that, they would just have to assume that someone abducted Mr. Clay and he was the victim of foul play.

Meanwhile, Mary Martha had mounted her jeep, determined to invade the field house. "Two days now we've skirted around the obvious. Lord knows those people up there just might know something. Least it won't hurt to try and find out."

Now she was taking charge, the lady in faded loose jeans and tight fitting tee shirt. Rachel and Rena wore crotch-tight hip-hugging jeans over youthful curved solid features nurtured by work in the underground mine. This morning they admired their brave companion, Mary Martha.

She drove them toward the field house. Rachel just had to vent her anxiety. "You gonna go right up there and ask those people about the old man?"

"You gonna come right out and ask them?" Rena echoed, fearing the unknown, a confrontation.

"Why not?" Mary Martha fired back, cocksure. "Nothing wrong with finding out, maybe old Cloy is up there with them. Something funny. They've never lifted a finger to try to find him. You'd think they surely know about him being missing and all."

"We shouda called. That would have been better, I think," Rena frowned from the back seat of the open air jeep.

The driver thought a moment. "Could be, but I'd rather meet them face to face. Better chance of seeing just what kind of people they are."

It was 7:30 when she parked behind the Land Rover and struggled through the limbs along the left side of the three vehicles parked in the overgrown driveway of the field house. The ornate brass door knocker made a loud hammerlike sound. She waited, then rapped it again. The third time she knocked four hard raps with her knuckles before turning to leave. For a moment she stood in front of the white Peugeot station wagon, just surveying the jungle of rambling roses, kudzu vines and tree-like shrubs.

The left twin front door of the old Weidimeyer house squeaked open on dry hinges and Jorge squinting at the sunlight, stepped barefoot on to the terrace. Obviously disoriented from being suddenly awakened, he wrapped the robe about him and was fumbling with the belt when he saw Mary Martha.

"Yes," he said softly, so as not to awaken his house companions. "May I help you?"

"Why, yes, yes, you just might," the woman replied, moving back toward him. "I'm Mary Martha Cosner from down the road here. No doubt you've heard about old Mr. Clay being lost."

"No, maam, I haven't heard about it. I'm sorry to hear. Does he live around here?"

"Yes, sir, he does, down here between Shaffertown and Leadmine. He's been gone since Thursday. In fact there's a big group of people hunting for him, the National Guard and a lot of others, and they haven't seen a sign of the poor old fellow."

"I am sorry, maam, but we wouldn't be knowing anything about him, we don't know anyone around here. You see, we don't live here, we come here only once in a while."

"Just thought I'd ask, no harm in asking you know, so thanks a lot anyway."

"Right, maam, I'll be on the lookout for him, okay?"

"Thank you very much then, I'll get along, got to keep searching." Her report to Rachel and Rena in the jeep was less satisfying to the curious coal miners.

Rachel questioned, "Couldn't you tell whether he was lying or not?"

"What did he look like?" Rena asked. "Did he look strange or what?"

"No, he didn't look strange, he looked darned sleepy is about all I can tell you. Talked a bit foreign, but he didn't look strange. In fact, he looked pretty good to me, you know, young and tall and . . . "

"Ah, come on now, don't give us that kind of baloney," Rena countered, "Why don't you tell us what you really think?"

"Well, to tell you the truth, I didn't see anything one bit suspicious. He didn't look any different than any other man who'd just crawled out of bed."

"Didn't you see anybody else?" Rachel countered, "Didn't he invite you in? Must not been very friendly."

"Nope, not another soul and no, of course he didn't invite me in or back for that matter. He had no reason to," stopping short at what she heard herself saying. "Why didn't he invite me in?" she puzzled. "Then why should he, it's not like as if they live here or anything." She continued thinking as she revved up the jeep.

Apparently Mary Martha's intrusion did not awaken the others. It did shake up Jorge. Now, the very thing he and all the others in the small group of naturalists tried to avoid had happened—contact with the capibaxias, the locals.

"Damn it," he thought, standing there in the dark of the hall, back inside, "they'll be back." It was this contact, this being exposed, especially since they had found the cavern, that plunged him into a chilling, trembling fear, forcing a trip to the portable john on the back porch.

Irenea stirred slightly when Jorge dropped the robe and eased down beside her. He shook, some from the cool morning but mostly it was fear. His reaction to the visit surprised him. Why should this bother him so? But it did. What would Dr. Roberto say? No way did they want contact with the locals. It would just ruin their privacy and their quest to be the first to publish a completely accurate documentation of the status of the rare big-eared bat. In fact the hideaway over these past three years had given them the edge on others who sought recognition among the exclusive group of scientists devoted to preserving rare and endangered species of plant and animal life.

Jorge shook as if it were January on the Horseshoe and the heat was off. He pulled on the zipped-open sleeping bag they used as a comforter, yet he vibrated, shaking his bedmate awake. Irenea thrust her arms around her lover, pulling his face into her soft gown-covered breasts. Yet he shook and Irenea comforted.

"My darling, are you really so cold? What is it? What is it?"

"Nothing," he mumbled, "it's nothing."

"You poor darling." She began rubbing his face and pulling him closer as her left hand slid down below. Like a sedative, her caring arm and caressing hand brought Jorge under control and for a while there in the dark room, beneath the warm cover, he lost his fear of being discovered by the former policewoman.

SIX

All they could do now was let imagination replace reality. Surely the people at the field house were suspect. Mary Martha's tranquil outward appearance defied the true nature of how a freckled-faced redhead is supposed to react. Rena and Rachel were far less restrained.

"You just wait and see," said Rena. "When the truth is known, if Cloy is ever found, it'll be somewhere around that old house."

"That's exactly what I was thinking, only place he could be, the way I see it," Rachel agreed. "I don't care what that guy says. He's bound to know something."

Mary Martha drove the jeep, hardly hearing their words, catching only the developing sentiment of her two companions. Suddenly she reacted, "Oh, now, be careful, my friends, better slow down just a little bit. It's easy to blame the unknown, you know. We don't have any right to accuse those people up there, just because we don't know anything about them."

"Well, damnit, they're the only ones we don't know about, and they are right up here in the middle of where the poor fellow would've gone," Rachel reacted, frowning and picking at the tight natural curls of her chestnut hair.

"Of course you're right, but that's also a good cop-out too, because when you look at the facts, we don't have any reason on God's green earth to suspect them, except that they are strangers up here, and you know how everybody around here reacts to strangers, right? They must be up to something, right?"

"Right!"

"Right!"

"Right! But we'd look pretty damned silly if we were wrong, wouldn't we?"

"You know what we mean, MM. You'll have to admit, there

is a heck of a good chance that they know something, that's all I'm saying," Rachel reasoned.

"Well, even if I did agree with you," the driver said calmly, "I think we should just keep our mouths shut about talking to that guy up there, until we know more than we do now."

Both Rachel and Rena agreed. "But, I think we ought to keep an eye out for what they're doing up there," Rena told them.

"Oh, I do too," Mary Martha agreed, "We need to do that, of course. But for God's sake, don't let's go setting off a panic, when there's no good reason for it. We don't even know how many there are, or anything. They just might be some of those wilderness people, backpacking and vacationing, and now that they know about the old man, they might enjoy helping hunt for him."

Colonel Apolla's searchers climbed and crawled along both sides of upper Horseshoe Run, their objective—the towering Hogback—looming in the foreground.

Amos, Ralph and Stripe retreated to Cloy's porch to wait. It was about 11:00 a.m. when they left Stripe and went across the road to Amos's to lunch. Mrs. Sell's hot blackberry cobbler dessert brought raves from the weary friends, and they continued to talk about it, retiring to the front porch, to cogitate what they could do next.

Down the road toward Leadmine, they heard an ambulance siren pulsating like a regular heartbeat. Not until it came nearer did it concern them, for within a minute it was in sight, red lights alternating, siren wailing, speeding toward Shaffertown. Now they knew what to do, follow it in Amos's truck. At the forks of the road at Shaffertown, the ambulance sat parked, rear doors open, a dozen soldiers hiding the cot on the ground. Amos and Ralph parked and hurried to the site. "What's the matter?" Ralph asked, anxious to see who was on the stretcher, hoping to see Cloy alive.

"Snake bite," the sergeant said, "Private Jancey, he got bit by a big rattler up there about two hours ago."

"Is he bad?" Amos inquired.

"No, looks like he'll be all right, swellin' a lot, but we got a tourniquet on it pretty quick. If we get him up to the hospital right away, looks like he'll be okay."

The first real hope they had had now was gone, and Cloy's whereabouts was still a mystery known only to the dog and he wasn't talking.

Mary Martha tried reading the Sunday *Baltimore Sun*,

which arrived in the morning mail. She sat staring at the paper beneath the hair dryer bag, but she could not concentrate.

The policewoman in her took over. "Why not give it a try," she thought, "That's what I need, that's exactly what I need, to learn for sure."

Rena and Rachel donned clean blue jeans and blouses, their to-and-from-work traveling clothes. At 4:00 they left, leaving Mary Martha an hour to work on strategy.

She was fortunate to find the four-party line free, but she had to be careful how she worded her request, to avoid tipping off the gossips, who delighted in listening to their neighbors' phone conversations. She dialed the Baltimore number of her longtime friend Terry, a police captain.

The local operator intercepted the call, "Your number please?"

"478-2129."

"Thank you, go ahead please."

She asked the police station operator, "May I speak to Captain Tolliver, please?"

"Terry?"

"Hey, that you honey bunch?"

"Yea, it's me."

"What you up to?"

"Terry, I need your advice. Please listen, don't ask too many questions, but let me brief you."

"Shoot."

"I need to gather some verbal information."

"Verbal?"

"Right, I want to plug in my lighter and put on the headset. Get me?"

"Got you."

"How about tonight?"

"You don't fool around, do you?"

"Nope, you know me. Tomorrow's your day off, right?"

"Right."

"Also Wednesday."

"Yeah."

"Plan on both days."

"Okay."

"See you at o-five hundred tomorrow."

"My pleasure."

"How about mine?"

"You got it. The coffee pot'll be on and breakfast a cookin'."

"Sounds good." She kissed into the phone, "Chow."

"Chow, oo-la-la, rum bun."

"Hush." She hung up, feeling certain the minute she spent getting things set had no local listeners, and if they did listen, it was doubtful that they understood what she had in mind.

The all-day search up Horseshoe to Hogback had been another dry run. "Hain't seen hide nor hair of 'im," one Green Beret complained as the exhausted hunting party tramped into camp that Monday evening.

Three hard days they had scoured, inch by inch, the territory frequented by the 74-year-old gentleman and his "faithful" dog companion. It would require another strategy session between Amos and Ralph and Colonel Apolla, about what to do next, the fourth day of the manhunt.

Mary Martha left a note on the refrigerator door announcing that Terry would arrive sometime before 5:00 tomorrow morning. "Don't be surprised when you hear him fixing breakfast," she wrote and signed MM.

All the time since Cloy had disappeared, worry had filled the immediate community. Yet, there were no tears shed, for Cloy just did not have close friends. For all anyone knew, Ralph was his nearest kin and even they were not buddies. The mystery surrounding Cloy's whereabouts supplied a form of excitement that usually passed right on by the Horseshoe Run valley. Truly, the last incident worth mentioning was when the storekeeper in Leadmine blocked the cemetery road and refused to let a funeral convoy through. Said the road was his property, and the church had no right of way to the graveyard. That did stir things up a bit, evoking some bad feelings against the storekeeper.

Mary Martha turned her jeep into the driveway and crunched to a stop behind the white Thunderbird. Before her feet hit the ground the floodlight high up on the corner of the house flashed on and Terry rushed out toward her, wiping his hands on the apron tied around his waist. A quick-kiss greeting was all Mary Martha allowed on the walk beneath the bright light. But inside with the door closed, she beamed at her handsome police captain and threw her arms around his neck for the kind of greeting reserved for lovers. Gradually the "hello, how are you?" kiss grew into a frenzy of foreplay and accelerated breathing.

Two minutes of ecstacy definitely would not be enough, but, for now it really should wait, Mary Martha thought, pulling back to look directly into Terry's half-closed, dazed eyes and whispering, "Oh, boy, do I ever need you." Touching her finger to his lips she continued, "But, darling, let's save it a moment while I get a shower and slip into something clean and much more comfortable."

"If we have to, sweetheart," Terry said drawing a long breath. "I've started breakfast. Smell the coffee?"

"Oh, yeah, I hadn't noticed. Sounds good. I'm starvin'," Mary Martha said, gripping Terry's hand and reaching up to give him a quick peck on the cheek with her swollen lips.

Terry went back to the kitchen and Mary Martha hurried upstairs.

When Mary Martha eased back downstairs she wore a slick skin-colored night slip beneath an ankle length, lightweight cotton blend robe. It was a becoming garment of ocean mist and pink apple blossom print. Her red hair hung loose around her neck and her eyes and face sparkled like freshly poured champagne.

"May I serve you, my dear?" Terry asked softly to avoid waking the other three housemates, who should be sleeping at 4:30 in the morning.

"I can't think of anything I'd like better," said Mary Martha, flirting as she slid into the dining booth. The robe slipped open just enough to show her white legs above the knees. "I'm ready, sir," she taunted.

Terry dropped two slices of bread into the toaster and brought two glasses of tomato juice from the refrigerator. "I fried some link sausage already, and all I have to do is scramble some eggs."

"What, no fried potatoes, too?" Mary Martha asked, coyly.

"Well, I figure it this way, honeybunch. If I feed you fried potatoes with all this other you'll go to sleep on me. No way, Jose, am I gonna foul up things like that. So there!"

"You know, I was just foolin' you. I couldn't eat 'em if you had fixed 'em. Too much. But I could take a cup of coffee," Mary Martha said, beaming at the man she loved but had not seen for fifteen days.

Terry served the hot scrambles, toast and sausage and joined Mary Martha in the quiet hour before daylight.

"I couldn't have done better myself," Mary Martha jokingly complimented Terry. "Believe me, it's a very welcome change to have someone else cook you a good breakfast."

"Kinda fun doin' it," Terry said grinning. "Cause I know what it's gonna get me."

"Get you! Give! Givin' all you got to the one you love is what it's supposed to be. And you say, get. You think of it as get, do you?" Mary Martha said, tongue-in-cheek, kicking Terry's leg with her bare foot.

"Look, you know I was just jokin'. I know I don't have to serve you breakfast to get it," Terry replied.

"I know, sweetheart, but don't you realize that you could look at it a little differently. You say, to get it, and I think of giving it. Don't you honestly feel that way, too? Know what they say, better to give than to receive."

"Just you wait a few minutes, you'll see."

The twenty-two minutes they spent over breakfast were devoted to a quick briefing on the mystery of the whereabouts of Cloy Clay.

Turning the subject to the moment, Mary Martha again complimented Terry's cooking. "Oh, my goodness, I was hungry, and your cookin' sure was a treat. Thanks a bushel."

Terry cleared the table and placed the dishes in the sink. He turned to face Mary Martha standing only a foot in front of him. She placed her right arm around his waist and lay her head against his chest. Together they walked toward the door leading to the hall. He tripped off the kitchen light as they floated toward the stairs.

Securely inside the huge bedroom Mary Martha quietly locked the door. She went straight to the bed and turned back the apricot-colored spread and flowered sheets. As Terry quickly undressed, she removed her robe and slid on to the bed. Terry approached the nightstand clad only in athletic shorts and switched off the light. He moved onto the bed and stretched out on his back like Mary Martha. For a long moment they lay there in the quiet cool morning, just an hour prior to sunrise.

Terry eased his left hand along the sheet and found Mary Martha's hand. They gripped and held hands, maneuvering fingers between fingers. Gradually Terry turned on his left side and reached with his right hand to touch the silky gown.

Many minutes later, calm restored, like that which follows a violent thunderstorm, Mary Martha whispered, "Isn't it crazy they named it the missionary position? Do you believe that?"

"Of course. When you think of it that way, makes you feel kinda righteous and good about it," Terry said, snickering.

"Well, I don't have to think of missionaries to feel that way."

"Oh, I do," Terry joked. "Yeah, boy, I do. That's why it's my favorite."

SEVEN

At 10:00 Tuesday morning, Mary Martha jumped awake. Bright sun rays bordered the light-proof blinds of her private bedroom. Each of the housemates had their own personal room in the big white weatherboarded house. This morning, Mary Martha awoke from deep pacified sleep, even if there had only been about four hours of it.

She could not resist waking her bedmate, kissing his neck and cheeks and lips, enough to arouse even a tired policeman.

Alice's note on the table reminded, "Call me at work when you know something. Feeling left out, you prunes, AA."

"We'll see her this evening," Mary Martha told Terry. "I'm taking off two nights and work the weekend. Have a big one comin' up, Kiwanis convention comes in Thursday night through Sunday. Hoods 'll have a picnic, unless we double the force, breaking in cars and siphoning gasoline. Keeping them out of the rooms is no easy duty either."

"You can handle it. Be a breeze for you compared to what you handled in Oriole town," Terry observed, taking a place at the table.

Brunch was drip coffee made from unadulterated limestone well water, orange juice and toast and margarine and fresh raspberry jam.

First Rena, then Rachel, joined them at the table. Immediately Rachel wanted to know what were they going to do today. "Where to now? Going back up to the field house?"

Their leader studied the question, avoiding a quick answer, wondering if she should include the other two women in what would amount to a stake out. Why not? After all, they were becoming like family, at least sharing a house. "Not really up to the house, but possibly a stakeout, so we can do a little eavesdropping."

"That'll be something, right in the broad daylight, eavesdropping," Rena said. "Have to sneak up close to do that."

"An then, it would have to be at night," added Rachel.

Suddenly it dawned on Mary Martha that her friends knew nothing of the plans, "Oh, for Heaven's sake, we're gonna use some mighty sophisticated equipment. That's why Terry came, all of a sudden, see, I called him yesterday and he brought just what we need."

That gave life to brunch, with Terry having to explain the power and the limits of the listening device.

It was a few minutes past 11:00 a.m. when they turned up the narrow rutted road, which, if followed, would zigzag up and over Hogback Mountain. Mary Martha gambled that this would take them to a logging trail, which would accommodate the jeep, and lead to a point above the field house. Instead they found a logging truck road, seeded to fescue to slow erosion.

This made it easy as eating fresh apple pie to drive to a site above the object of their investigation. From here they could see through the tree foliage, down upon the slate roof of the mansion. They felt secure that they were hidden from line of sight of the house, yet the distance was just a little farther than between goalposts of a football field.

Earlier, Mary Martha had sworn her housemates to "shut your mouth" silence. "No talking when we get up near the field house," she had warned. "All we need is for them to know we're nosing around and that's all she wrote, we'll be through."

Captain Tolliver laid the handsome black leather carrying case on the hood, and with Mary Martha assisting, soon established a sophisticated electronic listening post. The microphone dish was placed upon an aluminum tripod, exactly like the ones used by professional photographers. The cassette tape recorder was punched to record, the two headsets were plugged in and pulled on by the operatives, and both their faces formed that hear-nothing expression.

"Just water runnin'," Terry whispered.

"Yeah, let's move it a bit, ever so little," Mary Martha mouthed, tiptoeing about as if someone would hear her footsteps.

"There, just a little more," Terry told her, "now you're doing it, now oops, too far, fading, back just a hair, there, that's it."

A female voice, more woman than child, "So good. I just love it here, especially with you daddy, just you and me."

A man's voice, "It is nice that you like to do these things. You know, for God's sake, your mother doesn't."

"I know, that's why I like to do this, to do something you like so much, and to have you to myself."

The two intent listeners looked at each other and then to Rena and Rachel with that expression which said, "What have we here?" They continued to listen.

"I'm glad it was our turn to stay here today," the girl said, "I want to spend it alone, just you and me. Oh, daddy, I do love you so very much." There were obvious hugging and kissing sounds and the man said, "I love you too, very, very, very much." Then for a moment it was quiet before he continued, "Tell you what, sweetheart, let's have some breakfast now and then we can have a fun day, just the two of us, until the others get back."

"Okay, daddy, sounds neat, also remember we're to get dinner and have it ready by seven."

The eavesdroppers continued listening through granola crunching and coffee sipping and little conversation, just movements about the kitchen and table. So far, not a hint that the two knew anything about old Mr. Clay. After an hour of listening they decided to check out, until later that evening, when the others would be back. Maybe that would bear more fruit.

Alice joined Mary Martha and the police captain for the evening listening session. Rachel and Rena were at work in the coal mine. On the headsets it sounded like a party—lively conversation, rattling of ice cubes, and lots of laughter. Nothing of value to record, until suddenly the others were silent, with one man saying, "You know I told you about the old man they said was missing. Be something if we find him."

"Why?" asked another man, "what makes the difference who finds him?"

"We'd have to turn him in."

"Oh, no, not necessarily would we need to do that."

"Well, if they don't find him they're going to be up here again looking and asking."

"Let them look and ask, just don't ever leave the doors open to our sanctuary."

"I think we are going to find the little creature as we go farther. There has to be another entrance somewhere. It just feels more and more right for us to find them."

"What on earth are they talking about?" Mary Martha mumbled and frowned at Terry, each with their ears covered by the large rubber headset cups.

Down in the field house a man with a heavy accent began to tell about people vanishing, especially children, in the area where he grew up. "Sometimes you find them covered with blood and chicken feathers, hanging by the toes. Always there would be a torch burning there. People said it was a sacrifice to bring good health to the village."

"That was voodoo."

"Not so much, exactly, maybe some but I don't know for sure."

"My God, they surely don't do anything like that anymore?"

"Oh, I don't think so, but even here in the U.S. some strange things happen. You know some of the cults."

"Hey, hey, please let's get off this kind of stuff. Another round of drinks."

It was party time again and the eavesdroppers discovered no clues to the missing Cloy Clay. So, again they wrapped up the sound gear and headed out for home before dusk.

As she drove toward Leadmine, Mary Martha said to her best friend Terry, "Be a lot of fun to listen in on that bunch later on tonight, wouldn't it?"

"Be a waste. I've heard about all there is to hear, and I'm sure you have too."

"You're right, except I guess you always think you'll hear something a little different."

Alice, taking in all this, offered, "I guess I've missed a lot, no more than I've heard."

"I know it sounds fascinating but there just ain't all that many different ways," Terry reminded. "Would be interesting, though, to know if that man and his daughter sleep together."

"Just the thought of it makes me want to gag," Mary Martha said with disgust.

"What in the name of heavens you talking about now?" Alice exclaimed.

"We'll play the tape for you, see what you think," Terry told her.

EIGHT

"One more day and that's it," the colonel declared sounding as though time were rationed. "If we don't find him tomorrow it'll be up to the FBI or the CIA or God or somebody else to find him. Lord knows we've scoured this whole country, every inch of it where one might have walked in a day."

Amos and Ralph studied the map with Colonel Apolla and a half-dozen others. It was Amos who thought of it first and others agreed that the area on the right side of Horseshoe, up against Hogback above Shaffertown, had not been searched. The colonel agreed that some of the searchers should give that a shot and the others would fan out over the entire area they had covered since Saturday.

Four fruitless days and no promise that the fifth would be any more productive. Amos and Ralph, a thousand times it seemed, shook their heads in disbelief at how Stripe had changed. No way would he take them anywhere, just followed them and lay at their feet. Amos reminded, "That dang dog always used to smile at me, you know, wag his tail and smile, but not any more."

"Strange the way he's behavin'," Ralph agreed. "I can feel it. I'm gettin' convinced that we're not gonna find old Cloy alive. If he was alive I know that dog would go back to 'im and that's for damn sure."

The two of them pined on the porch of Cloy's house as night enveloped the valley. They sat unseeing as bats at regular intervals scurried out of the attic above the porch roof like fighter planes debarking a carrier deck and flew off into the dusk. Their drunken flight patterns were familiar to Ralph, who often enjoyed the sight but not this night. He stood up, his knees cracked, his face grimaced and he stepped to the edge of the porch. He looked to the sky as he did so many times before when Cloy was there. Even the whippoorwills calling to their mates and getting replies had no attraction to Ralph. One thing he did notice was the unusual hue of the jet vapor trail stretching across the Horseshoe Run Valley the color of a cherry popsicle.

Cloy's nephew was facing one of life's realities, the finality of death, and Cloy's apparent passing brought a fresh reminder that the same fate was only one, two or three footsteps into the future for both him and Amos.

Amos, too, was engrossed in deep thought nearing grief, for it was clear to him that Cloy must be dead. His heart told him how much grief lay on him. The lump grew in his throat until he could not swallow, the way he had felt during the sermon at his father's funeral.

At the big white house in Leadmine, Thursday morning brought a shocking discovery. Whether it was a prank or a threat was hard to decipher at that point for the occupants were too disturbed to think clearly.

Rachel noticed the blood when she passed the jeep en route to the mailbox. It shocked her so that she ran back into the house and screamed "Oh, my God! Look, would you. Just look."

Rena and Mary Martha accompanied her back to the driveway to see blood-streaked side mirrors on Mary Martha's jeep. They were large mirrors, three times the size of those on Rachel's Mustang.

"Fresh blood alright," Mary Martha allowed, touching a finger to a spot laced with brown and red feathers. "What did that guy up there last night say about blood and feathers and kids hanging by their toes?" she asked before remembering, "Oh, you two weren't up there last night. One of the men we listened to told about some such crazy stuff like kids being strung up by their toes and covered with blood and chicken feathers, some kind of voodoo."

They puzzled over this bizarre happening in the driveway before Mary Martha went to her room to awaken Terry and share her concern with him. Surely there was an explanation for the incident not associated with the people at the field house. However, she wondered if possibly they detected her investigative work and sent this warning.

Eventually Rachel went for the mail, still more concerned about the bloody side mirrors than the letter from her sister in Adrian, Michigan. Shortly, all four of them were back in the driveway searching for clues to the blood on the glass mirrors which even dripped on to the aggregates in the driveway.

The pickup dressed up with a fiberglass camper shell stopped and the mailman walked toward the group at the jeep. "I didn't see any of you when I went up, figured I'd wait till I came back down and have you sign for this letter. Which one of you is Mary? It's a certified letter. I need you to sign for it."

It was a thick letter from Aunt Christilina in the Friendship Manor nursing home at Friendsville, Maryland. Mary Martha had visited her a month ago and the letter reminded her that she must go see the dear old lady soon, in fact, should have gone before now. For the moment, the letter diverted her attention from the bloody side mirrors.

Time would come later to absorb the letter that would impact her life as much as being born so far back in the hills.

NINE

Progress in the cavern was slower this morning than on any of the three previous excursions they had made since Sunday. Footing was unsure in the clay slime of this heretofore unexplored connecting shaft. Gradually the tunnel narrowed to crawl space, forcing the explorers to inch along on all fours. Dr. Roberto could hear water running ahead and fresh damp air surrounded his sweaty face. The battery-powered miner's lamp gave ample light but where the small tunnel would lead was a mystery. From his prone-in-the-mud position the leader ordered his followers to hold up "um momento" until he had a chance to probe a few feet beyond the current tight spot. "Right now it's not for certain if this tunnel will be large enough for us, especially Felecia," he chuckled. "You, my dear, may have some problem up here, you know your hips."

"Kill him! Kill that Brazilian up there," Dr. Roberto's wife demanded as though she meant it.

"Oh, my dear, you are still back there and so close. I was just trying to see if you were keeping up."

"Oh, yeah, I know. I know your jokes. Just you wait till I find the right crevasse, in it you go."

"You wouldn't do that, now would you? Way back in here? Surely you fear not getting out of here without your brave leader."

"There are other ways to get even with a chauvinist, just you wait."

"Just so long as you threaten to me, then I must not have to worry so much." Dr. Roberto softened, playfully carrying out his diversion, attempting to ward off a suffocating attack of claustrophobia. "Ah, yes, yes, my dear, you have a way of turning the chauvinist in me into the animal you want me to be."

"Oh, my, you are a poet. Go ahead on in there and fall off the deep end, see if I care." Felecia trailed off, realizing that this was simply a charade allowing both of them to vent steam in a tight spot.

Carlos lay between the leader and his wife, followed by Jorge, Irenea, Kitty and her father, C. Baxter Bennington. This was the Assermanses day to keep house and be ready to attend to any emergencies which might develop in the cavern.

In a moment Dr. Roberto was out of sight from the others in his party. The slippery clay-lined squeeze tunnel made a sharp left turn upward and gradually curved like the chute of a silo-type fire escape at the corner of an old schoolhouse. The leader slid onto his side and curved around and down toward the water. Suddenly the floor of a large chamber caught him. A rushing creek ran past six feet to the right.

He felt shock, a serendipity of large proportions, equaled only by the moment Jorge led them into the cavern last Saturday night. This was as it should be, a whole new cavern world, a gallery filled with moving fresh air and the ideal habitat for the point of their mission—to find a colony of the nearly extinct big-eared bat. As far as he could see, some one hundred feet straight ahead, there was a great hall. Still on his knees, he slowly turned his head left and up to the ornate calcite dripstone deposits hanging from the cathedral ceiling. Quickly Dr. Roberto decided to include the others and turned, directing his headlight up the slick flume toward them.

Teasing, he called, "Now is the time for all good explorers to test their skills at riding a slickey slide. Come on, Carlos, clear the way for Felecia to do a belly landing."

"Coming, sir," Carlos replied sounding more distant than the thirty to forty feet up around and down into the greasy slick tube of a tunnel where the others lay.

Felecia's husband caught each of them as they landed head first, sledding on their vitals. Felecia was greeted with special attention by her husband but she shook off his caring hands and slid on by stopping just short of the creek.

Kitty felt ecstatic in the new surroundings, possibly due to the freedom she felt after escaping the slimy intestine-like link between home base and this unfamiliar but spectacular sanctuary. The others were content to sit and rest, thankful they had escaped the constricted passageway to discover a gallery of splendor. But Kitty was jubilant, dancing to a rock rhythm only she was hearing beneath her miner's cap. Her headlamp streaked across the water up to the icicle forms which tapered to single drops of vadose water sparkling like tiny clear Christmas tree lights. Note by note she bounced along the edge of the rushing creek.

It was a delightful few moments for both the adults and Kitty. Dr. Roberto was sharpening his focus upon the mission in these ideal surroundings for the last remaining colonies of the *Plecotus townsendii virginianus.* If they knew where the tiny big-eared bats yet lived, measures could be taken to protect them before they disappeared from the earth.

Kitty's thoughts were caught up in the lovely spot. She explored out and beyond the others' lights. It was an innocent venture and it ended abruptly when her heavy boot kicked a crusted edge of a calcium carbonate mound, throwing her heavily clothed body off balance toward the rushing creek. She screamed so loud her companions jumped to their feet to see her splash into the cold swift water.

"Hurry! Help! Daddy, please hurry." The desperate girl screamed from the deep water. Normally a good swimmer, Kitty was being dragged toward the dark beyond her light. She could feel the downslope taking her faster. "My God, hurry and save me," her voice trailed.

Her father, Dr. Roberto and Carlos ran to assist. Carlos unsnapped his rope loop readying it to throw to Kitty. The powerful flow pulled the girl toward certain death in the dark bowels of the cave nearly two miles from the comfort of the field house.

The men ran in vain catching only a glimpse of the girl as she flailed out of sight into the tunnel. A solid wall stopped them and there was no way to pursue Kitty except to follow in the creek.

Mr. Bennington appeared calm for the moment, "Let's think now just how can we best rescue her?" He yelled above the ocean-like roar of the speeding water being sucked through the round shaft.

Suddenly Kitty's father grabbed Carlos's rope, pulled the rope over his head and drew it tight under his arms. "I'm going in there. You just keep the rope taut and let me go as fast as you can."

"Maybe we have enough rope among us to let you see what's down in there. Could be a big pool in there." Carlos wondered.

"You keep your own rope for throwing to Kitty," Dr. Roberto told Mr. Bennington.

While the men hurriedly made rescue plans Irenea and Felecia joined them. Dr. Roberto looked about for a column on which to anchor the lifeline. There was none near the tunnel so they would have to improvise. The five of them would make anchor and gradually feed out the four fifty-foot sections which they had snapped together.

"Okay, Benny, if you are sure that you will chance it, it is time you go. We're ready," the leader told him.

Only two minutes had passed as they prepared for Bennington's frantic rescue effort. There was no way to know what lay ahead or even whether Kitty was still alive or dead, bashed against the rocks or suffocated in a suck hole.

Alone in the big old field house, Jorge's cassette of samba music providing a carnival atmosphere, Harry and Peggy Sue Asserman were enjoying the ultimate pleasure between man and wife. It had been an hour since they first ran the thirty-minute tape and girated to the drumbeat. Now feeling the urge for more such excitement, Peggy reached over and extracted the cassette, turned it and plugged it in to stage the atmosphere for another set on the air mattress.

They were ignorant of the developing tragedy deep within the cavern where they had spent the three previous days. Now they were engulfed by the lively music in the semidarkness of their locked bedroom, unable to hear the questioning shouts from outside. "Anybody home? Hey in there, anybody home?"

Three vehicles in the driveway and loud music in the house was proof to the colonel's Green Berets that someone was there. But after a few minutes of not routing anyone from the house, they moved on, not giving much thought to the possibility that Cloy would be there. They lacked the information the women had, and there was little cause to be suspicious.

Up Thunderstruck Creek, one of Colonel Apolla's Green Beret reserves moved along a tiny side stream in the continuing quest for the lost man. It was more accident than curiosity that led the private to find the cool exhaust from the cavern. He removed his cap and lay on his right side so he could maneuver his cheek to the clear shallow running water and drink a half-dozen refreshing swallows. He caught his breath and continued to satisfy his hot-weather thirst. Lying there resting, he noticed that cold air blew steadily across his face. This seemed a bit strange, for there was no wind in the woods today, and it was hot and still in the hollow. He could see only a few feet into the darkness under the rocks which formed the waterfall. A well-hidden cave entrance was what the soldier found secluded under the small waterfall, the access to Cloy Clay's cavern. But, the soldier did not link this piddling hole in the ground to the missing old man.

TEN

Dr. Roberto instructed Carlos to sit directly behind him and brace his feet against the leader's hips. Likewise, Jorge should sit directly behind Carlos. He asked Felecia to pull the rope taut across his lap and around his left hip, then across Jorge's lap and around his left hip. The women would keep the rope untangled and help to feed it through the men's hands.

"Now, listen very carefully," Dr. Roberto told them. "Let's listen to find out if we can hear Kitty down there."

With the roar of the water and the gusting wind in the tunnel, they could only imagine hearing her cries for help. No one could be sure. They could only hope.

Bennington sensed that the water would be terribly cold and he concentrated upon remaining upright in the turbulence. It would be important to keep his cap on to assure having the light. Going into the totally dark tunnel without a light would be futile. He kept reminding himself that he had to keep his wits if he was to succeed.

One big step and he was in the deep, and there was no bottom. Immediately he was up to his armpits in a swirling, rushing creek. His 160 pounds pulled hard at the lifeline and his colleagues eased the grinding rope around their bodies and through their hands. The first fifty feet fed out and they continued to see Bennington's light downslope in the tunnel. Before the second fifty-foot section was released, he was out of sight. The pull was greater and tension among the anchor crew mounted.

The brave man at the end of the rope struggled to remain erect. His feet occasionally touched bottom now, and he felt sure he was going down a steeper slope. Water lapped up around his neck and down the collar of the jumpsuit. It was no longer so cold, his body having adjusted to the skin drenching chill of the water, which actually was the same temperature as the air in the cave.

Those handling the rope braced, Dr. Roberto with his feet against the wall and the other men pushing against him.

"Hold tight, everybody, he's pulling awful hard. It is so much down hill in there," Dr. Roberto yelled. "Half of our rope is going and he is not stopping yet."

What each secretly feared was that the entire two hundred feet of rope would go and Bennington would still be hanging on at the end of it. What then?

The third ring and snap coupling came through the men's hands reminding that they were working on the last fifty feet. The leader had to remind his colleagues, "Everybody hold on ever so tightly. I am going to count down. We must go slower than before. We have to keep ten feet for holding, you know. Felecia, you tell me when it is coming near the end. Remember you are not to let go the end. Okay?"

Foot by foot, he counted as the rope pulled even harder. "Forty four, 43, 42, 41, 40 . . ." Aloud he shouted so they all could hear him and know when the end of the rope neared.

When the counting and rope release reached twenty the leader ordered a halt for the moment. His voice sounded the despair they all felt.

Kitty's father now hung suspended below the lip of a wide waterfall, water shooting over his head. His light cast on water several feet below. He could see that there was a huge chamber. There were numerous rocks and drip formations. The water fell into a pond or small lake the size he could not discern, hanging up in the pouring water as he was. The awesome sound of the water cascading into the dark below him was similar to a violent windy rainstorm.

He could see enough to realize that Kitty might still be alive provided she had not crashed into the rocks. However, it also was quite possible that she had been pulled into a swirl hole, also certain death.

Momentarily the anchor people prepared to give Bennington another ten feet, all there was, in case it might be enough to reach a spot in there where the girl might still be alive.

Bennington had to decide quickly what to do hanging there in the downpour above the water only the Lord knowing how deep it would be. Impulsively, he dug deep into the huge patchpocket and located the scout knife. He fumbled with cold stiff fingers to open the cutting blade.

Once more he ran over the rationale for doing what he was

about to do. No way could he go back, even if they all pulled, for the downdraft would be too much for them. Neither could he hand-over-hand pull himself back up over the falls against the powerful force of the underground river. He took a deep breath and slashed the knifeblade across the half-inch nylon rope, severing it just above and back of his head.

Instantly Bennington fell feet first into the lake and at the same instant Dr. Roberto fell backwards into Carlos's lap. The rope was free and Bennington was gone.

Realizing that their partner had freed himself, they frantically retrieved the rope and examined the end of it. Plainly it had been cut with a knife. "No question he's cut himself free," Dr. Roberto told them.

"What does that mean?" Felecia questioned.

"Maybe he saw Kitty and went to her?" Irenea offered.

"Little good it does for us to say what we think happened in there." Dr. Roberto tried to sort out just where this left them and what it might lead to. They all were stunned at these lightning fast developments that had brought a double-dealing tragedy down deep in the cavern. Until now the secret cavern had seemed just an ideal place in which to find a colony of big-eared bats. But for now, the mission was "dead in the water."

ELEVEN

Terry, the Baltimore police captain, had seen and heard and dealt with just about every known act of man, but the bloody mirrors on Mary Martha's jeep stumped even him. He could not believe that the people at the field house had detected or even suspected the investigative work he and Mary Martha had done. He wondered if someone was trying to scare the women out of the big house. Could be that some good citizens saw the place with four single women living in it as a house of sin.

"Right on target," he told his dearest friend. "This happened after I came. You know, a man staying here overnight would have to be frowned on by most of the people around here, don't you think?"

"Could be but I never gave it a thought," Mary Martha told him. "I don't think anybody would pay any attention to that."

"Ah, come on now, it only takes one like that guy who runs the store up there, you know, remember how he put a fence across the graveyard road. Could be a character like that."

Mary Martha thought for a moment as the two sat on the couch trying to unravel this new development. "I don't think anybody would go to that kind of trouble. I think if they wanted to run us out they might burn a cross on our yard or slash our tires but not blood and feathers like the guy talked about up at the field house. Besides, everybody around here knows us. We grew up here. It's not as if we were unknown women setting up a whorehouse or something."

"Well, anyway, it could be something serious," Terry told her. "And I think we better find out what it's all about."

"Right, but for right now let's just forget about it and go have a good lunch. How about a glass of Lambrusco, that'll help."

"Great, but I think we can find the answer with a little nosing around. Gotta find out today if we can, before I head over the hill tomorrow."

"Right now I don't much feel like taking on another search."

It was while they sipped wine at the breakfast nook that they heard the fluttering and cries of birds in the yard. Terry tried to see the cause of the disturbance, but the spruce tree outside the kitchen window blocked his view. They hurried outside to learn the awful truth. On each side mirror of the jeep, desperate cardinals, a male at one and a female at the other, fluttered and fought, picked and struggled at their own images in the reflection. It was a sickening, sorrowful sight to see the poor ignorant wild creatures grappling with the beautiful bird images fighting back at them.

They had to break it up, for it was too gruesome to watch. The brilliant red trimmed in charcoal black male redbird and his brown with red-tinged mate had to be chased away to break their hypnotic spell.

"How dreadful, really ghastly for such a thing to happen to those poor innocent birds." Mary Martha sighed.

"I know, I've never seen anything like that," Terry replied thoughtfully. "It's such a damned shame. They'll be right back to do it all over again, I'll bet anything."

"Well, they'll not do it on my mirrors again. I'll cover 'em, drape something over 'em."

"How about those tear off plastic bags you get at the produce counter, you really can't see through them very good. I bet they'd work."

"We've got dozens of 'em. I'll try that."

Following lunch Mary Martha and Terry departed for another hitch at the listening post. During the entire hour they never heard a voice down in the field house. The Assermans lay out of sight on the roof outside their bedroom soaking up sunshine, unaware that their breathing was being monitored all the way up against the hill. They also remained ignorant of the dreadful turn of events deep within the cave where the other members of their party were.

Terry turned off the sound gear and whispered, "Let's get the heck out of here and maybe we can give it a whirl tonight."

"I'm ready when you are," Mary Martha replied.

"How about right now, then?" Terry playfully called her hand.

"Oh, no, you don't, up here in the woods, no, we at least have to get back to the house and in that bedroom, not up here for heaven's sake. Could be someone spying on us too."

"Just thought I'd take you up on your offer, don't want to miss out on anything that good."

"Thanks a whole bushel but I can wait."

Driving back Mary Martha began to feel anxious to dig into the thick letter from her dear old Aunt Christilina. Thick as it was she may have to wait till Terry left before undertaking it.

Back at the house she was tempted to engage Rena and Rachel in a set of lawn bocci yet she felt guilty at being seen playing when the old man Mr. Clay was lost. She felt affected and concerned beyond reason since he was little more than a mere acquaintance to her. Well, he had always been very nice to her, but she guessed he was that to most people he knew.

Suddenly she thought about the birds and the mirrors. "Oh, for goodness sakes, Terry, I forgot about the grape bags."

"Grape bags? Oh, oh, I know, the produce bags," Terry recalled. "I did clean off all the blood and guts and feathers but they'll be back."

"Not if I can help it, I'm gonna keep those bags in the jeep from now on. That's just plain awful for those poor things. My God, what a thing to happen to such pretty birds." She was determined to prevent any more such bloody messes.

TWELVE

Exactly seventeen minutes had passed since Kitty Bennington fell into the raging underground creek. Now that her father C. Baxter had cut himself free and dropped into the lake, the others tried to recover from the shock and select a course of action.

Suddenly Felecia was wringing her hands and offering solutions, "We've got to get help," she told them shouting her words at a third faster rate than her normal slightly southern mode of speech. "Look, we can't handle this alone, we've gotta get help and quickly. I say we go get some special rescue help, that's exactly what we must have to deal with this. Roberto, honey, no use you trying to be a hero or anything like that when we don't have anythink to work with. You know I'm..."

Her husband interrupted her by grabbing her around the shoulders and pulling her face into his chest. "Honey, listen to me, listen, you're terribly excited right now, listen a minute, you may be right but let's think about all this for a minute. No need for us to act in a frantic manner. I have a feeling that Benny is okay in there for the moment. But we must get to him as quickly as we can."

"I think you are right," Jorge spoke up and then added, "Let's think real hard about this and see if we can deal with this ourselves. Maybe there is something we can do."

Felecia, not calmed by the caring arms of her husband, yelled through tears, "There you go, of course we can offer up each one of you brave men one by one until you're all down in there wallowing in the unknown."

"I agree with you, Fee, no sense in trying to do something we can't do," Irenea spoke sounding as forlorn as Felecia.

"Okay, let's all sit down here in a circle so we can share our thoughts better," Dr. Roberto suggested. "Let's turn off all our lights except one, make it some more easy to look at each other."

Felecia threw her arms wide gesturing, "Big deal, we're going to sit down here and have a seance, is that it? For the life of me I can't figure you guys. How on earth can you just sit down and think about this when we must get help?"

"Come on, now, my sweetheart," her husband tried to calm her. "Remember, dear, it's at least one hour back to the field house. You know how slow the travel was to come to here and if we go back to there and come back to here it will be a very long time."

"He's right, Felecia, it is a long way back there and even then we may not be able to help," Jorge tried to persuade her.

"Anyway you look at it time is wasting, and I think we must act quickly if there is any chance of saving them." Felecia pushed her point.

"Please understand, I know there is a great chance that both of them have by now perished," Dr. Roberto answered. "But also realize that if they are now alive, and there is of course at least a little chance that they are right now alive, then a few minutes or even a few hours may not be so much important."

Finally the five of them tried to heed the leader's reasoning. His lamp illuminated their faces as they sat in a small circle with boot soles touching in the center.

Nearly a minute passed before he began to tell them what seemed most important to do. "What we most need is to communicate with them, either one of them, Benny or Kitty. If we can do that, we can that way know how much time we have to rescue them."

"Now we need the walkie-talkies," Jorge reminded, since they had not made it a practice to bring them into the caves for there seemed to be no need for them up to this point.

"Maybe so," Dr. Roberto agreed, "but we don't have them and if Benny or Kitty both had a set the water may make them not work so good."

"They probably wouldn't work at all," Jorge said. "We don't have them and that's just it, so no use to even think about that."

"Let's think of what it is possible for us to do," the leader suggested. "If we can figure a way to try to communicate with them, that is what we have to try to do."

THIRTEEN

It took ten minutes to reach a decision. Dr. Roberto dos Santos helped them conclude that they would attempt to locate and rescue the Benningtons without seeking outside help. At least for now, that was their decision.

"It is for sure that we must make a trip back to the field house before we can proceed," he told them. "Is it agreeable that we remain here, all except Carlos? He can go to bring back the remaining ropes and the plastic."

Carlos had only moments before volunteered to make the journey, feeling certain it would be much faster to go alone.

Dr. Roberto suggested to Carlos, "Tell Harry that he should return with you to help bring some more food and to help us here if we must send someone down in there."

It was Irenea who provided the appropriate diversions to occupy the long, long two hours and ten minutes until Carlos returned with Harry and the supplies. She told them about growing up in Brasilia, describing how so many folks there became sick from isolation in the early years of the new capital city. "They went crazy. It was so different and it was so far to travel to Rio or to the beach. It was different some for us, for my daddy was a Deputado, from Espirito Santo. We could travel some more easy than lots of the others. I was fifteen when he took me with him to New York to the United Nations. We stayed there for two months while he was on a study commission for the Brazilian government."

"I've heard they had many suicides in Brasilia," Dr. Roberto told her. "I have only visited there three times and stayed at the Hotel Nationale."

"I am afraid what you heard is correct. Too many people just could not stand it. In the early days when I was a girl there was nothing to do. You know, so many people were used to going to the beach."

"It helped some when they built the lake, didn't it?" Jorge asked.

"Oh, yes, it did, but it was many years before they decided to do that."

"Yeah, I remember so well," Dr. Roberto said. "Remember, Felecia, on our honeymoon, how dry it was in the hotel. We had to hang up wet bath towels to make moisture in the air."

"Oh, yeah, we did spend a good bit of time in the hotel room, didn't we?" Felecia joked.

"That dryness has changed now," Irenea told them.

"I know," Dr. Roberto interrupted. "In fact they have a problem with fog at the airport."

"You're right. That's for sure. Now it is common for the airport to be closed in the mornings."

They continued to discuss Brasilia with interest since Jorge, Irenea and Dr. Roberto were natives and remained Brazilian citizens. Felecia had made only short trips with her husband to Brazil.

When Carlos and Harry slid down the chute into the huge room where the others waited, the urgency of the moment returned. Carlos reported bringing 150 feet of rope and he showed them the sheet of clear tough plastic and a set of walkie-talkies.

Harry said, "I brought some food when you feel you are ready for it."

It was a total team effort with too many hands trying to construct the simple but fail-proof floating exploration vessel.

Carlos showed them how they could use the plastic and attach it to the rope. Dr. Roberto vetoed using the walkie-talkies. "We can try first to send some paper and pen. It can work if it gets to them. If that does not this time work, we will then try the radio."

Carlos unfolded the eight foot by six foot plastic sheet onto the concrete-like floor to determine the actual size they would need.

"About half of that is enough, I think," he told them.

"We must make very sure that it is large enough before we cut it," Dr. Roberto cautioned. "We will send only the necessary items—the ballpoint pen and paper and the light, I think, is all we need to send this time."

"Send some food," Felecia suggested.

"I don't think so this time, sweetheart. They have food with them."

"Yes, of course, they have food with them," Felecia countered with a hint of sarcasm. "But did you ever try to eat a wet peanut butter sandwich?"

"No, I have not, but what they need is something hot and stimulating."

"I thought of that," Carlos reported. "I brought a flask of Scotch."

"Excellent," the leader commended. "And we will place the flask in the package. Is it the metal one?"

"Yes, sir, it is the metal flask from your bar case, sir."

"Now we must get our preparations completed. It will be so necessary to make the vessel completely water-resistant," Dr. Roberto said more as a self-reminder than to inform the others.

They determined that a section of plastic six feet by six feet was what they would use to carry the necessary communications materials to the Benningtons.

Mr. Asserman offered a plastic ice cube bag he brought and they used it to double-protect the writing materials. In minutes they constructed a crude but waterproof float. Several knots were tied at the end of the rope cut by Mr. Bennington. The large clump of knots was placed inside the bag formed by gathering the corners to make a sack. Nylon cord drawn tightly by a dozen wrappings around the neck of the sack secured the rope inside and it was hoped that this would keep out the water.

Now it was ready for the launching, the miners lamp shining ready to attract the attention of C. Baxter and Kitty.

Suddenly Jorge offered a suggestion causing the others to wonder why they hadn't thought of it first.

Under these circumstances, each of them could be excused from spawning any brilliant ideas. However, it is under pressures such as these that a great idea speeds to the rescue.

"We can fix an umbrella over the end of the bag to shield it from the water." Jorge showed them. Taking a soft plastic bag from his pocket and tightly wrapping it around the rope just above and draped over the puckered neck of the heavier plastic pouch. This was tightly bound by several windings of cord giving double insurance to this exploratory mercy mission.

Dr. Roberto commanded Carlos to help him manage the tether, thus assuring that the entire rope would not be lost in the raging water. Through his hands, the leader would try to sense developments at the other end down in the unknown.

Quickly they fed two hundred feet of rope through the tunnel and over the falls, yet there was no pull on it. Another fifty feet produced the same result even though the plastic vessel was floating in the lake below the falls. The pull of the surging water kept the rope taut.

They saw the light come over the falls and descend like a bubble elevator on the outside wall of a tall hotel. Kitty and her father had struggled ashore and were now together on a yard-wide beach where the water was calm. Their soaked clothes, though uncomfortable, trapped valuable body heat that would continue to be the predominate factor keeping them well during the long hours before rescue. They were grateful to be alive following such an experience. Now the light gave them hope following the longest three-hour period either had ever spent.

The bag danced in the water beneath the falls, a spectacle of beauty were it not for the emergency. How long would it take for it to spring loose and float free in the lake? The answer came in only a few minutes. The very thing C. Baxter wanted to happen, did. The glowing bag gradually inched toward the middle of the small impoundment. The light was celestial to the Benningtons, an assurance that their prayers were indeed being answered.

A few more minutes and all the rope they possessed stretched from Dr. Roberto's hands to the lake. "Well, that's it. I suggest we leave it thirty minutes and then we retrieve it."

"Can't we bring it back more quickly?" Felecia pleaded.

"Please, dear, realize that to open the bag and to close it again takes some time. We must allow for that."

Jorge agreed. "Even if they have the bag right now we need to allow the reasonable time to open the bag and write to us a message."

"It'll take a good while, Felecia," Irenea told her. "Even if it takes an hour, we will then know if they are still alive."

"A half-hour is what we will wait this time," Dr. Roberto said.

Mr. Bennington shivered as he held Kitty close to him and cradled her wet head against his chest. They watched the glowing vessel drift out and away from them. C. Baxter began to agonize over the decision he must make, whether to risk drowning in the lake or remain on the relatively safe ledge.

Right now both he and Kitty were much warmer than when they first climbed out of the water.

Fear of drowning was genuine to him, for he had experienced a frantic struggle in the lake. His heavy clothing, especially the shoes were almost more than he could manage. Fortunately, his cap and light had held firm on his head and he lucked on to Kitty. He had heard her cries and struggled to reach her. To dive back into the lake was an alternative he dreaded. Surely the floating light would eventually come near them.

It did exactly opposite. In fact, after floating to the middle of the pond the light started on a course to the other side. This stirred Kitty's father to action.

It had been twenty-eight minutes since the light arrived and all this time the two stranded members of the spelunking group watching and hoping for the miracle. But it was not to happen. Suddenly C. Baxter jumped up, unbuckled the belt carrying the batteries to his miners lamp and laid his cap with the light on the ground. In moments he stripped off every item of soggy wet clothes. In the process he told Kitty "I'm going after that light. I must get it. If they take it back they'll think for sure we're dead."

Kitty screamed as her father plunged into the lake and swam overhand toward the floating beacon. His naked body adjusted to the 54° F. water. Though not exhibiting the perfect form of an Olympic swimmer, Mr. Bennington was determined to win. He had to get that bag so that his comrades would know that he and Kitty were safe and waiting to be rescued.

Another ten strokes and he would catch the rescue vessel floating slowly toward a spillway. At that very instant Dr. Roberto's thirty minutes were up and hand over hand he began the retrieval. C. Baxter saw the awful results. Back toward the waterfalls the rescue bag went in short jerks.

"Damn, damn to hell," he swore from the middle of the deep impoundment. He treaded water a moment and looked toward his lamp back on the bank with Kitty.

Jerk by steady jerk, the rescue light ascended the steep wall of water cascading over the falls.

He swam back slowly until he reached Kitty and his waterlogged clothes. Even before he could pull on one item of his garments C. Baxter had to comfort Kitty. She cried uncontrollably until her father caressed her and repeatedly kissed her forehead. He assured her that their friends would not give up with only one attempt.

FOURTEEN

Mary Martha ripped open the envelope to read the turn-of-the-century handwriting penned by 86-year-old Aunt Christilina.

Dear Mary,
How are you? Fine I hope. This leaves me feeling worse than I was when you was here. I heard about Cloy being lost and all. That is a shame. I wonder have they found him yet? Your cousin Ora came over here from Cumberland and told me all about him being lost. She was here a Sunday I think it was. I have some things I want you to have that was give to me by your momma. She told me some things that nobody else knows and when she lived with me there before she passed away she gave me an envelope to give you. She told me never to give it to you before anything happened to Cloy. Now since he is lost and all I figured I better send it to you. Mary you come and see me you hear. You know I won't be having much more time. Some days I feel like its going to be my last.
Your Aunt Christilina

"What on earth is so much a secret that Momma couldn't tell me?" Mary Martha puzzled over the feebly written words.

She had waited until Terry left following their slow-paced mid-morning breakfast. Now she was alone in her bedroom where she and her man had spent another lovers night. Mary Martha was stunned at something so secret she had been kept in the dark about it until now.

Anything that mysterious required the security of a locked bedroom door, she decided, and promptly walked over and tripped the night latch. She returned and stood in front of the dresser mirror holding the letter from within the letter from her aged aunt. Shrugging, she decided to take the plunge and open it, ripping the yellow envelope with a metal fingernail file.

Inside were newspaper clippings, some snapshots, a silk

bookmark and a six-page letter on narrow sheets of lined tablet paper. She began to read:

My Dearest Daughter,

I don't know how to start this letter to you but a thousand times I wanted to tell you. When your daddy was living I never could tell you, then when he passed away I still couldn't do it. I guess I was afraid you would never forgive me. I have prayed and prayed for Jesus to forgive me for my sin. Jesus has forgiven me and I beg you, dear Mary Martha, I love you so much. As I near my last days I beg you to please forgive me too. I think I'll send you this letter to see if you will forgive me. If I don't send it before I go I'm gonna ask Christilina to give it to you after Cloy Clay departs this earth.

Mary Martha took a deep breath and moved away from the mirror and sank into the edge of the bed where the fragrance of love-making lingered in the air.

Again she read:

You know your daddy and Cloy both was in the Army. Your daddy was called before Cloy and he was over in France when Cloy came home on leave. They was both at Camp Lee, Virginia. Cloy was going to be shipped out when he went back. Cloy, you know, didn't marry Betty until he come back from the war. It was when Cloy was home on leave that it happened.

Me and Cloy growed up together and we never thought about marrin' each other. Least ways I never did. But when Cloy come home in his uniform and all and your daddy had been gone for about a month it happened. It was not planned that we would meet but Cloy was over to our house for supper. I was livin' with mom and daddy. He said he was going up on Thunderstruck the next day just to look around and maybe dig some ramps. It was in the spring and nice warm weather. Next day I told momma I was going to get a mess of watercress greens. I went for a long walk up to Thunderstruck maybe hoping I'd see Cloy. I was so lonely. I ran on to him way up there and we had a little picnic on a rock along a creek up there. Cloy took me in his secret cave. He had a big flashlight and showed me this beautiful great big room and the big waterfalls. It really was so beautiful in there but it was chilly. When we came back outside the air was so nice and warm and the sun was shining. We went up against the hill to a level spot and sat down and one thing led to another and we did something we shouldn't have done. I'll never forget the way we enjoyed that little time up there in the woods with the sun shining on us. But it was something I never could tell anybody. When I got back home I tried to protect myself from gettin' in a family way but it was too late. You have to know that Cloy was your real father but Cloy don't know and I don't think he ever suspected that he was. That was the only time we was ever together like that and he was the only man I ever was with besides your daddy. I should say my husband. And he always thought he was your daddy. And you know he dearly loved you. I love you so very much and I always had a special feeling for Cloy because he was your father.

Mary Martha was shocked at what she read and her face grew white, her arms became numb and her bare feet felt as cold as her fingers as her body reacted to the revealed secret.

"Oh, my God," she gasped, "That poor man never did know. My real father never did know."

Compassion gave way to anger. She was angered by the betrayal, a lifelong betrayal by her mother. The very mother she loved and trusted. "How could she do this to me? Me of all people, her own and only child?" She agonized. "How, Momma, how could you do this to me?" She cried softly and fell back on to the bed.

Moments later she opened her eyes to the ceiling. Her anger subsided and her eyes widened at her mind's new perspective. Maybe she was being too damned pure blaming her mom for making love in a root hole with Cloy Clay and never ever telling her about it all these years. What good would have been achieved had she known about it?

"I'm not so sure but what mamma did the right thing," she said softly, testing it in her mind. "The way it was, I never knew, daddy never knew and Cloy never knew. Only mamma lived with the secret and most of all it didn't bring any shame on anybody."

FIFTEEN

The next word to hit Mary Martha's troubled mind was cave. Her mother and Cloy went in a cave. It was a cave that Cloy liked so much that he took Gladys Cosner in it when they both were young during World War I.

"Of course he could be in that very cave right now and still alive," Mary Martha mouthed. She jumped up from the bed, stripped three tissues from the nightstand box and blew her nose and wiped her eyes. She prepared to go downstairs still not certain what, if anything, she would do with the new information. How much of it should she share with her housemates? Would she have to reveal anything to Mr. Amos and Mr. Ralph, Cloy's closest friends?

She took a few minutes more to reread her mother's letter and the newspaper clippings. One item was from the Leadmine column of the *Parsons Advocate* dated April 3, 1916. It read, "Private Cloy Clay is this week visiting his parents Mr. and Mrs. Omar Clay of this community. Private Clay is stationed at Camp Lee in Virginia. He will be going overseas when he returns to camp after his two-week leave."

Right now it seemed important to hide the letter to assure that no one would learn what had been revealed in the communication from Aunt Christilina. She was becoming convinced that her friends need not know any of the details. It would be better that way.

Downstairs she and Rena and Rachel prepared a snack. Several times the others tried to get Mary Martha to discuss the certified letter. She told them only a glossed-over description of what the puffy envelope contained. "Nothing important. Poor old lady, my Aunt Christilina is having awful problems of senility and she just had to send me some clippings and things she wanted me to have. She heard about Cloy and she is worrying about him being lost."

"What did she say about Cloy? Did she have any idea what

might have happened to him?" Rena asked hoping to get something specific from Mary Martha.

"No, nothing like that. She just seemed to be worrying about him and wanted to share her worry, wanted to talk to somebody. I've gotta go see her real soon, poor old thing. She's quite a lady but now she's gettin' so old and she's beginning to pity herself, you know, and that's such a shame when that happens."

"Nothing new then?" Rachel asked.

"Nothing new, honey. You're right, nothing new." Mary Martha was struggling with what to tell and what to keep.

A few minutes of small talk was sufficient to move their minds into another line as they fixed a snack, tea and graham crackers.

Colonel Apolla's Green Berets began pulling out of Cloy's lane, abandoning the search, at 12:30 that Thursday, the sixth day after their hunt began. Amos and Ralph saw them off and moved back out of the sun onto Cloy's porch, giving up on ever finding Cloy alive.

Today marked the eighth day since Cloy left home, went up the creek and entered the cave. If only Amos and Ralph knew, then they could attempt the rescue, but they didn't.

Amos dared to speak of the real world. "Ralph, you know we better make some plans to have a kind of funeral for 'im, don't you think?"

"Well, to tell you the truth, I didn't want to think about it, but I figure you're right." Ralph said slowly but puzzled.

"Maybe you'd call it a memorial service instead of a funeral."

"Maybe that's what it would be, wouldn't it?"

"Never been to one of them, where they weren't no body to view."

"Yeah, I've been to 'em. Pretty sad, no flowers or nothin' up front in the church."

"It would be kinda odd not havin' a casket or nothin'."

"Guess it'll be up to us to do it if it's gonna be done."

"Guess that's right," Amos agreed spitting across the porch and on to the dry yard grass.

"Maybe we oughta wait a couple of days before we do anything."

"I don't know, and then again, I was wonderin' where we'd have it."

"Suppose a person would have to have it up in Parsons at one of the churches up there."

"Maybe at the funeral home?"

"That would cost a bunch of money, I bet, to have it at the funeral home."

"I don't know, seems no reason to go to the funeral home when you don't have a corpse."

"I's thinkin' even be strange to have it in a church up town. I know danged sure Cloy wouldn't want to have his funeral up in Parsons. He stayed away from town as much as he could and people up there don't know 'im."

"What about havin' it right up here at Cloy's house? Right here."

"Yeah, here in the yard, and the preacher could speak from here on the porch."

"That way all th' people right around here would come, too."

Smiling, Ralph had a thought that amused him. "Stripe could attend if we had it here."

"Sure," Amos grinned, "Stripe could just lay here on the porch and pant and in a way he'd represent old Cloy, you know."

"Oh, well, let's just wait and if we decide to have a service I'd think we just might as well have it here."

"Maybe on a Sunday afternoon, people could bring a picnic and we could just have dinner and then a short service."

"Could have a little singin' and the like and some good talkin' about Cloy."

"Only'd be right, and I don't think we'd want to have any cryin' kind of talk, just somethin' good about Cloy and some good visitin' here amongst his friends."

"I think we'll wait."

The two youthful women coal miners seemed puzzled at Mary Martha's plan to go on a trek into the same territory so thoroughly searched by the Green Berets.

"What in the name of God do you think we can do up there?" Rena asked.

"Yeah, that bunch of men scoured those hills and hollers for five days now," Rachel reinforced.

"I know, I know, but just on a hunch something tells me we oughta give it a try. Haven't you ever had such a feeling? I just have one of those silly hunches that somehow they missed him."

"I think we'd be wastin' our time. We really ought to be gettin' the law to go up to that field house and find out what the devil's going on up there," Rachel said.

"Up there's where we're gonna find 'im," Rena continued.

"Look, trust me. You know, older and wiser," Mary Martha kidded. "Seriously, I have this crazy feeling, that's all." She lied.

"Durned wild goose chase, I bet, but it sounds like a fun hike," said Rachel.

"If we take some good food and cold beer I'll be in for it," Rena agreed.

"We can do that," Mary Martha told them. "Then we"ll drive up to the end of the lane past the field house and leave the jeep. Save a lot of walking. We'll go up Thunderstruck a ways. So, roll out in the morning and we'll go about eight."

"My Lord that's early after workin' till one in the morning, but we can do it this once," Rachel growled.

"Well, I'm gonna go out back and get me some sun to cover up the broken veins in my sexy legs," Mary Martha changed the subject and went off to think.

SIXTEEN

This time they would try walkie-talkies, anything when you're desperate, but how to make them work was the question.

Carlos showed them how to establish a two-way radio link between the dark recesses of the cavern to the safe chamber, which crackled with the rescue party's anxiety. "Tie down the on switch so it will be in the send mode. On this end we can be able to hear them yell to us."

Dr. Roberto agreed, "That just may work, but if it does not, they still may get the bag and then we can talk with them." He continued to insist that only one light be on now to save the batteries for the anticipated long time in the belly of the cavern, reaching from the field house along the Horseshoe to a minute tributary of Thunderstruck.

They soon resupplied the vessel, this time including, at Felecia's insistence, a tin of sardines and a tube of saltines. The whiskey flask, turned-on light and radio and again the writing paper and pen were the items to send down on the second try.

There it was again. The plastic bag glowing in the dark quickly descended the falls and into the murky tumult of the lake. The powerful pouring river of water over the falls pulled the vessel into the undercurrent like the turbulence generated by a paddle-wheel riverboat, and the light kept going under out of sight. It returned in seconds to be beaten under again.

This time it seemed much longer to C. Baxter for the vessel to be thrown free of the entrapment into the the serene glistening lake. This time he didn't wait for some force of nature to send light to his safe perch, a rock ledge beach of sorts.

Again he stripped and dove in to corral the rescue vessel, for this could be their friends' last attempt for a while to determine if they were yet alive. Beyond this it could take days to find them, but he was certain that eventually someone would come.

"This time I've got you," C. Baxter spoke almost as if talking to another person. Those five words came over the radio being held in anticipation by Jorge. "Hear that, would you?" Jorge yelled.

"I heard him," Carlos said for he was standing beside Jorge holding on to the rope.

Dr. Roberto had not heard C. Baxter, too much noise from the creek, and he was six feet from Jorge and the handset.

Jorge listened for more. He shushed all to be quiet. "Only water sounds," he told them.

"Oh, my God!" Felecia yelled out her pent-up emotions when Jorge took the handset away from his ear.

"Please, now let's listen some more. Let me have the set, Jorge," Dr. Roberto demanded.

For a few more minutes, he patiently listened, his right hand over his right ear and the set over the other. There were muffled sounds of talking, Dr. Roberto thought, but no words he could discern.

First C. Baxter had to labor into the wet clothes. The worst of it was putting on the heavy wet socks and the god-awful cold, wet insulated underwear, pulling hair up around the groin and freezing his delicate male extremeties. This was the second time around and this time he warmed the long johns before putting them on by blowing his warm breath into the crotch.

It was a tedious task to unwind the cord to open the plastic sack. As soon as they did, Dr. Roberto could hear them and he reported, "They're both alive. Ah, yes they are alive, indeed," he shouted. "I can hear them both talking about the walkie-talkie."

C. Baxter saw that the radio was tied on and he began to talk to his colleagues. "We are safe down here." Then he realized that he had to untie the string in order to hear. Again he repeated, "Dr. Roberto, we are safe. Kitty and I are alive down here, Over."

"Thank God you are now alive!" Dr. Roberto exclaimed. "You must tell me about your condition."

"We are fine, only cold but fine. Over."

"Kitty is also with you, right? Over."

"Oh, yes, right away I found her and except for being scared and cold is doing just great. Over."

"We sent some food. You know, I wish we could send you some dry clothes, that would be some help, don't you think? Over."

Dr. Roberto suddenly realized that only he could hear and he took the radio from his ear and held it out in the air for the others.

"I'm sure that would be impossible right now, but we'll be okay until we figure a way to get out of here. Over."

"We must determine a way. Oh, by the way, you see the flask? That may be a substitute for the dry clothes. But listen, tell me, do you think we can pull you one at a time back up into here with the rope? Over."

"That's the problem, sir. There is no way that will work. You see, there is a great big waterfalls down here and we are down below the falls. There is a large lake and we are on the side of the lake. Over."

"That does present for us a huge problem, but we must think of something. Right now, Benny, take some time to get a drink of whiskey into both of you and we will talk here about what we will do next. Over."

"Roger."

"Ten-four or whatever. We'll be talking to you in a few minutes."

SEVENTEEN

Alone in the house Peggy Sue Asserman agonized to the breaking point. She had to talk to someone. The telephone was one way and she dialed her friend in Arlington, Virginia. The operator, informed of which number on the four-party line to charge, let the call proceed. It rang in Executive Apartment number 525.

"Come on, for God's sake, Gwen, please be home," Peggy Sue anguished aloud. "Please answer me. I need you." There was no answer. She let the phone ring on and on, finally giving up. A look at her watch told her why. It was only 3:30 in the afternoon and her friend would not be home from work at the Pentagon until six.

Next she walked the floor, into the kitchen, back to and through the great hall of a living room, and then up to her and Harry's bedroom. On her sixth trip through the house she determined that she must reach someone, anyone, to get help, for by now more of her party could be drowned down in the cave.

The car, that was it, she would take Jorge's car to the village. Down there at the store they could help her, she thought. Where to find the keys to the Peugeot?

Nerves. Her nerves needed calming. She could think better, act better and feel a whole lot better with a drink. She poured a glass of scotch and drank a gulp straight, a second swallow and a third, grimacing, gasping for breath. Then she searched for the car keys.

She found them on the floor among scattered small change by Jorge and Irenea's unmade bed.

Dressed in short shorts, halter and tennis slippers Peggy Sue returned to the kitchen for another swig of whiskey. She rushed out the front door leaving it ajar and headed for the unlocked car. The seat of Jorge's station wagon was locked into the last notch to accommodate his long legs, a good six inches too far back for her. She yanked the top handle on the left side of the bucket seat and hunched hard forward, to no avail. Another pull and the seat back caved in on her, crushing her tightly against the steering wheel. Another hard pull on the lever freed the seat back and her body pushed it on to the rear seat forming a recliner.

"Oh, hell, what a car, damned foreign car," she fretted.

Now that she knew what that handle did she adjusted the seat to its proper notch then tried the flat-shaped lever just beneath the first one. She pulled it hard enough to break, she thought, and the seat sprang all the way forward. That put her in a driving mode, upright and snug against the large skinny steering wheel.

"The ignition, where is the ignition?" She searched the dash finding the lighter, the choke, ash tray, and the glass covered meters. There was no place for the key. The right side of the steering column had only one little lever. She pulled it and the horn blew a puny note. Still there was no place to plug in the key.

"What the devil?" she anguished. "Do you have to crank this French contraption?" By now the whiskey was working, flushing her face and popping the sweat in the sweltering heat intensified because the doors were closed and the windows were tight.

Peggy Sue Asserman slid out and stood looking at the steering wheel in disgust. Suddenly she spotted the ignition sticking out like a knot on a pine tree along the left side of the steering arm.

She quickly slid back into the seat and stabbed the long slender key with deep notches into the orifice. It penetrated about a quarter inch and stopped. She jammed and wiggled, twisted and pushed the aluminum ignition key which was being forced upside down into the slot. Angrily she gave a hard pull to extract it. The key was stuck. She forced a hard jiggle to free it. This was more than the precision car ignition key could stand. It broke off leaving a chunk inside the slot.

That was that, no car. The big station wagon with the Land Rover still attached to the trailer hitch was parked behind Jorge's station wagon.

Peggy Sue was not about to give up just because the car wouldn't start. Back inside she went, drank the last of the glass of scotch and made another whiskey-assisted decision. She would run down to the nearest house and tell them about

Kitty and C. Baxter being washed away in the cave. It was time to act. She could not wait.

Out into the weedy driveway she ran cutting across through the once spacious lawn. She reached a point near the lane through knee-high weeds and briers. There were hidden fence boards strung along the road bank. Suddenly Peggy Sue's left foot ground down upon an ugly rusty spike nail anchored in a grassed-over board. She fell headfirst over the bank with the rotten chunk of a board hanging on to her shoe.

Fierce pain shot up her leg. She kicked to free herself, breaking the chunk off from the twelve-foot oak strip of fence. Impulsively she drew her legs down over the bank and sat up in the road and the chunk came with her left foot. The awful pain intensified as she dragged the two-foot piece of lumber on the bottom of her left foot to where she could reach it with her hand. Then she saw the hideous spike punched up through the top of her shoe a good inch; covered with blood and glistening in the sun.

"Oh, my God, my God, Oh!" She screamed and fainted backward into the mass of weeds in the narrow roadbed.

It was her good fortune that a solid wall of trees across the road along Horseshoe Run cast a shadow protecting her from the afternoon sun. Otherwise she could have been severely burned lying there unconscious on her back in the road. Gradually blood oozed out around the nail saturating the flimsy white canvas slipper.

Six minutes passed before she awoke and slowly sat up. Again the earth turned black, her head throbbed and she fell over on her right side. A few more minutes and she recovered enough to feel the god-awful agony in her left foot and leg.

The whiskey boosted her courage and she tried to tear herself loose. It was certain that pulling the spike back through the arch of her foot would be terribly hard to do. The pain was one thing but the strength to do it was not in her arms. Eventually she maneuvered to stand on her right foot, holding the board and her left foot inches off the ground. Biting her lips, closing her eyes to the sickening sight of it she tried easing the board on to the ground. This caused the nail to grind past the bones, yet she pressed down shifting all her weight onto the left foot. She had to do it in spite of the agonizing pain.

Unstable, dizzy from the whiskey and shock, Peggy Sue with her right foot, stepped down on the board. The weight off of her left foot, its arch returned to a natural weightless state, forcing a slight withdrawal of the nail. This grinding in the hobbled foot nearly brought on another blackout.

Bravery beyond any point she had ever experienced surprised the dainty 38-year-old city woman, as she would recount later. Right now she was bent on freeing that foot and getting back into the house. Now the tragedy was hers and she forgot about the others in the cave. This was her own battle and she had to win, a fact she had not fully learned until that freshman year at college.

Facing up to the moment, Peggy Sue leaned right, pressing down hard on the board with the free right foot. Clinching her fists, her eyes squinted, her jaw locked tightly shut, the time had come to free herself. Thus, with one sudden yank it was done. The four-inch fence nail stuck straight up in the air, blood covered and ready to fell another unsuspecting soul who might sock a foot down upon it. This time it would be in the road where a car tire could be the next victim.

EIGHTEEN

Carlos was volunteered to stay at the radio while Dr. Roberto, Felecia, Jorge, Irenea and Harry worked their way back to the field house. They emerged from the cavern at 4:20 to find Peggy Sue asleep. Her foot was wrapped in a bath towel and a bottle of scotch sat on the floor beside her bed.

Harry thought it better not to wake her since it appeared that she might have sprained an ankle for there apparently was no blood.

In the kitchen they poured drinks to calm their nerves and to pamper their tired bodies. The rigors of the day, the uncertainty of how to solve their dilemma produced a somber mood, quite different from their usual happy-hour atmosphere in the big kitchen.

Dr. Roberto initiated a serious discussion on how to proceed. "Think with me for the moment. It is only my opinion but I think we were nearing another place where the cave reaches the outside. You can feel the fresh air moving in there. We could be only a short distance to the outside."

"Of course it could be close or it could even be a mile from where we were," Jorge reasoned.

"I think, Jorge, it was some more closer than a kilometer," Dr. Roberto asserted. "So our best possibility is to try to find that entrance to rescue them."

"Today?" Jorge questioned.

"Of course we must find it today or tonight, whatever it takes. We must find it," Dr. Roberto urged.

"I think we should inquire down in the village, maybe someone there will know exactly where it is," Felecia said emphatically.

"I think that is not so good an idea, dear. First we should try to find it ourselves. That way we will not be giving away our mission to the public."

"Mission, the all-important mission, that is the important

thing," Felecia taunted, resenting her husband's dedication to the scientific expedition at the cost of their stranded friends.

"First, I remind you that it is some obvious that no one around here knows of the cavern or they would have been in this area connected to the house. Secondly, I do consider it important to preserve the sanctuary just in case it is the home for the *Plecotus townsendii virginianus.*"

"Well, I'm going to keep out of this. No need for me to try to tell you, but I think there comes a time when you seek assistance from others," Felecia told him. Then with emphasis, "Especially when the situation is more than you or I or Jorge, all of us, can handle. Believe me I'm scared and I don't mind admitting it. I don't care what you say. We're desperate, you know, desperate is exactly the way I feel right now and nothing you've said so far makes me think I'll feel any better tomorrow."

"Drink up, you'll feel better, dear, and then we can determine what is best to do," her husband urged bringing a long period of silence to the room.

Irenea brought pepperoni and cheese from the refrigerator and each sliced what he or she desired for a snack. After twenty minutes of rest and refreshments, Dr. Roberto urged upon them a plan. "I think, Jorge and Harry and I should go on a search for a place to enter the cave. We can do this while it is yet daylight, you think so, Jorge?"

"Yes, sir, of course we can. How about you, Harry? What do you think?"

"I'm with you and we'd better go soon to allow enough time before dark."

"If we depart soon we can have over four hours before it becomes dark," Dr. Roberto calculated, looking at his watch.

They placed two battery-powered lights into a shoulder bag which Jorge carried and the three men set out from the house to look. In the yard they surveyed the hills and concluded that apparently the cavern curved on a level course beneath the mountain. Also Harry ventured that they should look for the opening up one of the streams where they might see the outcropping of limestone. They did not know the stream names, except the main Horseshoe Run. However, they set out for the largest junction a quarter of a mile up Horseshoe to where Thunderstruck branched off. They decided to follow the smaller Thunderstruck Creek in hopes of finding a place where they could enter and locate C. Baxter and Kitty.

Each man carried two sections of rope just in case they needed to use it in the rescue attempt. They talked, looked, sweated and panted in the still air of the narrow valley enveloped by huge hardwoods.

Gradually they scaled the rough creek bed toward their goal. They had walked for nearly an hour with no results. There was absolutely no place where water poured from a limestone outcrop. In fact, no limestone outcroppings were evident up the stream to this point.

Another hour of slow, steady walking with short rest stops and the stream became finite, only a trickle of water. It was then 7:00 and they were about two hours from the field house. Dr. Roberto concluded that it was time to begin the journey back. "A search up here in the night would not be profitable," he told Jorge and Harry. "We must make a special effort when it becomes morning. Surely we can find some place then."

"Do you suppose there could be more than one place, surely there must be somewhere in addition to the field house?" Jorge asked.

"There must be another place. I know we were near it in there." Dr. Roberto encouraged. "We can find it I am certain, almost, of that."

Twilight spread across the Horseshoe valley as the three tired men struggled toward their temporary home. It was dark when they entered the field house to relate their despair at not finding the cavern.

Peggy Sue told them of her injury. Dr. Roberto quickly asked her if she had taken her tetanus booster shot. "Yes, yes of course, I had mine in May," Peggy Sue told him.

"Yeah, we both had them at the same time, didn't we?" Harry directed to his wife.

"Right, but that won't keep it from getting infected, though," she told him, almost as if asking "will it?"

"No, of course not," Harry said. "However, you did put something on it, didn't you?"

"Yes I did, after a while, but as rusty as that thing was it sure might get some kind of bacteria in there."

"Long as you're protected from lockjaw. That nail could have been clean, out in the open air up here, so you never know, could be free of germs," Jorge pointed out. "You'll just have to watch it and if it starts swelling and aching you'll have to see a doctor."

"It's doing both right now. It's swollen and it hurts a plenty," she told him.

"Think we should go and see a doctor now?" Harry asked Jorge and then turned to Dr. Roberto. "What do you think?"

Before either could answer, Peggy Sue thought of Jorge's car. "Jorge I think I ruined your car. I don't think you can drive it now."

"What do you mean?" Jorge quizzed.

"I was about to drive down to the village and I tried to use your car and I broke the key."

"I have another set, okay?"

"Yeah, but a piece of the key is still in the thing."

"Well, we'll have to check on it later. Right now I need a drink and something to eat." It was not that they lacked transportation. There were additional vehicles, they were not stranded.

Food and drink appealed to the others and again they tried to relax in the midst of a developing dilemma that could very well require expert help to solve.

NINETEEN

Mary Martha rushed home at daybreak from her security head job at Canaan Valley Resorts. The only lead she or anyone had came in the letter from her mother. Now the search had become a personal matter in that now she was searching for her father, a fact that had not yet become real to her. It seemed only a dream. Today could change that.

She prepared the coffee to drip, went to each of her friend's rooms and tried to wake them. Then she took a shower, more to help her feel fresh and alert than to cleanse herself.

It was 6:30 when they drove off up the road toward Shaffertown. They entered the narrow lane leading to the field house, still the old Weidimeyer house to them, and drove slowly toward the dead end at the sycamore tree where they had parked before. Mary Martha spotted the piece of board with the long spike in it lying in the right car track. She asked Rachel to remove it before they proceeded. They could see the rear of the Land Rover behind the tall shrubs in the field house driveway.

When Rachel returned to the jeep she said, "I see they're still here. The cars are still up there."

"I know, probably still sleeping this time of morning," Mary Martha said not as interested in them now that she had new information.

Leaving the jeep at the end of the road, Mary Martha took the tote bag. In it she had placed two flashlights, a two-cell and a six-cell, a bottle of pure maple syrup, a can of evaporated milk, a tube of saltines and a soup spoon. Also she had included for them three apples, two oranges, a jar of peanut butter and three slices of bread. The vacuum bottle contained hot black coffee. On top of all this she had placed a folded thin cotton blanket.

"What all you got in the bag, a picnic?" Rena questioned, since the bag looked a bit heavy for their needs.

"Sure, some food, we'll have a picnic up in there someplace,"

Mary Martha lied. "Figured we just as well enjoy it, don't you think?"

Mary Martha led, taking them up Horseshoe to Thunderstruck. She pretended to question whether to go up Horseshoe beyond the junction or should they take the smaller creek, Thunderstruck. All the while she knew which way to go but she acted a bit before choosing the course she knew was the right one.

Limestone outcroppings were not a part of her knowledge regarding caves in the region. She was being guided by the bits of information revealed by her mother.

It was a comfortable 73 degrees before 7:00 as they picked their way among the loose creek rocks, avoiding the water in the small stream. They stopped occasionally, but when they did, Mary Martha was always a dozen steps in the lead. Finally, some ninety minutes after leaving the jeep, it looked right to her for them to change course. She suggested, "Why don't we walk up this creek here a little ways before we go on up Thunderstruck?"

"Is that what this creek is called?" Rena asked wondering how Mary Martha knew so much.

"Yeah, I've known for years that this was Thunderstruck. Crazy name, isn't it?"

"Wonder how come it ever got such a name?" Rachel pondered.

"Oh, I don't know, could have been from a lightning storm. Up here in the mountains it does thunder and lightning awful bad. Maybe someone thought it would be cute to call it that instead of lightningstruck. Probably was named by some guy who was up in here when a storm came up and lightning struck a tree close by."

"Kind of a good name, really," Rena agreed.

Now Mary Martha began a more intensive search. "Right up this creek is where it sounded like Momma was talking about," she thought, scrutinizing every inch of the steep bank bordering the six-foot-wide stream. Each step brought them closer to a small pool of water below a four-foot high waterfall. Native brook trout darted into the deeper water as the women neared the pool's edge.

Mary Martha stopped and Rena and Rachel caught up, rattling rocks with each step.

She spotted it. There on the left side of the falls was a hole in the bank beneath a solid wall of light gray stone. Mary Martha suggested they sit down and rest a few minutes, giving her a chance to have a better view into the darkness. "You see that hole over there?" she asked the others.

"Yeah, big enough for a bear to crawl in," Rachel joked.

"Just a washed-out place, looks like to me," Rena reasoned.

"That's what it looks like, doesn't it?" Mary Martha agreed, still trying to see back in it. Then she joked, "Could be a bear in there right now, you know."

"In a place like that here in the summertime, a bear wouldn't be in a place like that, he'd be out eatin' berries," Rena suggested. "Good place to hiberate in the winter time though."

"I'm gonna go over around there where I can get a better look," Mary Martha announced. "I've got a flashlight in the bag. Let me get it out and shine it in there."

"You don't plan on us being up here till night, do you?" Rachel questioned. "We've got to get back in time to go to work, you know."

"I know, but I'm used to carrying a light with me all the time up at the lodge so I just brought it along." She sat the bag on the rocks beside the water, extracted the two-cell light and took careful steps across the creek. She knelt down at the hole and exclaimed, "There's cool air coming out of there, kinda blowing out. Feels cool and damp."

Now she could see that the passageway beneath the huge rock immediately became larger. She snapped on the light and for certain this was a cave. Possibly the very cave her mother described.

"Come over here one of you, just one at a time, and take a look," she yelled.

Rachel came, took the light and looked. "Oh, yeah, it's a cave all right, big in there."

"Let me see," Rena demanded and they moved aside to let her see for herself. "That's exactly what it is, a cave back in there." She sounded excited as she started to move farther in to get a better view.

"No, no, wait a minute, honey. Let's wait, we don't want to go in there just yet," Mary Martha cautioned.

"I'm not gonna go in there anyway," Rena said. "I get enough of that kind of underground duty up there at Beaver Creek. I just want to get a better look."

Mary Martha was convincing, though, and the three of them went back to the other side of the creek to talk. She took out the coffee jug, twisted off the lid and poured it nearly full. They shared sips around as Mary Martha kept an eye on the cave. Feeling cold and anxious, she began to tremble.

"Listen, you two, do you suppose old Mr. Clay could have gone in a cave like this and maybe is still in there?"

"Oh, for God's sake, you suppose? I never gave it a thought," Rachel gasped. "Surely not."

"Why would he ever do a thing like that, go in a cave way back up here?" Rena questioned.

"I don't know, he could have. Never know what goes through some people's head. He could be right in there," Mary Martha asserted. "We just might be the ones to find him after all."

"Well, I'll just go in there and see, if that's what you think," Rachel volunteered.

"Would you?" Mary Martha asked, relieved at her offer. "I hate to admit it but I've never been in a cave before, scares me just a little."

"One thing, all three of us shouldn't go in there at once," Rena suggested. "Let's let Rachel go in just a little ways and check it out."

"Give me the light, I'll go in. Probably doesn't go in very far. I'll check it out then we'll know."

"Listen, I've got a bigger light if you want it."

"This one's okay," Rachel reasoned, then she questioned, "A bigger light? Did you know we were gonna find a cave? Is that why you brought all these lights and stuff?"

"Not really," she lied, "just wanted to be prepared in case we found something like this."

"Seems durned funny to me," Rena frowned. "I swear to God, I think you knew something."

"You come over and watch, just keep the big light and I'll go in there," Rachel urged.

Like a bear on all fours Rachel crawled in out of sight. "Hey I can stand up in here! Look, Mary Martha, I'm standing up. It's a big place in here," she yelled sounding as though she were hollering in a barrel.

"See any thing?" Mary Martha asked.

"Nothing yet just a great big place, oh, my goodness, look

how beautiful. It's really nice in here," her voice trailed as she walked farther away from the small hole in the bank.

"Come on back, Rachel. Come on back before something happens to you," Mary Martha yelled.

There was no answer. Mary Martha stiffened from fear. "What if Rachel had fallen in or something?" she thought.

Another minute and Rachel was back within ten feet of the outside. "I'm able to walk right to here. It's a big room in here. In fact I didn't go very far but it sure is nice in here, just a bit cold, but it sure is nice. Just like walkin' on Main Street."

"Come on out," Mary Martha urged.

"No use me comin' out, you all come on in. Sure looks plenty safe in here."

TWENTY

At nine Thursday night Carlos had become weary from waiting. He told C. Baxter on the walkie-talkie that he was thinking of returning to the field house to get some warm blankets and dry clothes for them. C. Baxter and Kitty urged him to go and return as quickly as possible.

"Bring some hot tea and cookies, too," Mr. Bennington urged, "but be plenty careful yourself. We'll be okay till you get back."

"If you're for sure, I'll go this moment and return back at about midnight," Carlos said.

"Midnight, well that makes no difference in here in the dark. Could be noon now for all I know," Kitty pined.

"It is nine o'clock now so I will go and return back. Maybe the others will be coming back, too. Dr. Roberto said they were going to look for another place to come in to where you are now. For sure, my friends, I will be back here to join you."

"Go on now, we'll be fine. See what you can learn from Dr. Roberto," C. Baxter urged over the radio as he and Kitty huddled tightly together to entrap as much body heat as possible.

In the field house Carlos found Dr. Roberto and Jorge studying an aerial photograph secured from the U.S. Forest Service. Painstakingly Dr. Roberto searched Thunderstruck Creek using a four-inch magnifying glass.

"Carlos, come here, get yourself a drink and I will be with you in um momento," he urged. "First, let me check one point further."

"When you finish, let me see if I can locate the Greenbrier outcropping," Jorge offered.

"Oh, yes, that is important. You do that, Jorge," Dr. Roberto continued to scrutinize every inch of the photograph for a clue to where they should go first thing Friday morning.

Dr. Roberto, Carlos and Harry sipped whiskey while Felecia

and Irenea helped Peggy Sue soak her foot in hot-as-she-could-stand saltwater.

Jorge studied the picture. Using the magnifier, he began at the field house and slowly moved along a contour at the base of Hogback across the upper branches of Horseshoe and around to Thunderstruck Creek. Holding the glass still, inches above the huge picture taken in April of '59, Jorge kept his eyes focused upon a meaningful spot.

"Hey, you guys, Dr. Roberto, look here," Jorge urged, placing his finger on the picture beneath the glass.

Dr. Roberto moved in, took the glass and began to study the spot.

"See those white rocks there in the bank along that side of the creek? See it?"

"Yes, I see it, that's limestone, right?"

"Well, I followed around from here and that's just about where the limestone seam should be."

"Has got to be it, don't you think?" Dr. Roberto studied bent over the dining table.

"That has to be it, crops in that small stream there just a little distance from the creek we went up this afternoon," Jorge told him.

"Well, that's where we will go first of things when the morning comes," Dr. Roberto said with renewed purpose.

That decided, they sat with Carlos and Harry and learned of Carlos's plan to return to the cavern to maintain radio contact with C. Baxter and Kitty.

Within the hour, Carlos began his journey alone through the passageways of the cave. He carried two vacuum bottles, one of hot tea and the other filled with steaming chicken noodle soup. The cookies he found were chocolate chip-coconut, a full bag of them. He moved quickly for twenty minutes until he suddenly thought of the ropes.

"I don't have enough rope to reach down there," he thought, remembering that his comrades had each taken their sections of rope for use in case they found another way into the cave. He would have to improvise, this time sending a package down in the stream without a rope attached.

"That should work just as well," he decided and rushed on to resume the vigil.

Dr. Roberto decided that he and Jorge and Harry should rest until morning and then they would return to the mountains. "This time we will find the other entrance, we must find such a place to bring them out."

Peggy Sue informed the other women that the hot soak had relieved the pain. "Wonder if it will heal without going to a doctor?" she asked.

"We should know by morning," Felecia assured. "We'll look at it then to see if there is any more swelling. Just may not get infected, treating it like this."

"Could heal right up," Irenea agreed. "May be clean and you are a healthy person, too, so you may not need to see a doctor."

"Whatever we have to do, we will do," Felecia told her. "Truth is, you should have seen a doctor just as soon as it happened. A big risk not seeing a doctor."

"If it starts throbbing again I'll give it another soaking," Peggy Sue said, encouraged that for the moment there was no pain.

When Carlos picked up the radio and called C. Baxter following the three-and-one-half-hour absence, there was no answer. It was all quiet down in there. Again he called, "C. Baxter, it's me, Carlos. I'm back, come on." Nothing. Again and again he tried but failed to raise a voice on the other end.

What to do except to keep trying, Carlos wondered, beginning to imagine the worst. Something unusual, he thought, for C. Baxter not to be counting the minutes waiting for his return and news from Dr. Roberto. But all of his attempts to contact the Benningtons were futile.

By 2:00 a.m., Carlos had reached a high level of frustration. "I should get the hell out of this place to tell Dr. Roberto of this awful happening," he mumbled, moving back and forth along the swift water like a harried coach at a soccer game.

Additional attempts to reach C. Baxter failed. Carlos continued to prance and reason. Eventually he settled down to sit against the wall by the tunnel and wait.

When Carlos awoke he heard C. Baxter's voice, "Carlos, Carlos, are you there? Come on, Carlos, Carlos have you returned?"

Carlos grabbed the radio, squeezed it to talk and answered, "Here, I'm here, my friends. I was worried."

"We are just fine, Carlos, cold but just fine. Over."

C. Baxter laughed, "I think I fell asleep for a short while. I know Kitty was sleeping and I think I went to sleep, too. Over."

"You must have been sleeping. You made me get some worried, I admit. Over."

"I think it is possible that you were sleeping when I awoke and called for you. I called for you many times. Over."

"You could be right. Let me see, I came back to here at about 12:30 and it is now ten till four. Over."

"In the morning?"

"Yes, of course in the morning. I returned in three hours and thirty minutes and I was trying to get you for most of an hour. Over."

"We are safe here, but eventually we must get out of this dungeon of a place. Over."

"They are trying very hard to find the place. You can be sure of that sir. Over."

"Say, Carlos, did you bring some hot tea?"

"'Oh, yes, sir, I did bring some hot tea and hot soup and a bag of cookies. Okay?"

"Good man, Carlos, my friend. Now how can you get them to us?"

"That can be some problem, sir, for I do not have enough rope. I think I can send them down without the rope."

"Just thinking about the hot tea makes me warm all over, but I hate to think of going in that cold water once more. No, the more I think about it I suggest we wait on the food. Okay?"

"You be the one to decide. I will send it when you tell me to, sir. Okay?"

"Let's just wait. I shiver to think of going back in that blasted water now that our clothes are beginning to feel some dry. We'll wait."

"As they say on the CB, ten four."

"Ten four, good buddy, we'll talk to you later, alligator, get some shuteye and all that kind of stuff, gonna back on out of here and put on a snooze cap myself, over and out."

Carlos smiled, relieved to hear C. Baxter trying to be cheerful even though there was no certain plan that would rescue the father and daughter. Fortunately, for the moment they were safe, awaiting Dr. Roberto to return with a plan to bring them back up over the high waterfalls or out through another hole. "Oh, well, all I can do now is wait." Carlos spoke into the darkness and settled back against the wall.

TWENTY-ONE

It was old hat for Rena and Rachel to go underground but Mary Martha found it more difficult than any of her previous policewoman duties. Yet she had to face up to it. She must go in to be there if they should find her real father, dead or alive.

Once inside, Mary Martha quickly adjusted to the magnificent fairyland surroundings. They used both lights to survey the majestic calcite formations high on the ceiling and along the walls of the huge chamber.

"Now I understand what Momma described in her letter," Mary Martha thought. "No wonder Cloy brought her in here. No wonder he liked this place. My God, what a beautiful place, like something no one around here has ever seen," she continued, overwhelmed by the awesome sight.

Off to the right in the distance she could hear the roar of water falling. "Sounds like Blackwater Falls," Mary Martha said, pointing her long flashlight toward the dark area.

"Has to be a waterfall," Rachel agreed. "Let's move on over that way and take a look."

Soon they could see it. "Fantastic, absolutely fantastic," Rena exclaimed. "Did you ever?" She gasped, moving out ahead of the others. Suddenly she felt the difference on the bottom of her thick-soled shoes. It was a film of slick clay on the floor as they went toward the falls. A vaporizing spray generated from the cascading underground creek. They could feel it wetting the hair.

"A fine mist similar to the air coming in off Curtiss Bay," Mary Martha thought, remembering her years on the Baltimore waterfront.

"Watch your step, you all," Rachel cautioned, stopping in her tracks until Mary Martha and Rena joined her.

Now they would be more careful, inching along in short well-planted steps. For the moment they directed their lights to the floor, forgetting about the waterfalls.

"Look, look, here's tracks," Rachel said. "Someone's been in here. Look at the tracks."

"Tracks?" Rena looked and was quickly convinced. "I'll be, real tracks."

Mary Martha squatted down to look and directed her light along the trail left by shoe prints in the mud.

It was the moment for Mary Martha to take charge. She dropped to her knees and scooted along studying each track. Then she saw the dog tracks. "Cloy's dog," she thought, "it's Cloy's dog tracks and that's Cloy's tracks, has to be."

"What on earth are you doing?" Rena asked as she and Rachel watched their friend study the signs in the mud leading toward the edge.

"Hey, look here, here's dog tracks, too." Mary Martha pointed, inviting them to come take a look.

"Whatta you make of it? Think it's been Cloy?" Rachel inquired, squatting beside Mary Martha and studying her face instead of the tracks.

"I'm sure it's been Cloy and oh, God, the tracks go right over there to the edge." Mary Martha exclaimed and moved three shuffles on in that direction.

Impulsively she fell forward onto her elbows, holding the long flashlight in her right hand. "You all hold on to my feet and I'll ease on out there where I can look down over the edge."

Slowly she crawled on her belly in the slick slime, Rena gripping her right foot and Rachel the left. "Come on, let me go on out here to where I can see. I'm not gonna fall in down here on my belly."

Inch by slow inch she progressed shining her light off into the distance until the beam hit the lake of rippling water. She slid forward another two feet and reported, "Look here, all this fresh dirt dug up. The dog's been digging. Dug a ditch here. See here." She showed holding her light on to the foot-deep cut in the edge of the bank.

"Do you suppose?" Rachel asked and was interrupted by Mary Martha.

"Yes, I know what you're thinking and that's what must have happened. Cloy's dog was here and dug this place."

"But do you suppose he?"

Again Mary Martha excitedly took over. "Hold me tight and I'll go out just a little more where I can see down. See over there, what a lake, must drop off here into the lake."

Carefully she pushed on her breast and now she could look over the bank which dropped straight down for about ten feet onto a ledge at the edge of the water. Her light came directly onto Cloy, his body curled into a letter C lying on his left side.

"Hold me tight and please don't let me go," she yelled and then, as if she had given up, she said, "Cloy's down there, right down here a few feet below me on the rocks."

"Is he dead?" Rachel asked.

"I can't tell."

"Can't you see if he's breathing?" Rena wondered.

"I can't tell from here," she said hiding the fact that her eyes were clouded with tears preventing her from seeing except in a blur as if trying to look at a road sign through bifocals.

Suddenly Mary Martha yelled to Cloy. "Hey Mr. Clay! Hey! Can you hear me?" But his body lay rigid, no sign of life.

"Listen, pull me back so I can get up," she told them.

Back on her feet, Mary Martha led them to the dry floor where they sat down to think about what to do and how to do it.

It was 8:50 a.m., Rachel reported, as Mary Martha proposed that one of them should hurry back to the house and call the fire department. Rena volunteered to go and Mary Martha gave her the jeep keys and then spelled out instructions.

"Tell them to get the funeral home to send the ambulance up to where we parked the jeep. You better wait for them at the forks of the road at Shaffertown. Oh, yes, better tell them we're gonna need a ladder, ropes, oxygen and a litter."

"What's a litter?" Rena asked.

"A stretcher, you know, one you can strap a person onto, carry them out of a place like this and down through the woods."

"We don't know if he's alive," Rachel stated, wondering about the preparations being made by Mary Martha.

"Let's just assume that he is until we know better. That way when they come we can be prepared."

"Okay, that's it then? I'll go as fast as I can but you'll have to remember it's gonna take several hours to get them up here with me having to go all the way back and call them and all," Rena reminded them as all three walked toward the light shining through the small exit.

Mary Martha and Rachel exited the cavern behind Rena,

stepping into the filtered sunlight beneath the towering oaks, sugar maples, and poplar trees. Rena hurried off downstream, traversing the rocks and water somewhat faster than when she came.

"Look at you," Rachel said to Mary Martha. "What a mess you are."

"Oh, my goodness, I am covered with mud." Then she thoroughly washed her hands in the creek. "I've gotta go use the bathroom," she told Rachel, feigning an excuse to walk up the steep sloping hill opposite the cave.

"What you going so far for, no men around?" Rachel called.

"Gotta get up away from the creek. I don't want to pollute the water." Mary Martha fibbed. Up out of sight, she soon approached a level spot. "Just like Momma described. Here's where I was made," she thought. "Right here and the sun is shining in just like she said it was that day forty-seven years ago."

A strange feeling grasped her entire body as she thought of what happened between her mother and Cloy, and suddenly she did have a genuine urge to use the toilet. Rather than spoil the spot where the youthful couple made love, she moved out around the hill, trampled down the weeds, undid her belt and zipper, dropped her jeans, pushed down her snug-fitting panties and squatted, urinating on the dry leaves.

Within ten minutes she joined Rachel by the creek. Mary Martha took out the jug of hot coffee, poured the cap full and handed it to Rachel. They shared the hot black coffee, neither talking nor sharing their thoughts.

Soon Mary Martha urged that they go back inside, instinctively wanting to be near her father. Even though she knew that for the moment there was nothing she could do, she was compelled to be in where he was.

This time they explored along the left side of the great room until they could see the waterfalls. Mary Martha directed her light up beyond the lip of the falls where the beam hit another high ceiling, revealing a huge room.

"Listen, did you hear that?" Rachel asked. "Listen now real good."

They both heard the echoing yell. "Up here, we're up here," the voice resounded amid the roar of the water hitting into the lake below.

Repeatedly the yell came. It was a man's voice, they were sure.

"That can't be Cloy," Mary Martha reasoned.

"No, he's back over here to the right. He's not that far away," Rachel said.

"I better answer, don't you think?" Mary Martha suggested and then she hollered at the top of her voice, "Where are you?" and listened for a reply.

"Up here, we're up here," they heard. "I see your light."

Now they could see another light against the ceiling above the falls.

"I see you, I see your light," Mary Martha yelled and listened to the echo bouncing from wall to wall around the entire open area.

Twenty minutes downstream Rena ran head on into three strange men wearing miner's caps with lamps. Dr. Roberto politely greeted her and listened as she told of her urgent trip to get help.

"It is possible that we can help," Dr. Roberto offered. "Do you think so?"

"Yes, I believe so, but do you think I should go on to call for the ambulance?" Rena asked.

"I suggest we go to see first and then we can determine if we need other assistance."

Rena led Dr. Roberto, Jorge and Harry back up the creek and into the cave. En route she realized that these must be the men from the field house.

Inside the cave Rena started to tell Mary Martha about this turn of events when Dr. Roberto took over.

"I am Dr. Roberto Drews Vieira dos Santos and this is Jorge Gerhardt and Harry Asserman. We are temporarily living at the old Weidimeyer house. Your friend here explained that the missing old gentleman is in here."

"Yes, sir, he is in here. I am Mary Martha Cosner and my friends are Rena whom you have already met and this is Rachel. We have been looking for Mr. Clay. We live down in Leadmine Village."

"Well, let us see if we can assist."

"It is very slick so you must be careful to not slide over the bank," Mary Martha told him.

"Jorge, you and Harry can hold me with the rope and I will attempt to go to him."

Quickly they snapped a rope to Dr. Roberto's belt. Mary Martha pointed to the spot. Dr. Roberto went forward toward the bank while Jorge and Harry anchored the rope. They suggested that the women should also grasp the rope to assist in the rescue.

"He is right straight down from where you are. It is about ten feet down there," Mary Martha informed.

"I see now. Wait please until I attach the rope to my belt in front so that I can face the wall." Dr. Roberto said preparing to make the descent.

Carefully the Brazilian made his way, selecting protruding rocks to secure his shoes. Soon the rope was creased in the mud on the edge of the bank. Gradually they let him down until the line became loose.

"I am down now. You can let loose of the rope." Dr. Roberto yelled from beside the water where Cloy Clay lay lifeless on the rocks.

It was totally quiet in the cave except for the windy sound of the water pouring into the lake for what seemed a long time until Dr. Roberto yelled. "He is living. He has a pulsebeat. Yes, he is still alive!"

The women all breathed more freely but Mary Martha was ecstatic "Oh, can you?" she started, then "Can I help in any way?" "Can I come down there where you are?"

"I think so, if you wish. Maybe we can determine some more about him. Help her down, Jorge, you and Harry, put a rope on her and I will help her down."

Mary Martha retrieved her tote bag and soon was let down over the bank into Dr. Roberto's arms, steadying her to prevent her from slipping into the lake. The rocks were slick as ice from the continual spray coming from the falls.

Immediately she slid her left arm beneath Cloy's neck and lifted his bare head off of the muddy rocks. She felt his bearded face and gently rubbed it and began whispering to him, "Mr. Clay, can you hear me, Mr. Clay?"

Dr. Roberto knelt beside Cloy and began to rub the old gentleman's muddy hand, gently squeezing it, feeling for life.

Slowly Cloy's eyes opened then blinked shut in the blinding light.

"Oh, you poor man," Mary Martha said softly. Then she turned to Dr. Roberto and asked that he take some things from the bag. "Get the blanket and spread it over him. Then let's get some of the other things so we can give him some nourishment."

"Maam, I have some whiskey. It would be the right thing if we can give a sip of whiskey for energy."

"Yes, let's do that. There is a spoon in my bag and some milk and syrup and other things."

Dr. Roberto gave her the soup spoon and poured it half full of whiskey. Gently Mary Martha lifted Cloy's head higher and pressed the spoon to his closed lips. Dr. Roberto assisted to pry the weakened man's dry lips apart to permit the whiskey to enter. The impact of the strong spirits made Cloy squirm and moan.

Next Dr. Roberto cut two holes in the can of milk and poured the spoon half full and added some maple syrup. Mary Martha eased this into Cloy's lips, draining the contents into his toothless mouth. Then they waited.

Old Mr. Clay responded to the TLC administered by his daughter. Mary Martha held him as a mother caring for an infant. She talked to him softly asking him if he had any pain, was he hurt, and did he want more food. Cloy seemed to understand her but his answers were not informative.

She asked Dr. Roberto for more milk and syrup and Cloy licked his lips, appearing to like the taste of it. They gave him three more spoons of it.

"Think he should have a cracker now?" Mary Martha asked Dr. Roberto.

"I think maybe not yet," he answered. "Just let him rest a while and we will then give him some more of the liquid."

Now Cloy's eyes remained open, he appeared conscious, responding to the food and Mary Martha's nursing.

Dr. Roberto, realizing that Cloy was mending, suggested that Mary Martha continue the care and he would temporarily depart to join the others. She urged him to go, suggesting that it would be important that they determine how to remove Mr. Clay from the ledge and take him to the hospital.

Dr. Roberto scaled the cliff aided by the rope and the four rescuers pulling him back to the safe, dry area above.

"The girls here told us they heard someone calling off in the distance over there," Jorge told Dr. Roberto.

"Of course, it has to be C. Baxter and Kitty," he told them. "We saw their light up there on the ceiling, way up in there."

The response came quickly. All of them heard the man hollering. "Up here, we're up here!" It echoed around the walls amid the roaring waterfalls.

"We have found them," Dr. Roberto shouted.

"We can rescue them from here," Jorge urged.

"Of course. We should be able to do it from here some much better than the other way," Dr. Roberto agreed, walking toward the far end of the hall. When he neared the end of the room beside the falls he looked up, his light striking the glistening wall. He saw exactly what they had searched so hard to find. He was certain that the cluster up near where the top arched and along the roof were bats taking their daytime sleep.

"I must not dare to mention this to the women or anyone other than our party," he thought. "We can determine if it is our precious *virginianus* species when the others are not here."

He was too close to the waterfalls to hear C. Baxter hollering for help. But he could see that they should be able to apply their experience in rappelling and spelunking to bring their comrades out safely.

Back with the others, Dr. Roberto assured Jorge and Harry that they could perform the rescue before the day was out. "We can do it ourselves, I am sure."

"That is important, sir," Jorge agreed. "We do have the necessary equipment in the Land Rover."

"I agree," Harry said. "We can do it, not easily, but we can do it."

"The lake is up there where they are," Dr. Roberto concluded. "A lake up there and a lake down here," Jorge commented, looking relieved at what they had found.

The task ahead would require a greater test than any of the party had previously experienced. Their confidence in their ability to do what was necessary was bolstered by the relief they felt in finding this new entrance to the long, winding limestone cavern.

What they did not yet know was that this discovery would unveil the mystery surrounding a legend perpetuated by the local people. It began that first year when John Minear settled St. George and built the fort to provide refuge from the warring Indians who used the area for a hunting ground.

TWENTY-TWO

If haste makes waste it also can cause neglect, and Rachel was guilty. When she and Jorge went to the field house to secure support for the double rescue operation, she failed to call Amos and Ralph. She called the Parsons volunteer fire department and suggested they bring five or six men plus the ambulance but not once did she think of calling Cloy's nearest friends. Right now she felt buoyed by the presence of the three knowledgeable strangers she met in the woods.

This was the first day since Cloy disappeared that Ralph and Amos had not met to worry and wonder what to do about it.

In the field house Jorge introduced Rachel to Felecia, Irenea and Peggy Sue. He told them of the discovery and the plans to initiate the rescue.

"What about Carlos?" Felecia asked. "How we going to get word to him?"

"A very good question," Jorge acknowledged. "But I think we can reach him on the radio as soon as we make better contact with C. Baxter. Then he can come out."

"In that case we are going back with you," Irenea suggested, informing him Peggy Sue continued to improve without any sign of infection.

"We must be there with you," Felecia insisted. "This is what we need to do and we surely can be of help, too."

Rachel went back to the phone to call Alice at the charcoal plant. "We did it, we found old Mr. Clay," she announced and listened to Alice yell for all in her office to hear. "They found him, they found Cloy Clay!"

"For heaven's sake, don't tell everybody. We'll have the whole county in an uproar."

"Is he dead?" Alice asked.

"No, no, he's still alive up there in a cave," Rachel told her.

"Listen, dear, I've gotta go, we have to get back up there and get him out and to the hospital."

"Listen, is he bad? Has to be bad off after all this time?" Alice questioned, tying Rachel to the phone.

"He is bad, I think. He's barely alive, the way it sounds to me. Now I didn't see him down in there but Mary Martha is with him and he's alive. That's all I can say."

"What about a doctor, you callin' Dr. Samuelson? Don't you think you'd better get him up there?"

"I wasn't gonna call him, just the fire department and the ambulance. They're callin' the ambulance."

"I'm gonna call him, see if he can go with the ambulance."

"They'd be on their way by now, I bet. Never thought about the doctor. Mary Martha didn't say anything about that."

"You go on. I'll call the doctor, maybe he can catch 'em."

"Well, I'll be up here at Shaffertown at the forks of the road waitin'."

"See you later when you get up here to town. You all will be comin' up here, won't you?"

"I don't know, we'll just have to see, depends a lot on how long it takes and all. Gotta work tonight, you know."

"See you then, bye," Alice ended and immediately dialed Dr. Samuelson's office.

Rachel left the field house and walked down the lane to the blacktop road to wait. Jorge collected appropriate gear from the Land Rover. There would be enough items to require three people to carry it all—rock hooks, spikes, hammer, all the rope and a six-foot inflatable rubber raft.

It was noon when Jorge, Felecia and Irenea reached the cave and went inside. Dr. Roberto suggested it best to complete the removal of Cloy before they attempted to reach C. Baxter and Kitty.

"Why do we have to wait? Help is coming for him, but no one is helping our people," Felecia said, looking her husband in the eye as if accusing him of being foolish.

"There are good reasons, dear," he said, not wanting to talk so much about the strategy in the presence of Rena.

"I assume you know what you are doing," Felecia relented not too happily.

First to arrive at the junction where Alice waited in the noonday August sun was Dr. Ben Samuelson in his International Scout, a four-wheeler he used to traverse the hills and hollows, hunting and fishing when he could find the time.

It was only a short wait longer until the fire department's red emergency wagon and the funeral home's gray ambulance arrived. In addition to the doctor there were eight other men.

Rachel rode with Dr. Samuelson and led them to the end of the lane where they parked end-to-end behind Mary Martha's jeep.

By ten till one they reached the cave, the firemen carrying a litter and lights and Dr. Samuelson toting his black satchel.

The crowd inside now multiplied until there were sixteen gathered in the big room plus Mary Martha and Cloy below.

Dr. Roberto, having surveyed the situation, proceeded to organize the operation. He suggested that first the doctor should be lowered to Cloy's side to evaluate his condition prior to any attempts to move him.

Jorge and Harry lowered Dr. Roberto to Cloy and then assisted Dr. Samuelson. Dr. Roberto helped to steady his descent.

The examination required several minutes with Dr. Samuelson administering one injection to relieve the pain he said he was certain was present.

"There are some broken bones, severe bruises and his general state is guarded," Dr. Samuelson informed Mary Martha. "You have done the very best you could have under the circumstances."

The mud-slick floor in the vicinity of where Cloy lay, down over the cliff, prevented the firemen from moving confidently to bring him out. Also, they wore no lamps, thus they were continually in their own shadows from the other lights. In spite of the obstacles Cloy was strapped on to the stretcher and gently lifted up to the main room where the floor appeared dry and calcite granules crunched beneath the heavy shoes.

It took a bit of clever maneuvering to thread the body on the stretcher through the bunghole exit of the cavern but that too was accomplished by the careful firemen.

Once, outside, Dr. Samuelson asked the litter bearers to wait a moment. He wanted to look at Cloy in the daylight. He observed Cloy's emaciated corpse-like condition—cornstarch skin, sunken eyes and hollow jaws.

Cloy opened his eyes, looked straight up and mumbled. Mary Martha did not understand the old man's attempt to communicate. She leaned closely to his face and said softly, "Mr. Clay, what is it you want to tell me?"

The frail old man slowly closed his eyes and Mary Martha imagined a gentle toothless smile forming on her biological father's face. But the words did not come again. Apparently, the weak, frail man had no strength and his mind would not function even to repeat what he had tried to say just moments before.

Dr. Roberto and Jorge followed the crowd out of the cave and stood aside, watching as the doctor listened with the stethoscope to Cloy's faint, irregular heartbeat. The professional's stoic face told Mary Martha that Cloy was even worse than she had believed when she held him for so very long down in there beside the lake.

It was time to go, Dr. Samuelson told them. "We must get him to the hospital. He is a very, very weak man. Let's go."

The women, Dr. Samuelson, the firemen and ambulance attendants all began the long rock-littered walk down Thunderstruck Creek.

TWENTY-THREE

This time the ambulance passed Amos's house more slowly than before, lights flashing and siren wailing, but Amos dared not think that Cloy could be in it and alive. He and Ralph sat on the porch, protected from the sun, following another of Ruby's hot midday dinners.

Mary Martha rode with Cloy, hovering over him like you'd expect a daughter to do. But Mary Martha would have insisted upon riding with any old man teetering between death and life, just in case there was something she could do. And truth was, she knew from extensive training and firsthand experiences a great deal more than the accompanying medical technician.

Dr. Samuelson followed the ambulance after warning the driver to cool it on this trip. "No need to rush. A few minutes aren't gonna make any difference now. And you know that damned one lane of blacktop and a million blind curves between here and town make it ideal for a head-on. Been enough of them up this way."

The youthful driver did hold it down but at 35 mph around the curves on the Leadmine road made for a rough ride to Parsons. The EMT and Mary Martha held on and watched Cloy. Cloy's head rolled back and forth with the curves.

"My goodness, lady, you sure did get muddy up there," the medic said as he took a good look at Mary Martha.

This caused Mary Martha to make a close survey of herself. The long sleeved plaid-checked shirt was crusted over her breasts; the legs of her jeans cracked and flaked with the dry gray clay.

"Boy! You sure are right. You'd think I'd been drug through a mud hole, wouldn't you?" Mary Martha smiled.

That ended their conversation as they wrestled with the road and Mary Martha again forgot about herself and began to think of the ordeal endured by Mr. Clay. "What a way for the poor old fellow to end up, the way he must have enjoyed going in that lovely place. It's such a shame," she thought.

About three miles down the road Mary Martha laid her head onto Cloy's face to listen and feel for breath. There was none. "Oh, my God," she yelled. "We've gotta do something. He's dying."

"Stop! Stop the vehicle," the medic called to the driver. "Doc Samuelson is right behind us. We'll get him."

Mary Martha knew Cloy couldn't wait even for the doctor. She must try to breathe life into her dying father. She grabbed Cloy's wrinkled, whisker-covered lips and squeezed them together as though she were gathering the top of a lunch bag for a bag-bursting prank; she then pushed her lips over the pucker and began to blow. Step by step, as she was taught and as she had practiced at least thirty previous times, she literally put the breath of life into her father's frail body.

Dr. Samuelson climbed aboard, injected Cloy's arm and urged Mary Martha to continue. He jerked Cloy's shirt open and slapped the stethoscope onto the sunken chest.

"Oh, yes, now you're doing it. Yes, siree, we've got a heartbeat now." Dr. Samuelson said encouraging her. "Yeah, we've got a faint one but it's steady. Put him on oxygen. I think that'll see him through till we get to the hospital. But be sure if he gets worse be sure to stop." He shook his head as he looked at Mary Martha, plastered with mud, "You sure did get messed up up there in that cave. Good bath would do you a lot of good."

TWENTY-FOUR

Now the spelunkers went into action. Dr. Roberto and Jorge hurried back inside, pleased that no issue was made regarding the others who were stranded up over the falls and out of sight. Nor had they revealed their mission in the cavern—to find the habitat of the brown big-eared bat.

The four others gathered around Dr. Roberto to hear his plan of attack. He said enthusiastically, "They were some very nice people, the capabaxia's. We will now be able to talk with them more about the area. That Mary Martha seemed so much a quality person. She knows much about the area."

"Possibly we can visit the old gentleman in the hospital," Felecia said encouragingly.

"Yes, I agree," Dr. Roberto said. "But now we must scale the wall beside the waterfall. That will take us to where C. Baxter and Kitty are waiting for us."

The rescue operation would require skills they had practiced in other caves and on the outside, too. Jorge and Harry previously had scaled the Nelson Rocks across the mountain in Pendleton County. That limestone country near Germany Valley and Seneca Rocks also was a prime area for bats. What they learned, however, was that the *Plecotus townsendii virginianus* had long since retreated to more remote locations. This they hoped was one of those places where humans did not frequent and where the hardwood timber provided the bats an umbrella of protection and insect population suited to their particular appetites.

Jorge volunteered to attempt the climb after it was decided that the logical approach would be to go down to where Cloy fell and skirt around the lake to the wall.

First, they tied the rope to a huge calcite post some fifty feet from the edge of the bank. This gave them a permanent anchor and each was able to scale down over the cliff after coupling two rope sections. Next they took careful steps along the water's edge to the wall where they encountered a profusion of spray. Once there it was apparent that one could go around the sheet of water and climb upwards on the jagged rocks behind the falls.

Jorge began the ascent, picking and choosing where to grasp with his hands and to secure the toes of his heavy shoes. His own light plus Dr. Roberto's provided back lighting to the water resulting in a picturesque scene visible to the women up in the great hall.

Slowly Jorge climbed to the upper limit where he encountered the water pouring over the lip of the lake. It was necessary for him to edge left and out from beneath the water. His shoulders and back were gradually being soaked by grape-size drops and rope-like streams of water leaking from the overflow.

The most difficult task lay above his head—how to draw his manly frame up, around and over the rim. To do this he would have to use the rope onto which he had snapped the rock hook. Now some forty feet above the foaming water Jorge prepared to snag the rocks or whatever might hold his entire weight, permitting him to pull up over the top.

This presented a high level of risk. For if he should slip without the rope being attached it would surely mean injuries and possibly death from the free falling down over the jagged rocks into the lake.

Jorge studied his precarious position and decided to take some precautions. First, he drove a twelve-inch spike into a crack in the rocks just above his head leaving three inches on to which he looped his rope and drew the slipknot tight. He gripped the rope in one hand, feeling certain this would hold him should he slip and fall. Next he attempted to loop the coil of rope with a sharp rock hook attached up and over the rim. The swift water thwarted his try and washed it back over thirty feet below against the rocks.

Again he gathered the rope into a coil and threw and again it came swishing back down. This time Jorge edged left, trying desperately to clear the rushing water, heaved with all his might and the hook caught something.

For a moment Jorge had to rest. The three attempts plus the climb had sapped his energy.

There was too much noise from the water falling into the lake for Jorge to try talking with Dr. Roberto and Harry, who anxiously watched his struggle. It was a painful experience for them, too. They leaned, crouched, climbed and moaned at Jorge's every move.

Soon Jorge felt ready to move on upward. He was sure he could do it if the hook was securely snagged. From here he would have to depend upon the rope looped between his legs and snapped to his belt. Inch by inch he pulled, aided by his toes on the rocks. Finally there was no way to avoid the water which rushed over his right shoulder. Now he could see over the top, his eyes level with the glistening water. Also he could hear C. Baxter's repeated calls off to his right.

"Over here, over here," Mr. Baxter called, swinging the light back and forth like a railroad switchman in a freight train yard.

Hanging there, Jorge called back enthusiastically, "It's me, Jorge, I'm coming."

He prepared to go the last four feet up over and into the lake. "If that thing holds, I'll be coming," Jorge said aloud, talking to himself, preparing to give it all he had. But progress was slow, slick, wet and dangerous going, gaining six inches and falling back four. Yet the wet rope held, his hands did not slip and his muscular arms gradually pulled him for his feet no longer found the ledge. Breast first in the rushing water, Jorge was encouraged to see that the crest on the lip of the falls measured only three to four inches. He steadied his weight with his right hand on the rope. With the left he grabbed the rocks on the edge and found a place to grip. This provided a secure hold to support a heave that lifted him up on to the edge on his belly. He drew his right leg up and brought his knee on top of the rim rock.

When C. Baxter saw that Jorge was up, some three hundred feet from where he and Kitty waited, he called to Carlos on the radio, "They're here. Jorge is now up in the lake. Over."

"Do you think I should stay here until he comes to the radio where I can then talk to him? Over." Carlos said anxiously? He was undecided what to do without further word on how the rescue was to proceed.

"I suggest you wait," C. Baxter told him. "Jorge will be here soon. Over."

"Keep me informed and let me talk to Jorge when he comes to you. Over." Carlos patiently urged.

"Roger, Carlos, over and out." C. Baxter signed off for the moment.

Jorge sat on the edge, his feet dangling down in the deep water, pondering his next move. Finally he hollered loudly to the women over in the lower great hall. "Get the raft and attach a rope to it and drop it down over here to Dr. Roberto." His voice echoed in the vast, open cavern.

Apparently they understood for he could see them go into action. Jorge attached his other fifty-foot section of rope to the anchored section and dropped enough of it down along the side of the waterfalls to reach where Dr. Roberto and Harry waited.

It took about ten minutes, taking frequent rests to hand over hand pull the heavy package up around the edge of the water to the lake. Carefully he unwrapped the raft and tripped the inflater which gradually blew up the kit into an orange six-foot boat. Now came the tricky part of the entire operation—avoiding the swift current that could sweep the vessel and its occupants over the falls, plunging them more than fifty feet to the lake below.

It took a bit of doing to loosen the hook snagged to a jagged edge in the bottom of the deep water. Once accomplished Jorge heaved the rope twenty feet out along the left side of the lake wall. He watched it disappear, waited for it to sink to the floor and pulled. Hand over hand he retrieved the line until the hook caught. This provided the necessary security for Jorge to belly over and into the raft. Then he pulled the tiny craft out into the quiet body of the lake. He pulled up the hook anchor and threw it and the attached rope out to the tiny ledge where it lay free of the water. This left the tail in the wash over the falls.

Jorge gingerly maneuvered his lean frame around in the flimsy boat, bringing his back to rest against the front edge. He could propel himself by rapidly paddling with his cold hands. Backwards he sailed to where C. Baxter and Kitty stood on the ledge directing the miner's lamp out in Jorge's direction.

The anxious father and daughter grabbed the raft and steadied it for Jorge to come ashore. They hugged and patted the Brazilian in the custom of his people when greeting friends following long absences.

"You found a new entrance," C. Baxter said eagerly.

"Yes, we found it with a bit of help from some local people," Jorge said, stopping short of giving details.

"Our wait seemed a long time but thank God we are safe now," C. Baxter said, sounding grateful and religious.

"Yes, we are all thankful that you are safe. Are you completely well?" Jorge directed his comment to Kitty who looked bewildered, not speaking or sharing her father's excited and grateful attitude.

"I'm okay, I guess," she said, calmly hinting of self-pity. "Sure, she's okay," said her father hugging her with his left arm. "We're on top of the world now that you're here to get us out of here."

"Right," Jorge said smiling through gritting teeth, knowing the realities of where they were. He knew that skills gained through numerous caving experiences greatly enhanced their chance of succeeding. On the other hand, this was their first attempt at fighting a waterfall of the height and spill of this one.

"What about Carlos?" Jorge suddenly asked. Until now they had forgotten him waiting alone up beyond the second high falls.

"Oh, yes, Carlos. We must call to him," C. Baxter said. He grabbed the radio, gripped and called, "Carlos, Jorge is here with us. Over."

"Bless the Mother Mary, they found it," Carlos said profoundly. "The Lord is blessing us. It is better than I even dreamed. Over."

"Yes, you did sleep, Carlos, I tried some times to call you when you must have been dreaming. Over," C. Baxter explained.

"Only for some moments I slept. Please now let me talk to Jorge."

Jorge took the radio and listened as Carlos continued, "Jorge, you will be able now to take them out from where you are? Over."

"Roger, Carlos, we can do it from here. It will take some time to go down over the falls but we can do that fine. Are you still in good shape?"

"Oh, yes, I am doing fine, but I want some very much to see the daylight again, over."

"Okay, Carlos, I think it is time for you to return to the field house and have a good cold drink for me. You will be there long before we arrive even if we are successful to get outside. It is going to take us a while and then the walk back to the field house from here will require much of two hours. Carlos, you should go now to see some sunshine. Over."

"I'm departing this moment."

Jorge helped Kitty into the raft, a task like walking on a water bed. He said he would take her to the far side of the lake above the spillway. Again he paddled the craft with his cold cupped hands. Kitty was assisted onto the ledge by the water to wait for the return trip bringing her father.

This was the easier part of the rescue attempt. From here, about thirty feet from where the water poured over the lip like beer from a pitcher, Jorge had to make careful preparations. One by one, Kitty and C. Baxter would have to rappel down the falls and wall to the other lake where Dr. Roberto and Harry waited.

Kitty will go first, Jorge first thought, then quickly changed his mind. "Kitty, I suggest that your father make the trip down first. He is some more experienced at rappelling such a high wall."

"I'm experienced but never in a waterfall," C. Baxter said, thinking and recalling. "Well, yes, I guess I had some experience in that falls up there when you all left me dangling. Man, I thought I was a goner, thought I'd drown. Honest to God, water went in up here at the collar and down into my boots to the end of my boots. I'm telling you that was some experience. You mean I'm gonna be doin' that all over again?"

"I think so," Jorge replied, half smiling. "I think it will be some the same, but down here I believe you will some easier be able to get under the water."

"Whatever it takes, we've gotta get out of here, right?" said C. Baxter.

"Right," Jorge agreed and then began helping C. Baxter to prepare for going over the falls.

Everything worked as planned until C. Baxter reached the lip, then about everything happened that could happen. Only God knows why the hook tore loose, but it did.

C. Baxter had floated and maneuvered along the edge, steadied by the rocks jetting from the wall. This close to the falls the wall went straight into the water leaving no ledge as there was where the Baxters had found refuge.

There on the lip, balanced on his belly, Mr. Bennington could see Dr. Roberto's light down and off to his right. To his left and straight out was a scary total darkness. He dared not panic. "Hell, this is why we do this kind of thing, crawling around in slimy caves, is to get this very kind of thrill and to test our skill," he said aloud, boosting his determination to go on and to settle his sudden flareup of nerves. He was unusually jumpy and felt guilty for feeling that way.

It was time to go. The water poured swiftly around his heavily clothed body. Fortunately, this time he would not have to swim. Rappelling down the wall beneath and beside the river of water would keep him clear of the lake below.

C. Baxter carefully turned on the slick rock lip of the giant bowl and tried to hoist himself with his hands to a sitting position, his back to the dark open area above the lower lake, his front facing the expanse of water where he and Kitty had met their waterloo. His right hand slipped on the tricky slick rock surface, throwing him onto his right rib cage. With his left hand C. Baxter grabbed the rope, which from the beginning was attached to the heavy leather belt, and yanked it to stop his sure fall off the rim to the deep below.

Somehow, known only to God, the hook became dislodged and C. Baxter's lifeline rope was free in the water. Sure as the stars shine in the heavens and the rain falls on St. George, he slid backwards and plunged headlong over the spillway, swept by the rushing water into awesome darkness. It all happened so quickly there was not time to see his life flash before him or to do anything to prevent the fall or assist the landing. It was sudden and sure and he dropped like a floating log until the hook caught on the rim rock. That stopped the fall and C. Baxter's belly felt the awful impact from the lifesaving belt.

For what seemed a half hour but was in reality only ten seconds C. Baxter's body was suspended, dancing on the surface of the great curve of water dumping into the lake. Quickly he broke through and swung back against the jagged rocks behind the water.

Jorge sat helpless in the boat. He saw what had happened but it had occurred so quickly there was nothing he could do to help. He couldn't even tell if the rope had caught or if C. Baxter had fallen directly to his death. He knew that his fallen companion could have hit rocks at the foot of the falls and been crushed like an egg falling from the countertop to the kitchen floor.

Kitty had failed to see or to realize the possible tragedy. Realizing this, Jorge was careful to not excite her about it. He was, however, plenty worried.

C. Baxter thought he might have wet his pants from the

scare. Wet as he already was, it didn't matter much. Fortunately, he was not hurt, just scared as hell. Now he could get his bearings and go on down. That was easy. It took only five minutes to join Dr. Roberto and Harry at lakeside.

"You are safe, old boy. How about that?" Dr. Roberto said eagerly, hugging C. Baxter and inquiring, "How is Kitty?"

"She is just fine, only tired and a bit scared, but fine," C. Baxter assured him. "Now Jorge can help her to come down. But God, I do hope so much that the rope holds better than it did for me."

Jorge proceeded to do what he had to do. He prepared another rope. This time he drove a spike into the solid wall to serve as the anchor. He pulled Kitty into the raft. Slowly he allowed them to float along the edge to the spillway taking care to avoid dumping over the lip by carefully gauging their drift with the anchored rope.

This time he personally managed Kitty's drop over the falls by controlling the rope. He released it inch by inch through his crotch and over the rimrock until she was safely below with the others.

Next Jorge lowered the inflated raft with Kitty's rope. C. Baxter retrieved it. He then stuck the CB radio into a huge pants pocket and slid over the rim feet first on his belly. Five minutes later he too was back down by the lake with Dr. Roberto and the others.

TWENTY-FIVE

Carlos climbed the ramp into the field house, feeling dirty as he imagined mangy dogs felt, from the trips and the long hours of waiting in the cavern. He yelled, "Anybody here?" and listened, feeling certain there was.

From down the hall came Peggy Sue's voice. "I'm still here, Carlos. The others are gone, but I'm here."

"Peggy Sue, you all right?"

"I'm okay I guess, well as can be expected," she answered, a bit low key, not really sure of how she felt, propped up on her mattress reading.

"I'll be on downstairs," Carlos called, trying to avoid being seen as scroungy and dirty as he felt.

"Carlos, when you can I want you to look at my foot," Peggy Sue said, sounding as if she needed his judgment regarding the progress of her nail puncture injury.

"I will return um momento, maam. Just a short time."

"No hurry," Peggy Sue said, hinting every so slightly that she wished that he would come see her now.

Carlos went straight to the large wall cabinet in which the scotch was kept. He took an open bottle to the table, got a glass and ice and poured a hefty drink. He sipped and the ice tinkled in the full glass as he went out to the back porch. He grabbed the washpan from the nail on the wall and stepped off the porch to the stream running from the cavern out through the springhouse. Back on the porch he parked the pan on the table and went back inside for a towel, washcloth and soap.

When Carlos returned to the porch he stripped out of his heavy shoes and jumpsuit and peeled off his shirt and began to lather up from head to waist. It was cold water, even in the summertime, but Carlos relished it as though he were a dusty robin splashing in a patio birdbath.

He emptied the first pan of soapy water into the weeds and

rinsed the pan in the stream before filling it again to rinse the upper half of his muscular, hairy-chested body.

Now the lower half had to be washed, right there before the birds and the bees and butterflies and magpies. What the hell, he thought, the porch faced the hill and nowhere else. Carlos felt isolated enough to drop his pants and long johns on the floor. He stepped up to the table close to the washpan and lathered the soap between both hands. This he spread all over his penis and scrotum and thick black pubic hair. He lathered the cloth and scrubbed the entire private area between his legs and along the crack. Vigorously he scrubbed, and rinsed and wiped downward until he was clean between every toe and the soles of his feet. Then he quickly stepped off the porch into the hot sunshine for a drydown.

So eager was Carlos to get a bath that he completely forgot to bring clean underwear. In fact he needed all clean clothes. So he pulled on his dirty pants and laid everything else out on the weeds to dry. Oh, how he did love this hot weather. He leisurely strolled barefoot toward his room up the stairs and down the hall past Peggy Sue's room, to dress. Then he would look in on Peggy Sue with the sore foot.

"Carlos," Peggy Sue called, "can you come here now?"

"Coming in just another minute," Carlos answered, splashing on cologne and spraying a fog of deodorant under his arms and between his legs. His room was at the end of the hall three doors from Harry and Peggy Sue's room.

When Carlos entered Mrs. Asserman's room, even though invited and urged to come, he felt as if he was invading her privacy—the seclusion of a bedroom of a married woman, the wife of a friend at that.

He shook off such a thought and walked toward her, feeling clean and free even if there was that lingering uneasiness of being alone with an attractive woman reclining on a fine air mattress bed.

"Carlos, I'm so glad you're here," Peggy Sue said smiling from her position propped up against the wall. Her bandaged injured foot was stretched out toward him and she wore a sleeveless thin negligee draped over her left knee. That leg was drawn up and her foot was planted on the bed as a prop.

"You want me to look at your foot?" Carlos asked with concern.

"Yes, I need you to see how it is doing. I feel like it is getting better but I need you to look closely and see if the swelling is going down and if it is still red."

"Sure, I can do that. You want that I take the wrapping off?" Carlos said, intentionally avoiding looking at her, an attractive 37-year-old brown-haired lady, in bed to boot.

"Go right ahead, please, just take it off and look," Peggy Sue said, looking at Carlos as if to say, "Come on, don't be afraid of me."

Carlos knelt by the bed intent upon doing what she asked. "Go ahead and sit down on the bed, that floor's too hard on the knees, I know. Get comfortable, after what you've been through, it'll take a while," she said, acting quite friendly.

Carlos sat down facing her and carefully lifted her foot and lay her leg across his knee.

This parted her legs and lifted her gown off the bed as it flared from her left knee and across her right leg. Suddenly Carlos was aware of the nakedness this position revealed. He had a clear view of her mass of neat chestnut brown pubic hair.

Momentarily Carlos felt that the lovely lady was watching his eyes. He glanced to see that Peggy Sue was watching his trembling fumbling fingers.

"Careful, Carlos, it is a bit sore you know, but just go ahead and undo the bandage and let's look at it," she said.

"Yes, of course, I am not used to doing something like this but I'll get it."

Soon he had unwound the cloth. He looked closely at the wound in the sole of her foot and then at the top where the big rusty spike had punched through. The merthiolate stained red the area near the punctures.

No way could he avoid frequent glances at the lady's beauty spot. Finally Carlos said, "Maam, it looks real good to me. I don't see any swelling." But he could feel an enormous swelling taking place within his own body. After all what would you expect from a clean, healthy, muscular man, a Latin at that.

"Let me see," she said reaching with her hands as she bent forward to lift her foot up in a position to see the bottom of it, throwing her partially exposed bosom within two feet of his startled face.

That maneuver slid the nightgown tail up further exposing her naked white lower body.

"It does look good, doesn't it?" Peggy Sue said reassuringly.

"Yes, it looks fine. How does it feel?" Carlos asked, shaking from the close encounter of the most human kind.

"It really doesn't feel sore," she told him, seemingly oblivious to the awful temptation she was throwing at Carlos.

"You know, I think, maam, that I would leave the bandage from on the foot now. It would be some more better for it," Carlos said getting more control of his emotions.

Then, just as if she had not shown, nor had Carlos seen, everything a woman can show, Peggy Sue stretched both long feminine legs onto the bed and draped the slick bedroom skirt to below her knees.

Carlos was immediately both relieved and disappointed.

He picked up the half glass of watery scotch and moved toward the door then turned to look back to find the lovely lady looking at him and ready to speak.

"Carlos, would you make me a drink and bring it please?" she said persuasively. "I think I'll need it if I'm going to try to walk on that darned foot."

"Of course I will, maam, be glad to. I was going to fix me a new one, too," Carlos said eagerly.

This additional gesture of Peggy Sue renewed his manly emotions. Carlos proceeded downstairs to the kitchen with rapid-fire questions flashing through his mind. Is it possible that Peggy Sue really didn't mean to tempt him like she did? Surely she was unaware of how much she showed him? But how could that be? She had to know. Didn't she remember that she did not even have on a skimpy pair of panties? Oh, what the hell, he thought, what difference did it make anyway? Just because you see something as tempting as a box of fine chocolates who says you have to eat any of them? Can't adults just be adults and let sex be only a beautiful fulfillment of love?

Carlos's mind answered quite quickly with "No, no, no, you damned fool, a man is a man is a man, you foolish Brazilian, of all people a Brazilian just doesn't think or act that way. What in the hell is wrong with you, you coward? Where's your manhood anyway?"

Then how in the name of good conscience could he actually make love to a good friend's wife? Would he end up feeling as scroungy as he had felt before taking that refreshing soap and rag bath? Then what is a man supposed to do? Just suppress the exploding manly urge and go off like a whipped tomcat with his tail tucked between his legs and cry around about what he passed up?

As he poured the drinks Carlos braced to face up to the enticing Peggy Sue. "No, sir, I'm going right back up there and be the perfect gentleman," he continued in his mind. "I'm not going to go to bed with a friend's wife. I'll take her the drink and I'll tell her that I think she should get up out of that bed and walk. That's what I'll do."

Carlos stirred his drink and drank it like lemonade, emptying the glass. He fixed another and headed up the stairs, a drink in each hand, wondering if his resolve would hold once he entered that bedroom door.

TWENTY-SIX

This had to be the second most important day in her busy useful life. Mary Martha stood outside the door of the little room in the corner next to the nurses' station. Even if she were allowed to be inside with her dad there wasn't enough space—two beds, Dr. Samuelson, a nurse and a nurse's aide filled the small room.

Right now Cloy was the only genuine emergency needing the heart monitor perched on a shelf at the head of his bed. Two IV bags hung on the rod extending from the bedpost. Oxygen was flowing from the tall tank in the corner into both of Cloy's hair-filled nostrils.

Mary Martha felt like a rock in the middle of the road with the nurse, aide and doctor forced to skirt around her in the narrow hall leading to the space at the end of the corridor that nurses had to call their station. The pharmacy and supply room in a small cubicle opposite the nurses' station were drawing staff traffic too. But Mary Martha either had to stand here in the hall or sit downstairs by the front doors in the waiting room. She chose to be just outside Cloy's room, ready to pop in the moment she was allowed.

Alice came and stood with her, whispering questions, and Mary Martha whispered answers. Presently the door opened and Dr. Samuelson stepped out.

He responded to Mary Martha's searching eyes with, "He's a tough one, I'll tell you. He's coming around. Gonna take a while but he's responding just fine. Wanta see 'im? You can go on in. Maybe you shouldn't stay very long right now, let him rest."

"But what about his heart?" Mary Martha asked, searching Dr. Samuelson's eyes for the true answer.

"It's doing all right. He's so awful weak and I'm sure his blood count is dangerously low, but I think his heart will be strong enough for us to build him back up."

"But you know what happened in the ambulance," Mary Martha said searchingly. "That might happen again before he gets built back up."

"Definitely, that can happen," Dr. Samuelson agreed. "But we have him on the heart monitor and he's right here at the nurses' station so if anything does occur we'll be able to respond."

Quickly he stole a glance at his watch, signaling that he must move on to other pressing matters and a waiting room full of people needing his attention, as he was the only family practice physician in the small county seat. The other physician, the hospital surgeon, was a native of the Philippines.

Mary Martha also looked at her watch, rolled her eyes toward the nurse sitting on the steam radiator, dragging on a cigarette and took two steps toward her. "Do you think Mr. Clay will need me or someone to stay with him?" She asked, holding back a gnawing desire to demand that the nurse get rid of the coffin nail she was sucking on. No question the fog of irritating tobacco and paper smoke would waft right into Cloy's room and right into his ever-so-weak lungs.

"Maam, I think we are quite capable of taking care of the patient," the nurse said defensively, not looking directly at Mary Martha but drawing deep on the cigarette.

"I'm sorry but I didn't mean to imply anything, just wondered if you needed someone to be with him?"

"Well, th' shape he's in we're gonna have to watch 'im round the clock anyways so no need for nobody else." The fortyish, yellow-haired nurse said.

"Well, then let me give you my phone number, one at home and one at work. Got something I can write on?" Mary Martha asked patiently, moving into the circle of smoke. "I'll need a pencil, please."

"Here you go," said the nurse pointing to the pad and ballpoint pen on the edge of the small desk.

"This number is at home and this one's at Canaan where I work at night. If you call there be sure to insist that they get me. I'm a security person up there."

"I'll stick it up here where it can be seen. I'll tell 'em to call you if he gets really bad," the nurse said, now trying to match the concern in Mary Martha's eyes.

"Now, I want to know the moment he turns worse," Mary Martha insisted.

"You his daughter?" asked the nurse.

"Well, no, no, I'm a friend. He don't have no relatives real close," she said shifting into her native lingo and verbal fractures.

"We'll call you if somethin' happens," the nurse said, looking at the clipboards holding patient charts, an obvious attempt to dismiss a person she perceived as knowing too much and caring just enough that all hell would break loose if the staff at the hospital goofed.

Alice held back, watching and admiring the older and wiser Mary Martha, awed at her spunk and surprised at the depth of her concern for the old man Clay. Then the two were off and down the creaking stairs, each step edged with a metal strip to hold the worn linoleum surface in place.

In Alice's car Mary Martha laid her head back, trying to relax for the first time in what seemed a century. Everything, it appeared, had been packed into these past few days, especially the last two since reading that letter in which her mother had exposed the family skeleton and pleaded for Mary Martha to have a forgiving heart.

"Home, James," Mary Martha said, joking but not smiling. "Get me home to a hot shower. I've gotta go to work."

"You have to work tonight?" Alice said, forgetting that her friend had important duties on Friday night.

"Gotta go. Kiwanis Convention is in at the lodge and I've gotta be there," Mary Martha said emphatically. "I've only got two others on duty tonight and they're not used to those big events. Yeah, I must be there."

"Too bad you have to work. I'm gonna go to the VFW Dance. Some of us girls are going, payday you know."

"Sounds like fun, you be careful now," Mary Martha said maternally to her housemate, who was certainly young enough to be her daughter.

"My Lord, it's good to lay back and relax a bit after this day," Mary Martha confided, closing her eyes to the beauty of the sunny afternoon in the Cheat River valley.

Rena and Rachel were in the car ready to rush off to work when Alice's car approached the driveway. After quick exchange about Cloy, they were gone.

In the shower, Mary Martha shampooed her curly hair and lathered her white skin, rushing so much she forgot to enjoy it.

All she could think of now was Cloy and getting to work on time.

Like a bolt of lightning, a flash hit Mary Martha's wet, sudsy head. "My good God, what about those other people?" she thought, stiffening and jerking the lathered washcloth from its cleansing duty. "I never for a minute gave a thought to those other poor devils up there in that cave. For heaven's sake, I can be so thoughtless," she said angrily. "I've gotta check on them."

Dripping wet, Mary Martha rushed to the phone in her bedroom, threw the wet towel down on to the bench in front of the dresser and sat down to search for the number. She grabbed the hand set and listened to the chatter. Quickly she laid it down and waited a few seconds and picked it up again and listened.

"Somethin' strange about it, that's what I say," the woman said excitedly.

"I bet anything someone's taken the old man up there and dumped 'im over," said the other woman.

"Wouldn't sprize me none," said the first voice.

"Had to been some of them hippies been runnin' round here this summer, bands around their heads and flowers in their hair," said the second woman.

Mary Martha pressed the button down and held the receiver suddenly noticing herself in the mirror, beads of water on her breasts and her hair tight to her head. She stood, jerked the towel from the bench and began massaging her dripping hair.

Again she tried the phone, easing her finger up to hear the continuing chatter of the excited, uninformed women still fantasizing about who and why Cloy Clay was done in.

Patience had always been one of her virtues but right now the circumstances sliced Mary Martha's tolerence to see-through thinness. She just had to do it so she said, "Please, folks, may I have the phone just one minute before I have to go to work?"

"Well, would you ever," one woman said disgustedly. "The nerve. Is this an emergency?"

"No, maam, it is not any emergency like someone dying or anything but I need the phone for only a minute to attend to some important business before I must leave for work. Is that all right with you?" Mary Martha said as calmly and politely as she could while biting her tongue to keep from telling both of them to take the phone and shove it.

"Well, I suppose if you only need a minute we could get off," one said, now more calmly than before.

"But we're not half done talkin' yet and we pay a plenty for this phone," the other said more harshly.

"Ah, let her have it and I'll call you back in just a minute when this person, whoever she is, gets her important call made." This time the phone line party underlined "person" and "important" in her attempt to ridicule Mary Martha the intruder on the gossip line.

Mary Martha dialed the field house number and Jorge answered, "field house."

"Hello, I'm the person you all helped today up in the cave."

"Oh, yes, how is the old gentleman?" Jorge asked with concern.

"He seems to be doing quite well. I just came from the hospital. He's so very weak. Now the purpose for my call was to see if you were successful in getting your friends out," Mary Martha told him.

"Oh, yes, maam, it took us some while to do it but we all got out without any injuries."

"Oh, I'm so glad. I'm really relieved to hear that," Mary Martha said with feeling, anxious to end the conversation due to time.

"Maam, your name is Mary?" Jorge asked.

"Yes, Mary Martha."

"Maam, I do so much appreciate the call. We will be wanting to know how the old man is doing. Please keep us informed," Jorge said carefully avoiding inviting her to the field house. Such a gesture would have to be discussed with Dr. Roberto. The whole stance of their presence in the area was now altered and they would have to talk about fraternizing with the capabaxias.

TWENTY-SEVEN

The telephone call from Mary Martha only slightly interrupted the celebration under way at the field house. Dr. Roberto was anxious to know the nature of her call and for a moment all of them stopped to reflect upon Jorge's report.

"The old gentleman, the lady who cared for him, her name is Mary Martha, she said he is stable now but very weak," Jorge reported moving back into the circle standing in the huge barren kitchen.

"How anyone could live that long is a marvel to me," Felecia said shaking her head in disbelief.

"He is a very strong man," Dr. Roberto said authoritatively. "It is almost a certain fact that a less old man would have decided to die."

"Please, sir, don't talk about dying," Kitty said, nervously grabbing her father's arm, showing the first sign of breaking down as the reality of her own trauma surfaced.

Quickly Felecia stepped forward, raised her glass and said, "I wish to propose a toast. First, I am so very thankful that we are all here safe in spite of the awful trials we have been through."

Responsively, like a square dance set, all seven others swooped toward Felecia, clanged their glasses and held them high, yelling "evviva, evviva."

Peggy Sue sat on the bench at the table, still favoring the punctured foot by not standing with the others. Right now she felt left out.

Impulsively she climbed onto the table and stood, her head nearly touching the ceiling beam. When Peggy Sue shot her glass into the air, it crashed against the oak timber, splashing scotch and water onto the table and the floor. Yet she held on to the unbroken heavy tumbler. Standing there, arm outstretched, she was no Statue of Liberty even though there was a resemblance. Indeed she was a beautiful woman, full breasts beneath a skimpy halter, neat hips covered with white short shorts. She demanded attention for her toast and said, "Listen, you all, I have a toast. Believe me I never, ever have been through so much in my entire life nor have I ever been so fulfilled either," she said, hesitating before continuing. "Having you all back safe is such a beautiful feeling. Believe me I panicked. I just couldn't take it, you all being in there in such trouble. But now here we are." Her eyes searched the group for their understanding of how she felt being left alone during the traumatic occurrences in the cave.

When Peggy Sue said she was fulfilled Carlos swelled a bit inside, feeling certain that reference was a compliment to him.

When Peggy Sue finished shouting her toast, the entire group rushed to crack their glasses yelling much like a group of cheerleaders at a basketball game. Then Harry assisted his wife to step down. She favored the injured right foot which was still protected by the neatly wrapped bandage which Carlos had removed earlier in the afternoon and redone later.

"Okay, my friends, let's have another round of drinks," Jorge urged, eagerly attempting to fuel the jubilant mood of the group now reveling in a highly successful day. "Dr. Roberto, has this been a successful day or has this been a successful day?"

"Your American expressions are to me very appropriate, Jorge, for today we used skills we learned from much practice to rescue our dear friends, C. Baxter and Kitty, and the old man, what was his name?"

"Clay," Felecia said. "It is a strange but simple name that lady Mary told me—Cloy Clay. Unique, don't you think?"

"That to me is a strange name," Dr. Roberto agreed, looking puzzled.

"But what a nice short unassuming name, so much like the people of this region here in the mountains," Felecia said spawning a smile at what she just had to say to her husband. "Now isn't that much to be preferred to the god awful long family tree names you Latin-lover Portuguese-speaking mixed breed of pups in Brazil carry throughout life? Seems only one reason for such long names, just has to be to impress everyone with their high status you try to lord above the poor nobodies you relegate to lifelong status of servants."

"It is so evident that we love the other for us to give such best comments," Dr. Roberto said, taking full credit for past raspberries he had given his wife.

Fact was that both realized a certain satisfaction from hurting the one they loved. Well, it really wasn't so much the desire to hurt as it was to even the score or to get ahead of the other. For Roberto and Felecia, it was a way to vent steam generating from anxieties. True it was somewhat of a contest between two persons who had accepted most of the other's faults except on those occasional moments when it became necessary to trip the popoff valve and let fly with some sly, cutting remarks that chopped a few inches to a foot off the other's ego.

Carlos flinched inside at Felecia's remark about servants, for that's what he was, sort of. But in the United States, his status was more like a member of the family or a partner. He was paid quite well for his work and he had plenty of freedom to do what he desired. In Brazil, however, it was different, for there your role was cast, servants were servants and were destined to remain so. Carlos realized that Felecia meant well and the fact that she said what she did in his presence was proof that she did not see him as a poor illiterate servant.

"Is it now possible to change the subject?" Dr. Roberto said, pointedly directing his comment to his wife. "If you do agree, may I speak a toast to our mission?" Then hesitating and looking to each individual, deliberately seeking their undivided attention as he so often did, he lifted his glass and began. "Today is the second best of days in my life. Today we found the perfect colony of *Plecotus townsendii virginianus*. No other expedition can show such outstanding results as we have discovered this day. It is possible the little brown big-eared mammals may live in this great valley forever."

"Evviva, evviva," the others yelled and broke into joyous laughing as they clicked glasses with their mission leader.

Dr. Roberto then followed up, directing his next comment to Jorge and Irenea. "And you, my friends, make possible our discovery. You found the secret entrance to the cavern. If we did not find this cavern, it is some possible that all our time would be spent in caves on the maps. They are ones that spelunkers would be exploring for the pleasure. That is where we are different, you know. We go into the caves to find the rare species. And now we can be certain of the greatest find in all North America."

"But, Dr. Roberto, you must give some due credit to the

ladies, you know, that Mary Martha and the others. They showed us to the primary haven where our lovely *virginianus* species make their home," Jorge said respectfully. "I'm not so very sure we could have found that hidden entrance."

"I must agree with you. It did make it some more easy," Dr. Roberto said agreeably. "I must wonder how they found it."

"Leave it to a woman," Felecia said slyly. "When there is a major task to perform or a discovery to be made, we women are known to perform admirably."

"And if it had not been for those women, Daddy and I might still be lying up in that cave a-shivering from the cold and not knowing how to get out of that wet place," said Kitty, supporting Felecia.

"You women do stick together," Dr. Roberto shook his head, immediately switching to a new route in conversation. "I cannot disagree with that but it now is time to look to tomorrow. It is time to examine our treasure. Tomorrow we must go back and make certain to carefully count the population. This will make it possible to prepare the accurate report of our findings. That will make it possible to have the journal article before any others. This we must guard with the most secrecy. We must not reveal any of our mission to the women or any others. It is my belief that this is going to be a making-of-history discovery. And only the true scientist can appreciate what means this discovery to the base knowledge on such rare mammals."

"You know, this reminds me of the most appropriate expression I heard Dr. Gordon Lippert of George Washington University say," Jorge the graduate student notes wisely. "He said the future is now, if you know where to find it."

The entire group was impressed by Jorge's pronouncement and Dr. Roberto said, "Very, very appropriate to our situation, Jorge, indeed appropriate. Now, please, let's all enjoy a most deserved evening for we are on the threshold of greatness in the scientific world."

"You mean it will be more important than the worldwide collection of hummingbirds that Dr. Rushi has in his museum at Santa Teresa?" Irenea questioned, recalling how impressed she was during her visits to the mountain village in her home state of Espirito Santo.

"My dear, there is no comparison," Dr. Roberto said sternly. "The professor is not in any sense of the word a true scientist. Oh, yes, he does have a great collection of hummingbird specimens and even the many species of live hummingbirds drinking from the bottles of sugar water. But true science, well, I must tell you it is only a show, like collecting photographs or paintings or even rare and precious stones. No, to include him in this as a scientific discovery is like mixing avocados and bananas.

"What we are doing is true science. We are determining the true environmental conditions which must be present to accommodate a nearly extinct species of bats. Our study includes all of the factors and will be documented for all mankind to know. We are truly saving these delicate creatures from extinction from the face of the earth," he lectured passionately.

"But, Dr. Roberto, I know what we are doing is a great piece of work," Jorge agreed. "However, to say that Professor Rushi is not a scientist is being rather harsh. Oh, I know that many scientists in Brazil have discredited Dr. Rushi for accepting all that money from the American philanthropist to build his musuem and to underwrite his hummingbird work. But he does have the greatest collection of hummingbirds in all the world. In fact, he is recognized as the world's leading authority on hummingbirds. I think it is more because he is a radical that so many scientists in Brazil have tried to discount his importance to science."

"No, no, no, that is not the reason," Dr. Roberto said angrily. "That man is, what do you call it about a woman, he is a prostitute in the scientific community. He is truly not a true scientist. He is only a collector. There is a great difference."

The others were uneasy at the leader's outburst. His serious sermon on the subject was about to destroy what had begun as a joyous occasion, much like throwing a wet burlap sack on a campfire.

Felecia stepped in to change the scene. "My dear, dear, ever-so-serious husband. Please do save your feelings about Professor Rushi for a later time. Now, please, let us all enjoy a great evening. Come on, let me freshen your drink. Let's all drink up."

She pulled her man to the counter and the ice and the bottle. "We can talk about the hummingbirds another time and at another place. By the way, I do somewhat agree with you about Dr. Rushi. I think he has let his popularity go to his head and in so doing he has taken on the government. I don't much appreciate him trying to do that. So, okay, enough is enough."

TWENTY-EIGHT

All evening she had been too busy to think much about her father. Now it was past midnight and the Kiwanians were settled in for the night and so far no phone call from the hospital. Her head told her, "No news is good news." Her heart told her to call and find out how Cloy was doing. Heart won.

The nurse said that Cloy was stable. "He seems to be sleepin' comfortable. I just five minutes ago replaced an IV bag and took his pulse and temperature. I don't think he woke up when I put the thermometer in his mouth, least he didn't seem to be awake. No, he's steady, just about the same as he was when he came in," she said kindly. "He is so very weak, you know."

"Yes, I know," Mary Martha sighed and thanked the nurse then added, "Oh, by the way, will you please call me here if he turns worse? I'll be here till after four then you could get me at my home number. You have that, don't you?"

The nurse confirmed that she did before Mary Martha hung up and hurried off to walk past each door of the 240 guest rooms. This took her outside into the cool, damp night air.

It was 2:23 when the phone rang in Mary Martha's office in the basement of the lodge.

"Captain Cosner speaking," Mary Martha said officially.

"This is the nurse at the hospital you talked to a while ago. Thought you should know that Mr. Clay is convulsing. He's shaking and trembling and he's mumbling and talking things I can't understand. Seems to be hallucinating."

"Well, how are his vital signs?" Mary Martha questioned calmly. "How about his pulse?"

"It comes and goes," the nurse said.

"His blood pressure, how's it compared to when we brought him in?"

"Weak, real weak, it's 60 over 30."

"Is the doctor there?"

"I called the doctor's assistant. She sleeps here in the hospital."

"What does she say?"

"Here, I'll put her on and let her tell you."

"Hello, I'm Anna Lansing. The patient is experiencing some reaction. To what, I'm not sure."

"Have you called Dr. Samuelson?"

"Yes, I called him just a few minutes ago. He's coming."

"He's really bad, is he?"

"Well, I don't want to alarm you but right now I'm stumped as to what could cause this. The poor gentleman is struggling so we're having to hold him. He has torn out the IV and he's hard to control."

"Oh, please be careful with him. Please be gentle. He's such a fine old gentleman. Please don't hurt him," Mary Martha pleaded. "Can I be of some help?"

"Yes, maam, I think it would be best if you were here. We are doing our very best to help him but he is hard to control even in his weakened condition."

"I'll be there as soon as I can make it. You think Dr. Samuelson will be there soon?"

"Yes, yes, I expect him any moment," Ms. Lansing said.

"Thank you so very much for calling me. I'm leaving right now. Be about a half hour before I can get there," Mary Martha told her and hung up.

Quickly Mary Martha contacted both her security persons, one in the patrol car, the other walking the rounds of the huge parking lot assisted by a well-trained dog.

Driving through the park she dared not go as fast as she wanted to, but steadily wound through the wooded area by the beaver bogs. It was not that she feared exceeding the 15 mph posted speed limit, for it was her job to write speeding citations. But realistically, it was her fear of hitting one or a dozen deer blinded by her jeep lights. From dusk till dawn you could count at least fifty whitetail deer grazing the golf course and at numerous points along the two miles of park road leading to the highway. You had to be careful to avoid slaughtering the beautiful wild animals. It was a real hazard to motorists. In fact, some broadside crashes had thrown the struggling beasts into the air and through the windshields of the speeding cars. Mary Martha knew firsthand what damage a deer wreck could inflict, for all too often she had helped to clean up the mess—

blood and hair and guts and hysterical park guests bathed in shattered glass.

When she reached Route 32 it was different. There were a lot fewer deer and the road was straight along the floor of the Canaan Valley. And tonight the moon was hanging above the horizon of Canyon Mountain. Now she could step it up to 50 and feel safe at the accelerated speed.

At 2:55 a.m. Mary Martha topped the stairs by the nurses' station at the hospital. Cloy's room was full of caring attendants—Dr. Samuelson stood between her and the two nurses, one on each side of Cloy's bed.

Impatiently she eased up behind the doctor, laid a hand on his arm and asked, "He's still struggling?"

"Oh, yes, maam, he is having a terrible reaction to the medication we gave him to help him sleep," Dr. Samuelson said, turning halfway around to address her.

"What can you do? Can't you do something to calm him down?" Mary Martha inquired.

"That's just it, that's the problem now. We'll have to wait till the effects of that medication wears off, I'm afraid. His system just won't tolerate it," Dr. Samuelson told her.

"How long will it take?" Mary Martha asked.

"Depends, just depends on how soon his system will pass it off. We've stopped that medication for him. Some patients can handle it and others can't," Doctor Samuelson said stepping back to allow Mary Martha to move up near the nurse on the right side of the bed.

"Nurse, would you like me to relieve you? Want me to help with him?" Mary Martha said softly, leaning over the bed to where she could see Cloy's glaring eyes.

"Here, hold his arm, try to keep 'im from throwing himself against the rail here," the short chunk of a woman said, moving back and squeezing past Mary Martha.

Oblivious to the nurse across the bed holding Cloy's right arm and guarding the IV, Mary Martha took over.

"You poor darling," Mary Martha said softly, touching her fingers to Cloy's forehead. "Please close your eyes for Mary. Please, I'm here with you."

Suddenly the little man's head shot up from the pillow throwing Mary Martha's hand aside. Cloy began to babble as his head fell back to the pillow. The wild stare in his eyes matched the nonsense he shouted.

Mary Martha caressed his wrinkled slim bearded face with both of her caring hands while holding his head to the pillow.

"You poor soul," she said lovingly, moving in close bringing her face to his. She laid her cheek against his like a mother would to her sick child. And for the moment, this calmed the pitiful old fellow. She held him tight to her face and gently rubbed his other cheek with her left hand. Softly she whispered, "Oh, you are so awfully weak and sick my dear, dear man. We must get you well. You will get well, please."

TWENTY-NINE

This was the day they had worked toward for the past three years, the day when they would begin the careful analysis of the colony of *Plecotus townsendii virginianus*. Dr. Roberto woke to the enthusiastic songs of the robins, cardinals, sparrows and a dozen other early-rising happy birds. Dawn had begun only moments before he slid off the air mattress bed and hurried downstairs to start the coffee. Next he progressed to the back porch and breathed in the clean foliage-filtered air of this warm summer morning.

When he finished in the toilet, again the scientist stood and listened to the delightful sounds of morning in the mountains. As he listened he took long deep ceremonial breaths as an athlete would when preparing for the pole vault competition at the Olympics. To Dr. Roberto dos Santos, today's event was far more important.

After a few minutes he went back inside where water was boiling ready to make his second favorite beverage, Brazilian-style coffee. He spooned twelve measures of powdered coffee from the two-kilo bag into the boiling water and stirred it. Next he gradually poured the hot coffee mix into the hornets' nest-shaped cloth strainer. The result was a rich brew made for real coffee lovers draining into the twelve-cup glass urn which sat over the slight gas flame.

He decided to let the coffee steep for a moment while he rousted the others from deep morning sleep or whatever it was they were doing.

Jorge and Irenea bounced out quickly, yelling their approval of what a great day this was going to be. Felecia moved about much more slowly. Harry came downstairs without Peggy Sue, reporting that she still had quite a sore foot. Carlos was quick to the coffee and eager to help Dr. Roberto with the exciting bat survey. C. Baxter came down still clad in pajamas and suggested that he and Kitty really did not feel up to going back in the cave so soon after the ordeal they had experienced.

"If you really need me, Dr. Roberto, I'll go," C. Baxter said pensively. "But if you don't need me, I'll stay with Kitty. She continues to be somewhat in shock."

"I believe, Benny, that the rest of us can today collect enough information," Dr. Roberto agreed.

Jorge and Irenea set out breakfast: a chunk of cheddar, chipped ham, hard rolls, plain yellow cake, bananas, orange juice and of course, the coffee. Irenea heated milk which each of them used liberally as they did sugar to prepare the Brazilian-style coffee to its exquisite peak of flavor.

"Delicioose, just like having a breakfast at the Hotel San José back in Victoria," Dr. Roberto said after taking the long first sip of the yellow coffee drink.

"You sound like you never had a good breakfast at our house," Felecia said curtly. "I fix the same things and you never say anything like delicioose, or even that it's almost okay."

"Of course I enjoy your breakfasts, but my dear, it is this day making it so good for me. Does it not excite you? Does it not make you feel the better now that we have found the Virginia big-eared bat in so large numbers here in this isolated haven for them?" Dr. Roberto asked, eagerly soliciting his wife's approval.

"I guess I can forgive you today for I realize how much this means to you. I know it is important, really," Felecia said, understanding the way her husband had longed for this discovery.

Following breakfast, Dr. Roberto proceeded to organize the group, running down a checklist of items they would need and who would be responsible for specific duties to be performed once they reentered the cave.

"Jorge, make for sure that you have so much film as we need, "Dr. Roberto instructed.

"How about six rolls?"

"Yes, yes, we will use two cameras, one for the slides and the other for the print pictures, so we will need someone other to use one camera," Dr. Roberto said, "Irenea, it is your duty to use one camera."

With all details checked and duties assigned, Carlos was the supply person. He understood how he was to function, making ready anything the others needed, including food. The scientific persons would be totally occupied going about their prescribed duties. They would work quietly and quickly to minimize their intrusion in the environment of what appeared to be a huge colony of *virginianus* females tending to their offspring.

This was an important point of which Dr. Roberto had to remind the others. "We must remember the reason the colony is located in this cave is that there has been some little disturbance of the ideal habitat. It is our obligation to be extremely quiet and to finish our work in a limited time, maybe in two or three hours or even less."

The leader was repeating what he had told them many times before. However, this time it was instruction for what was a day unlike any others for the scientist, obsessed with making a discovery worthy of international attention.

All the way up Thunderstruck Creek Dr. Roberto led by a dozen steps. Felecia kept him in sight through repeated demands that he slow down and let everyone take an occasional rest. This morning, Dr. Roberto was oblivious to the gorgeous surroundings—the gray slick beech trees, the shagbark birches, the tall stately tulip poplars. And the startled native brook trout could have jumped up his pants legs without him even noticing. He was indeed preoccupied with a vision of his future, basking in glory among the elite of the scientific world.

Upon instructions from Dr. Roberto, Carlos led the way into the cave, crawling backwards like the lively crawfish that darted about in the small creek. He dragged the huge canvas backpack into the bear-sized hole in the hill. The boss followed closely behind, shushing the others to nothing but whispers.

Inside, they used only one light. Dr. Roberto insisted that another day of disturbance like the rescue mission yesterday could make the bats decide to seek a new home. And that was just the problem—this could be the last such discovered and unspelunkered cave in the ideal setting amoung the beeches, oaks, hemlocks and maples.

Dr. Roberto and Jorge had read every available piece of literature on this dying species of big-eared bats. They knew that here in the eastern United States the *Plecotus townsendii virginianus* species seemed destined to perish unless the caves it used received protection. That for certain was why less than ten years ago it was placed upon the endangered list. Caves seemed to be the primary haven where they hibernated throughout the harsh winters of the Appalachians. But females required daytime privacy in the caverns to raise their young. This cavern, it seemed to Dr. Roberto, could be the end of the road for the tiny, fragile, elusive creatures that flew so crazily through the night.

It was indeed a precision operation from here on. You might have thought that Dr. Roberto was functioning as both producer and director on location during the filming of a motion picture. And Jorge was the cinematographer. Painstakingly Dr. Roberto laid out every aspect of the tasks to be performed—a precise count of every tiny big-eared bat within selected squares on the grid. The sectional sheets of paper such as used by architects were spread upon the cavern floor near the great expanse of wall.

Dr. Roberto asked Harry to record the figures on each ten-square section of the grid. "Give the squares numbers in sequential order, please," he told Harry. "You understand, I will be counting the number of specimen on a corresponding grid in the binoculars." Dr. Roberto whispered directing their light to the paper on the ground.

One additional light was to be used for the close specific work on the wall and ceiling of the great hall-sized room. This was the same room into which Cloy Clay had made occasional visits for so many years. Apparently no one else had known about this cave, except Cloy.

Dr. Roberto asked Carlos to bring the powerful hand lamp. It was equipped with a red filter which would protect the bats' light-sensitive eyes.

"You stand close, you know, like before, and we will move the light from the floor to the top very, very slowly," Dr. Roberto instructed Carlos, when suddenly he remembered one last significant detail. That was to mark the wall at ten-foot intervals so that each upward sweep would be done by columns. He told Felecia and Carlos to stretch the tape measure and chalk mark at breast height the sectional dividing lines.

Felecia moved to the second section and began to mark at the end of the tape but the chalk broke. Carlos directed the light so she could recover the pieces of chalk. He carried the tape reel and walked closely so the light would help her locate the half-mark she had made. It was then that they both saw what broke the chalk—markings cut into the limestone wall.

Carlos walked back to Dr. Roberto and asked him to come and see what they had found. Reluctantly the scientist came but as soon as he saw the graffiti on the wall his interest swelled. Slowly he eased his fingertips along the chiseled lines which were as neat as if the length of the soda straw had been pressed into soft cement.

Inch by careful inch Dr. Roberto intently studied the markings all the while attempting to verify that these were indeed ancient forms of communication rather than the work of modern day graffiti writers who just possibly could have left their forms of art as some kind of protest even in this secluded spot of natural beauty. Was there no end to where some people would go or what they would deface under the guise of being lovers of the wilderness?

THIRTY

The roller coaster ride of Cloy's fragile life kept Mary Martha glued to his bedside. During the past six hours her father had died and been resurrected six times. She feared, not frantically but earnestly, that there would not be a next time. And if there were no next time then the old fellow would never ever know that she, Mary Martha Cosner, really should carry the name of Mary Martha Clay.

She wanted him to know. Would it help him? Would he understand? Maybe he would be excited back to life if she told him, Mary Martha worried, as calm overtook the frail body housing the ever-so-fragile life.

Several cups of coffee for Mary Martha and three hours later Cloy's condition stabilized. He had a steady, stronger pulse and he stopped flailing his arms onto the bed and lunging his head up off the pillow. All morning he jabbered, but most of it made little sense.

It was almost noon Saturday when she decided to go home. Mary Martha tried to call to tell her housemates where she was but each time the Leadmine line was tied up. She gave it a final try as she passed through the waiting room. Immediately there was the rump, rump, busy signal meaning the line was out of order, as it frequently was, or that someone who had waited his or her turn to use the four-party phone was now on the line.

"To hell with it," she said disgustedly, slapping the phone back in its cradle.

Outside it was another gorgeous summer day. All the way home she alternated between elation and tears of sorrow for poor old Cloy. All at once her tangle of thoughts screeched to a halt. "What is wrong with you, Mary Martha Cosner-Clay?" the new character in her mind said. "Look, dear one. Why are you acting so crazily? All right, so Cloy, your father, does die. Is that so bad? He lived a good long life, didn't he? He was an honorable man, wasn't he? And, about you being his daughter, well, what good is that going to do? Answer me that. Now what's happening to you?" the male voice continued authoritatively. "Is it that you are thinking only of you? That's right, you want to have a life with your real dad, now isn't that about the size of it? You're not so much concerned about that fine old man, truly wanting him to live, as if you really had an unconditional positive regard to him. No, you really have all the regard for yourself," the new commander of her mind said.

"Ah, come on now," Mary Martha said aloud as she crossed the Dry Run Bridge. "That may be partly true. It would be nice to have a while with my natural father, getting to know him better, and doing things for him and him doing things for me. What's wrong with that? I can hope, can't I? And damnit, I do care about him, for his sake. He's my father."

"Ah, ah, ah, there you go again," the voice in her mind said. "I wonder, would you care so much if Cloy Clay wasn't your dad, or would he be just another old man lying up there in the hospital bed? Fact is, he could still be back up in that cave, dead by now, if you hadn't learned that he was your dad and found clues in the letter where he might be."

"You're probaby right," Mary Martha said, searching her conscience, "fact is, I know you're right. Who am I kiddin'? But durnit, I do want him to live even if it's only for me. I don't care, I want him to live," she said, crying aloud. "Oh, God, please let my father live so I can bring him home and we can have some good talks and all." She had to wipe the tears away so she could see the road.

It seemed that the very act of wiping the tears made room for a big smile. "I don't care, I want him to live and I'm not going to worry if he dies. At least I got to do something for my real father, and for that I am grateful." Mary Martha said, pressing harder on the accelerator as she was anxious to get home. She sped along the narrow, curving strip of blacktop draped in trees and summer shade.

THIRTY-ONE

News of Cloy's rescue made the wire services and by now millions around the world knew about it. And that unique name triggered numerous comments and conclusions that Cloy Clay had to be an Indian with a name like that.

Jae Weidimeyer-Rossi read the short story that Saturday morning on page 3 at the bottom of column 5 in the *Los Angeles Times,* dateline, Leadmine, W.Va. (UPI). Immediately she called her mother in Connecticut to report the event and ask if the Leadmine village mentioned in the story was close to her grandparents old place.

"Of course it is," Mrs. Weidimeyer said emphatically, becoming excited at hearing of Cloy Clay. "I know him, yes, I know Cloy Clay, we go back a few years but I knew him when we used to spend the summers there at Foredsa. He used to work for your grandfather."

"Momma, you know what I'm thinking, bet you'd never guess," said the business-like, attractive movie producer of Wilshire Boulevard. "I'm thinking, what a story, make a cliffhanger, spine-tingling movie."

"That's you, the chip off the old blocks as they say, your grandpa and your daddy, too," Sheena Weidimeyer said proudly to her enterprising only child.

"I'm sure we can develop a love angle and a dash of sex, but the story, my God, momma, this story is made for Hollywood," Jae said, getting excited about this event which she sensed was hers, one associated with her roots, one in which she could personally take a commanding hand in shaping the script.

"You'll have some Hollywood fun with the love and sex, for I don't think that guy Cloy had any love life, best I recall," Sheena Weidimeyer said from her fashionable home in quiet comfort sixty miles off Broadway in Connecticut.

"Momma, I must get this story, got any suggestions of who

to contact out there?" Jae asked. This was the first time she had ever consulted her mother about a movie idea, as she had always been afraid of being influenced or restricted by her strong, opinionated and conservative family.

"I do have a suggestion that just might get you some firsthand information. It's a start, I think," Mrs. Weidimeyer offered cautiously, fully expecting her independent daughter to reject it and try to come up with something better.

"Okay, momma, this time I'll listen. I'm dead serious about this story and I know you have the connections on this one. You lived there."

"Oh, yes, I lived there, your papa and I spent our best honeymoon there at Foredsa," Sheena told her, sounding excited and youthful as she reminisced about a happier time in her glamorous life as a moviemaker's wife.

"Momma, what's the connection? Who do I call?" Jae pushed enthusiastically, sitting behind her cluttered desk. She had a yellow, sharpened soft-lead pencil in her left hand and another in the straight blonde hair above her left ear. The thin oval black frames of her eyeglasses and her bun hairstyle were compatible with her last celebrated birthday, her thirty-ninth, held three years ago.

"There's a Brazilian fellow renting the old place up there in West Virginia. He told me he heads a small group of cave explorers. Let me see, I have his name here. Let me look, it's here on my desk somewhere," Mrs. Weidimeyer said hesitantly while lifting her eyeglasses from where they hung on a gold chain over her heavy bosom. "Here it is—Dr. Roberto Drews Vieira dos Santos."

"My God, what a handle," Jae reacted.

"He suggested I call him Dr. Roberto. His address is Executive Apartments, Penthouse 1, 1650 Columbia Pike, Arlington, Virginia.

"A phone number?"

"Yes, two of them. One is his Virginia number and the other one is at Foredsa."

"Give 'em to me."

Mrs. Weidimeyer recited two numbers, the second one with the 304 area code for West Virginia. "That's the number at the field house, that's what they call Foredsa."

"Field house! That's beautiful, I mean beautiful. Good

God, it's exactly what I need, couldn't write it any better myself."

"Well, I caution you darling, don't get too carried away. But maybe it has a possibility."

"Momma, I'll talk to you later. I've gotta get on to this while it's hot," Jae said as if ending any other business conversation.

"Well, listen, keep me involved in what you're doing. I do know a little of the area and I know a lot of what it was like at Foredsa. Oh, I loved that place. Been a long time since I was there, kinda dreaded ever going back, wanted to remember it as it was then, when your father was living," said Jae's mother holding her daughter a bit longer.

When Jae hung up she dialed Arlington and talked to a maid who informed her that Dr. Roberto was away and would not return until the end of another week. Was he at the field house? Jae asked, but the maid was not permitted to tell. Her answer was that he was on vacation. Next she dialed the number at Foredsa, or the field house to the spelunkers. A recording told her, "All circuits are busy. Please hang up and try again."

Again she dialed, punching the buttons more determined than before and this time contact was made, accessing the West Virginia system, a major accomplishment aside from reaching a clear line on the rural circuits. This time the Leadmine line was at least momentarily open and Jae's call rang in on a cocktail party for the group celebrating the greatest day of Dr. Roberto's search for the secluded habitat of the big-eared bat.

Jorge took the call from Jae Weidimeyer-Rossi, answering "field house."

"This is Jae Rossi of Weidimeyer Productions. May I please talk to Dr. Roberto?" she asked briskly, reflecting her eager impatience to get a lead on the story that she meant to have for her very own.

"Yes, maam, Dr. Roberto is here, just the moment until I get him," Jorge replied.

The jubilant scientist took the phone and announced, "This is Dr. Roberto Drews Vieira dos Santos."

"Dr. Roberto, sir, this is Jae Weidimeyer-Rossi in Hollywood."

"Weidimeyer-Rossi you say. You are related to Ms. Sheena Weidimeyer?" Dr. Roberto questioned.

"Yes, yes, sir, Ms. Sheena is my mother. She tells me that you are using the old family place there in Leadmine."

"Yes, maam, we use it as our field house, a good place for our work," Dr. Roberto told her.

Quickly Jae jumped in, "Sir, the purpose for my call is to inquire of the old man Mr. Cloy Clay, whom they found in the cave. Can you please fill me in a bit?"

"Maam, I know only a small amount about the Mr. Clay. He was alive when we helped some women who found him."

"You say some women found him," Jae said almost bursting with this new angle, a detail she needed, sweet serendipity. "Listen, sir, I'll want to talk to you much more about this but, sir, who were the women? What are their names?"

"I have some trouble with the American names. Jorge!" he yelled, "Jorge, come here! Here, I must give you Jorge."

"Yes, what is it you want to know?" Jorge asked as he placed the receiver next to his left ear and cupped his hand over the other ear.

"Sir, Dr. Roberto said that some women found the old gentleman, Mr. Cloy Clay. What are their names? Do they live nearby? Why did they find him? What relation are they to him?" Jae fired away at Jorge, not giving him a chance to answer between questions.

"Wait, wait just a moment, not so very fast. First thing, I know the name of one lady and she seemed to know Mr. Clay quite well. Her name is Mary Martha," Jorge told her realizing that he either had not heard or did not remember her surname. "I just now realized that I do not know the lady's last name, I'm sorry."

"How can I reach her? She have a phone?" Jae pushed.

"She must have a phone but I don't know for sure. She said she lives down here in the village. That's all I know about her. It is possible I could contact her and ask her to call you?"

THIRTY-TWO

Jae Weidimeyer-Rossi's phone number in his pocket, a glass of scotch in his hand, Jorge became the messenger of the determined movie-maker who sensed that this was that unique story she must pursue. "It is so very urgent that I talk with her about that Mr. Cloy Clay," she impressed upon him. And he, to escape her pleading, had agreed to contact Mary Martha with the message from Jae.

First, Jorge had to be reminded that the Peugeot wagon was out of commission, a chunk of ignition key stuck in it, and the GMC wagon remained hooked to the Rover. He'd take the Rover, he decided. He went outside, unhitched the vehicle, lifted the tongue and tied it to the grill.

Jorge thought he knew which house was that of Mary Martha and her friends, yet he wasn't absolutely sure until he saw the jeep in the driveway.

Mary Martha needed the nuisance of such a call about as much as she needed another parent on the deathbed to worry about. It was not in her nature, however, to ignore a plea for help.

At least Jorge now knew her last name, she said to herself, thinking about him having to drive down instead of calling, all because he didn't know her last name.

"I'm surprised he even remembered my first name, but he did," she beamed as she walked to the phone. "Nice-looking fellow, that Jorge."

Two kids imitating grownups were on the line. For a moment Mary Martha listened then broke in, "Excuse me, excuse me," she said softly. "Please, will you all soon be finished? I need the phone for only a moment, then you can have it back, okay?"

"Why do you need it?" One of them smartly asked.

"I need to make a business call and then you can have it

right back, okay?" Mary Martha said still feigning a patience she lacked after thirty-two hours without sleep.

This time the kindness paid off and the kids gave in. Within seconds she and Jae Weidimeyer-Rossi were into a twenty-minute conversation. And not too surprisingly they made a good match—Jae just a few years younger but both independent and experienced in the ways of the world.

Before they hung up, Jae had arranged with Mary Martha to meet her at Randolph Field at Elkins.

"I'll call you with the time soon as I get the flight schedule," Jae told her, making sure she had the numbers for Mary Martha at work, at the hospital and at home.

THIRTY-THREE

While Mary Martha slept, Ralph came from Thomas and took Amos with him to see Cloy. They found the wiry little man asleep, yet they sat with him awhile. A nurse's aide brought another chair so Ralph could sit between the beds. Amos sat at the foot of Cloy's hand-cranked hospital bed.

Cloy continued to have the steady drops of sugar water tapped in, but the other IV bag was gone. The tubes remained in his nose but for the past hour, the nurse told them, Cloy had been doing fine without the oxygen.

"He's so much better right now," the nurse said. "He really had us all scared there for a while. He was really bad. Thought we'd lose 'im."

Cloy's friends stayed about an hour and Cloy continued to sleep, occasionally jumping and twitching, mumbling and babbling, but apparently getting necessary rest. When they agreed it was time to leave they drove by the fire station and out Main Street to the VFW. Occasionally they had relaxed in the private club but today they felt like they deserved a bit of a reward after what they had endured. And now that they felt more comfortable about Cloy's welfare, a tall stein of Old German would be quite appropriate. Fortunately, the beer drinking crowd did not associate Ralph and Amos with Cloy, but the club was buzzing with Cloy's story.

Almost every person in the club had helped in the search led by Colonel Apolla or was with volunteer firemen when they rescued Cloy.

One barrel-chested, red-faced fellow seemed to overpower the rumble of the fifty or so other voices when he twisted around on the barstool and bellowed, "By God, I say the old bastard oughta died in the damned cave iffen he had no better sense 'n to go in one, old as he was."

It was strange how no one challenged him or even seemed to hear him. Apparently that was because it was early in the drinking day, for had it been later in the evening on Saturday, the fellow's blast would have been met with a challenge of fists or a cussing match.

Private conversations following the outburst were quite the opposite that of the drunken fellow's point of view. One said, within hearing of Ralph and Amos, "I think it's damned great that the old sonofagun had the gumption to get out and sang and go in caves and the like."

"Hell, yeah, exactly what a lotta young guys oughta be doin' steada ridin' round in a 4-wheel or a tote goat every place they go," said a gray-haired fellow of the same vintage as Ralph and Amos.

The two old friends found genuine solace in the smoke-filled barroom, with a pool table, miniature bowling alley, three pinball machines, a fancy jukebox and three window-type air-conditioners. They ordered another round, exchanging their dripping mugs for fresh frosted ones and two more bags of beer nuts.

The noise level made it some difficult to carry on a reasonable conversation but the two old friends tried.

"Amos, did you know there was a cave up there on Thunderstruck where they found Cloy?" Ralph asked.

"No, I never knew there was but I always figured there should be with the limestone goin' around the mountain like it does," Amos said loudly, leaning across the booth to make sure Ralph heard him.

"Nearest cave I know is up Maxwell Run, way up there back of the Sugarlands. Some nice caves up there but not up Thunderstruck. Hell, there's not even any coal mines or nothin' like that up our way," Ralph said thoughtfully, holding the mug of beer ready to take another cold swallow and searching Amos's eyes for the answer to why Cloy was found in a cave.

"Damned funny thing, funny as hell for old Cloy to be crawlin' in a cave when there wasn't supposed to be such a thing up there anywhere," Amos observed.

"Well, in a way you're right, but you're wrong in another way. Ever think about that? Guess there had to be a mine or a cave up on Horseshoe somewhere. You know, Leadmine had to get its name from somethin' like that," Ralph said, reviving an idea seldom mentioned in recent times.

"Legend, that's all that is, someone probably thought that one up. Oh, they might have found the Indians back there with soft metal objects or somethin', but Lord, by now somebody woulda' found it, you'd think, if there was such a place," Ralph said, obviously struggling with the puzzle of it all.

"Well, my old granddaddy always said there really had been a place where the Indians dug out ore. Of course by the time they named Leadmine it was only a legend," Amos said philosophically.

"Wonder who ever gave it that name, anyway?"

"I figure it was the Minears or the Parsonses or maybe the Maxwells or some of those early people that settled Saint George. They had to fight off the Indians," said Amos excitedly. "Even built a fort and yet some of 'em got killed and others were captured and taken into Ohio."

The dialogue between the two good friends began to sound like the script of a Saturday matinee Western.

THIRTY-FOUR

Jae Weidimeyer-Rossi arrived at the Elkins-Randolph Airport in a twin engine plane she chartered at Dulles. She had taken the red-eye flight from Los Angeles and rather than take the one Sunday commuter that would drop into the bowl at Elkins after three short-hop stops at other small airports in the hills, she had grabbed the charter and rushed on toward the story. She shouldered her one bag and hurried toward the terminal. There Mary Martha and Alice waited, knowing instantly that the lone woman passenger rushing toward them was the movie person from Hollywood.

Within minutes they were on the road toward Parsons, Jae insisting that she had no need for breakfast, even at 8:00 a.m. Sunday.

"I've gotta have a cup of coffee and a donut or something," Mary Martha said. "There's a coffee shop up here at the forks of the road."

"Oh, if you're gonna stop I'll have something, too." Jae said.

"Come on, let's go in and take a few minutes to get squared away. Besides it's kinda rough drinkin' coffee, bouncing along in this jeep," Mary Martha reasoned.

"I'm absolutely, positively famished," Alice said interjecting herself into the conversation from her perch in the back seat. "That pizza Bob and I had about midnight is done went and gone," she clowned, speaking as she thought West Virginians were expected to sound.

During the breakfast stop, the conversation focused upon Jae's probing questions. "How come Mr. Clay got lost? Why did it take so long to find him? Who found him? Did the people at the field house help in the search?" And, "Is he still alive?"

"Oh, yes, he sure is, he's a tough one, indeed," Mary Martha beamed, which might have seemed a bit strange, considering that she was not supposed to be related to Cloy Clay, only one of many people who knew him.

"Think we can stop and see him? He is in the hospital, isn't he?" Jae pushed.

"Of course we can see him, in fact I must go see him anyway. He's in a private room so we can go on in," Mary Martha told her.

When they passed the Kingsford Charcoal Plant Alice leaned from the back seat and told Jae, "There's where I work. I'm secretary to the plant manager. Ever use any of our charcoal?"

"Gosh, I don't know. I'll bet I have, but didn't notice."

"Our home office is also out in California. I talk to 'em about every day. They're in Oakland," Alice said, feeling a kinship to Jae.

"Yes, that's up near San Francisco. Well I'll be, they're located all the way back here," Jae commented as they moved past the acres of metal buildings, the mountain of sawdust and the flaming smokestacks.

When they topped the stairs to the second floor of the hospital the door to Cloy's room was closed. Mary Martha eased the door open to find Cloy getting a sponge bath. So, they would have to wait a moment and Jae continued with the questions, asking about the small hospital, the population of Parsons and how far was it to the field house. Presently, the door opened and the nurse's aide pushed by with the plastic pan of sudsy bath water.

Mary Martha had cautioned Jae that Cloy was quite weak and that right now would not be the time to involve him in conversation about his misfortune. Thus, the visit was polite and brief.

"Mr. Clay this is a lady who wants to meet you. She is Jae Weidimeyer-Rossi," Mary Martha said, placing her hand on his bony arm, lying limp on the bed beside his frail emaciated body.

"Who you say it is?" Cloy asked, his voice cracking. His hearing had deteriorated during the past two years.

"It's a lady whose family used to live up at Shaffertown, Mr. Clay," Mary Martha shouted, leaning over him.

First he looked at Mary Martha, then turned to Jae, puzzling, "You used to live at Shaffertown?"

"My grandparents did," Jae said, stepping closer. "My

father and mother spent a lot of time up there at Foredsa. I used to go there when I was a kid. Don't remember much about it."

"You wouldn't be a Weidimeyer, would you?" Cloy asked weakly.

"Yes, sir, I am Jae Weidimeyer. My father was Alex Weidimeyer," she shouted. "Did you know him?"

Cloy's lips twitched nervously and he slowly smiled and said, "I reckon I did. Knew him for years back there before the second war. Yes, that's right, I don't think they ever came back much after the war."

"That's about right. I've never been there that I can remember, although they tell me they used to take me there when I was quite young."

"Mr. Clay, her name is Jae, you know, like Jay Rockefeller, and her married name is Rossi. She lives in Hollywood and makes movies," Mary Martha said, patting the old man's sallow cheek.

"She'd be a makin' movies all right, that's what her granddaddy did, was make movies," Cloy said with a hint of a smile. "Made a lotta money at it. Yeah, they had the money."

Jae shook her head and pointed out, "Not that way these days. It's hard to make what people will pay to see. You have to find the right story, today."

Mary Martha, afraid that Jae would plunge on about filming Cloy's story, stepped into the conversation. "Listen, Mr. Clay, we have to go right now, but we'll be back real soon, okay?"

"Don't stay away too long. Got you to thank for findin' me, you know," Cloy said looking directly into Mary Martha's caring eyes.

"Okay, Mr. Clay, you keep on gettin' well. You'll be out of here real soon," Mary Martha told him, patting his bony shoulder as they departed.

Dr. Samuelson stepped into the hall, spotted Mary Martha and called, "Mrs. Cosner, just a moment, I need to speak to you." He stepped close and in a low voice said, "Best I can determine, Mr. Clay has some broken bones in his pelvic region or in his hips, can't tell yet. But the old boy's coming around quite good, so about tomorrow we'll get him into X-ray and find out about the broken bones. Otherwise, I think he's doing great for an old codger. Tell you, he's tough. I swear, I think that would have killed me, in fact, I know it would have. I'd have starved to death the way I like to eat," he laughed.

Quickly, before the busy man departed, Mary Martha introduced Jae to the doctor, reporting only that she was visiting because her folks once lived in the county.

They took the one-car width blacktop strip that crooked and turned over the hills and dales between Parsons and Leadmine like toilet paper streamers thrown from the top of a football stadium down over and among the spectators.

"Oh, my God, did you ever see anything like this?" Jae exclaimed, when they topped Alum Hill and entered the southern edge of Holly Meadows.

"You like this, huh?" Alice said. "I didn't know anybody else would feel that way about this place."

"Honey, my camera eye is rolling all the time, and this, this is absolutely movie-making landscape. It's so beautifully different. You know what I mean? It's, well, did you ever see anything like this valley and the hills in the movies? They're just different the way they shoot up. The whole place is, really, something else," Jae raved excitedly as she cut the cloth for her movie.

The eleven miles to Leadmine with strikingly different scenes around every turn churned Jae's creative juices to overflowing.

"Believe me this isn't all of it," Mary Martha told her as they approached Leadmine village. "Here's where we live, we'll stop for a while before we do any lookin' around. Okay?"

THIRTY-FIVE

Mary Martha wheeled the jeep into the driveway at her roomy white home in Leadmine. She fully expected their guest to go straight to the bathroom for a shower and then to bed. But those were the least of Jae's priorities.

"Something cold to drink?" Mary Martha asked, once they were inside where cooler, protected from the hazy sun of August.

"I'd love some juice or unsweetened tea or something like that," Jae told her as she walked anxiously about the kitchen.

Mary Martha's urging that she have a seat and get comfortable was lost on Jae. She was much too fired up about the story to relax now. The answers to a hundred questions had to be found. Now that she was here, so close to the heart of it all, she was eager as a foxhound sniffing a fresh track. She had to get onto the trail.

"Ah, come on now, let's sit and talk a bit, see what we should do and who you should talk to," Mary Martha said firmly. "We'll help you any way we can and I know the people around here will enjoy talking to you. I'm sure a lot of the older folks remember your family."

The steady one poured Jae a tall glass of apple juice and served it to her at the breakfast nook. Then she poured some for herself and called toward the stairs for Alice. "Alice, check on Rena and Rachel. Tell them to come on down here a minute."

For the moment they were alone, sitting at the table. "So you're the one who found Mr. Clay? Right," Jae started.

"Well, yes, I guess so," Mary Martha said a hint defensively.

"How come you? Oh, I know the others, your housemates, helped but it was you." Jae probed, searching Mary Martha's face for the answer. "You found him after the big search was called off. What made you do that?"

"Oh, I guess it was just because we kinda got into it, the challenge, I guess," Mary Martha lied.

"Were you close to Mr. Clay? I mean, you surely knew him quite well to be so interested in finding him?"

"No, not really," Mary Martha said truthfully. "I knew who he was and all but I really didn't know him to visit or anything like that."

"Are you related to him?"

"Oh, no, no, I'm no relation." Again Mary Martha lied and it showed. For her neck reddened and her nose twitched, her heart pounded and she had trouble breathing.

Jae was a pretty good lie detector. "It does seem a bit unusual for you to show so much concern for the old fellow. Lots of children don't show as much feeling for a parent," Jae said thoughtfully, then held back a moment.

There was a long moment of silence before Mary Martha decided to stop lying and redirect the conversation. "We worked as a team and it was kinda fun putting some of my police training to work. Anyway since I went with him to the hospital I've tried to follow up with him. But now let's see, where do you think we should start?"

"How about the cave? That's the focal point of this story, the cave where Mr. Clay was found."

"Okay, that sounds fine," Mary Martha said, obviously unsure that that was the starting point.

"Don't you agree?" Jae questioned, reading Mary Martha's brow.

"Well, I do and I don't. First I agree that the cave is a key part of it but there's so much more to it than the cave. I mean, no question you'll need to see the cave, but then there are so many things that you will want to know about Mr. Clay. And I think you'll want to talk to the people up at your place, you know, the people up at the field house."

"Yes, I know I'll want to talk to them and I do want to see Foredsa."

"Foredsa?"

"Yes. Oh, you don't know that it's called Foredsa? That's what my family always called it, Foredsa, after Henry Ford and Thomas Edison. They once visited here and my folks knew them pretty well, so my grandfather named the place Foredsa. Quite a man, my grandfather. He died in '49 but he's still a big name in Hollywood."

"You've never been back?"

"Never. I was too young to remember it. I've seen pictures

and heard a lot about it but I don't remember it. Bet it doesn't look like much now after all these years."

"You're right, it does look rundown, but the big house looks pretty good, even now."

"Maybe we should go up there first. A good place to start, get my bearings."

"Then there's Mr. Clay's home, you'll want to see it and you'll want to talk to his nephew Ralph and his best friend Amos. They know Cloy real well. They're the ones that got the search party up." Mary Martha felt some relief that the others might become involved, serving to lessen the burden on herself.

"Where's the dog?" Jae pushed to get more questions answered.

"Oh, I guess he's still up there at Cloy's, probably lying on the porch. Poor old mutt, he's been lost without Cloy, they tell me."

Alice bounced into the kitchen followed by Rena and Rachel. She introduced them to Jae interrupting the strategy session by pointing out their occupations. "They work in the coal mine."

"Coal miners!" Jae exclaimed. "You attractive young women work in a coal mine? Now that is interesting?" She appeared to be as taken by this new information as she was in the Cloy Clay story. Somehow she would want to incorporate them into the movie. "I'll want to talk to you about that," she told them as the movie camera mind rolled on.

"Tell you what, we can go on up the road and take a look around if you'd like," Mary Martha said before suggesting to her housemates that they might prepare to cook out about two in the afternoon. Turning to Jae she said, "We'll come back for lunch and by that time we'll be able to decide what else we need to do."

Mary Martha went straight to the phone by the refrigerator and tried to call Jorge or Dr. Roberto to announce their visit. Like so many times before, the line was loaded.

As they drove up the lane to Foredsa, Jae dodged the brush like a native. At the driveway to the old home she said, "I have a feeling I've been here before. Guess it's the pictures and then again I just may remember it from my childhood, you know."

The vehicles were there and the occupants were too. Jorge, clad in shorts and T-shirt, greeted them cordially.

Mary Martha introduced Jae. "This is Jae Weidimeyer-Rossi. I think you all talked by phone."

"Of course. You must come in. We are having a slow morning, each person fixing his own breakfast." Jorge said. "Come on in. Dr. Roberto is working on some papers. Dr. Roberto, we have the pleasure of visitors, Jae Weidimeyer-Rossi and you know Mary Martha. By the way, I am embarrassed to not know your last name," Jorge said to Mary Martha.

"Cosner," Mary Martha said, smiling as she was reminded of what a hunk of man she thought he was that first time they met.

They moved into the grand old kitchen now functioning as recroom, family room, living room, studio, parlor and kitchen. It was filled with a special aroma of Brazilian brewed black coffee.

Dr. Roberto greeted them and graciously invited them to have coffee, which he served and then sat with them.

"I have not yet met your mother," Dr. Roberto said to Jae. "But we have talked some times by the fono. You know this place?"

"No, sir, no, I have seen pictures, but I haven't been here since I was a small child," Jae replied.

"We like so much this place because it is private and most appropriate for our vacation times," Dr. Roberto said.

"It once was a very fine place. My grandparents loved it here, possibly for the same reasons as you do, sir. My parents used to come here. But after the depression came I don't think they ever came back."

"It seems such a great waste," Jorge said, puzzled. "Surely if you had known it was so nice a place you would have come."

"Possibly. Then again I have lived most of my life in California. Seems like I've always been busy and it is a bit far to come for only a day or two. Then come to think of it, my folks never seemed to want to come back. They talked about this place as if it were far in the past. Mother never talks about it any more," Jae said, seeming a bit puzzled by this fact which she had never quite realized until now.

Small talk out of the way, Jae jumped into her mission—to pursue the recent intriguing episode in Cloy Clay's life. "Dr. Roberto, I understand that you folks helped to rescue Mr. Clay."

"We did help some, but Mary Martha here discovered him and we helped her and the others," Dr. Roberto said, avoiding credit.

"They are spelunkers so they have the right equipment and they are experienced in doing these things," Mary Martha said, revealing more information than Dr. Roberto wanted to share.

"It is a vacation hobby for us," Jorge offered. "We do this for the enjoyment."

"Yes, you see we conducted a rescue of two members of our party who went over a crevasse into the water. It is a part of our, what do you say, our recreation." Dr. Roberto said, revealing only the minor part of their real purpose for spelunking.

Jae found this intriguing. Expert spelunkers could provide the authentic rescue scenes for the movie. This one was going to be filmed on location. "Dr. Roberto, I need your advice, sir. I am here to determine if the story surrounding Mr. Clay's tragedy might make a good motion picture, a feature film if you will. You and your group can be very important to this project."

"In some way we may be of assistance, maam, but it is not my desire to make movies. We try to avoid propaganda or, as you say, publicity."

"Sir, what I need is for you to take me to see the cave and to give me advice on how to get the most realistic views of the interior. Is it spectacular inside?" she asked excitedly.

This line of Jae's thinking stopped Dr. Roberto's train of thought. And his silence attracted stares from the others.

"It, is, absolutely, gorgeous. Like nothing I have ever seen," Felecia said as she approached from the hall. "I told Roberto that it's no wonder the old fellow went in there, like going into a great cathedral. I'll tell you, you don't need stained glass windows to give you that feeling of being in the presence of the Almighty, in there."

"My dear Felecia," Dr. Roberto said, intentionally interrupting his spouse's grand description. "Please, dear, we have important visitors. Please, I want you to meet Mrs. Weidimeyer-Rossi. She is the daughter of the owner, you know Mrs. Weidimeyer in Connecticut, the one we rent the field house from."

"My name is Jae, maam."

"My name is Felecia. I am delighted to meet you."

Thus, for the next few minutes the conversation steered clear of the cave while Jae explained to Felecia that she was in the area to study the Cloy Clay story.

"A fantastic story," Felecia said. "Oh, you are a movie producer, I'll bet. That is just terrific. I really think that's a great idea. A movie set in West Virginia. There hasn't been many of them. That'll be a chance to let people see what a beautiful place this part of the country is. I think it's a great idea, the Cloy Clay story and all."

"I think so too, but the only reason I'm here is because of the story and a chance for an exclusive. Believe me it's not because it is in West Virginia," Jae told her candidly. "The human endurance, the tough gritty character, the suspense involved in all of it. Where in this story I'll find any humor or, the must ingredient—sex—is beyond me, but surely it's there somewhere if we just dig deep enough to find it," Jae said, almost as if planting seeds to grow into revelations. At least it might cause those in her presence to think of what she'd be looking for and point her to the real sources.

It was time for Dr. Roberto to attempt some fancy footwork to avoid revealing his secret mission and to safeguard the sanctuary of his precious colony of endangered big-eared bats.

THIRTY-SIX

It was the last night of the Kiwanis convention at Canaan Valley State Park mandating that Mary Martha be there to supervise security. But some contacts had to be made quickly to further feed the tiger in Jae's hungry mind. No doubt a few hours could be spent with Amos, Cloy's nearest neighbor. Possibly Ralph would come and Jae could talk to both of them.

Mary Martha made the arrangements on the way back from the field house. She introduced Jae to Amos and his wife Ruby suggested that, if it was okay with them, Jae would come back at six to talk a while. Of course it was okay with them—talking with a real Hollywood person sounded better than spending the evening watching Hee Haw on television.

Back at the house and the big shady backyard, the charcoal was white hot, ready to cook chicken halves into a sumptuous barbecued meal. Alice was the outdoor chef. Rena and Rachel prepared all the fixins in the kitchen.

"I don't know about you, but I'm gettin' into a pair of shorts," Mary Martha told Jae as they walked toward the grill where Alice stirred the basting sauce.

"Sounds terrific if we're not going anywhere," Jae replied, still sounding antsy.

"Now, look, my friend," Mary Martha commanded, "Right now we need to take a few minutes, at least, to relax and think about your project, see if there are others you should talk to. So, how about a nice tall glass of cold California white wine? Bring any shorts with you?"

"Not one pair," Jae said disgustedly.

"Well, we've got enough fannies around here wearin' shorts that you won't have to do without," Mary Martha joked. She went straight to the kitchen, poured two glasses of wine and asked Rachel to help Jae find some shorts.

In the meantime Amos called Ralph and told him about Jae

and her plans to visit. Ralph said he would come. "Might be a bit later than six but I'll be there."

During the next two hours, Jae's mind was diverted from the project by her inquisitive hostesses, who wanted to hear about Hollywood. Rachel launched into the subject by asking "Is Robert Redford really as handsome as he looks in the movies?" That and a hundred other questions kept Jae occupied all through the picnic and then some.

Rena and Rachel had to work a Sunday night this week. So Jae's need to be chauffeured threw a curve into Alice's regular Sunday night date. That duty fell to Alice until she resolved it by asking her boyfriend to come for her rather than meeting at the VFW. This freed Alice's car for Jae.

That evening with Ralph and Amos and Amos's wife Ruby gave a lot of information to digest. For they gave her inch-by-inch, minute details about Cloy and about the search.

"You say his place is just across the road here?" Jae asked Amos.

"Oh, yes, maam, that's where it is, see right across there back of those trees is the house," Amos pointed from where they sat on the porch.

Ralph suggested, "Maybe you'd like to go over there and look around."

"Oh, I really would," Jae said. "Can we go now?"

They walked the some three hundred yards out Cloy's lane lined with rusty barbed wire fence and high weeds.

This trip cinched it. Here was the story: the dog, the quaint house and the gorgeous valley. Jae could envision old Cloy sitting on the porch, although she never for a minute planned to use him in the movie. For, to portray Cloy, the right actor or actors would have to be used. How many, she still was not sure, but she knew there would have to be one representing Cloy's older years and quite possibly there would need to be one actor to play Cloy as a young man. She would have to see if any of the early years would be important to the story.

During the hour before dusk Jae, Amos and Ralph sat on Cloy's porch as he would be doing were he out of the hospital. And Stripe lay on the porch as if waiting the moment Cloy would come home.

Amos was the first to mention the possible connection between the cavern where Cloy was found and the legendary leadmine from which the village got its name.

Jae grabbed that tidbit like a hungry trout leaping for a deer fly.

"What makes you think that?" she asked eagerly.

"Well, ever since I was a boy, I remember 'em talking about there just had to be a mine up in here someplace. And there's never been any mines up in here. But now that they've found that cave, I figure it has to be it." Amos said seriously, wishing ever so much that he could take a chew of tobacco. But that was something he and Ralph would not do in the presence of the lady from Hollywood.

Ralph reached to his hip pocket and pulled out the paper pouch, an act as much from habit as it was for the satisfaction of chewing. Suddenly he realized his error and stopped short of opening the pack.

"Oh, please go ahead and take a chew, no problem with me. I think it's a lot better than smoking," Jae said.

"I used to smoke but quit back there a few years ago. Believe me I get a lot of satisfaction out of chewin'," Ralph said.

"I never did smoke," Amos said, "but a good chew is a lot of company, especially when you're outside."

"You guys go ahead and chew. I think it's kinda manly myself," Jae said, wondering if she really meant that.

Then Jae got back on track. "My heavens, if that leadmine is for real or even if it isn't, that makes a whole new dimension to this story. Anything written about it?" she said.

"Well, yes, there is," Amos said thoughtfully. "Hu Maxwell's *History of Tucker County* tells about the Indians coming up the Horseshoe and returning to the Cheat River with lead. The way they tell it they had about enough time to come up to here and return. So as the story was handed down, people named the creek up the road here Leadmine. They call it Leadmine Run. That's how come the village was called Leadmine, after the Run."

"That history book, when was it published?" Jae asked.

"I think it was in the eighties," Amos said, puzzling.

"1884," Ralph said. "I don't have a copy of it but I've read it. It's a big book. They've got it in the library up at Parsons. That's where I got it. Got a lot of interesting things in it, I know that."

"Homer Floyd Fansler's *History of Tucker County* is full of stuff too. It was done back a few years ago. Boy, it's a big book, too," Amos told her.

"How about a historical society or any group such as that? Is there one around?"

"Yeah, sure there's one I been readin' about in the *Advocate*. There's a woman headin' it up. Let me see, what is her name?" Amos said turning his head to squirt tobacco spit off the porch. "Who's that woman who heads up the Historical Society?" he asked of Ralph.

"Oh, that's Clara Bennett Baker. I don't know for sure if she is head of it now but she's the one that started it a while back when she and her husband moved back to Hambleton. I believe he's retired from the government. They used to live in Washington, I know."

"They would be good ones to talk to about this, don't you think?" Jae reasoned.

THIRTY-SEVEN

The first rain in thirteen days swept quickly up Horseshoe Run and hit Leadmine with a barrage of fierce lightning and violent thunder. "Rain before seven quit before eleven." The old saw espoused by optimists of the valley promised a sunny Monday.

About ten minutes into the storm an inordinate burst of thunder broke into Mary Martha's deep dream-free sleep. She jumped awake sitting straight up in bed bewildered by the darkness in the room. It took a few seconds for her to realize that this was not her bedroom. She remembered that her guest, Jae, was upstairs in comfortable privacy. Mary Martha was sleeping on the fold-out sofa in the TV room that once served previous hostesses as a parlor, the pride and joy of the house.

Mary Martha squinted at the face of the wall clock in the shape of the state and learned that it was 6:50 a.m.

"Whooey," she blew, "What a short night." Short indeed. For it was only about two and one-half hours since she had gone to bed and immediately fallen into unconscious splendor. As she lay back down and listened to the noisy storm, she hoped to drift into hours of Sunday morning recuperation. But the rattling windows and keen flashes robbed her of that much deserved and rightfully earned satisfaction.

"Well, I better get up out of here. I'm sure Jae will want to get at it again and I'd better get the coffee on and get myself cleaned up," Mary Martha said, stretching and forcing a half-positive attitude about the obligation she felt to be helpful.

Already Jae was up and in her bathroom. No doubt the storm woke her, too, a good three hours before her normal rising time.

Over coffee Jae told Mary Martha about her fruitful visit with Ralph and Amos. "You know the leadmine is what intrigues me. They think that cave may be the legendary leadmine," Jae said excitedly.

"Could be but I doubt that," Mary Martha said thinking about it a moment. "On the other hand, who knows, it really could be it, I guess."

"Why don't we go back up Foredsa and talk to that Dr. Roberto and Jorge and tell them what Amos and Ralph said about it? Maybe they saw something that would indicate that there was really lead in there," Jae suggested.

"We can do that. But you know, the person who knows the most about that cave has to be old Mr. Cloy, don't you think?"

"Well, let's go see him, too," Jae said.

"I agree but I want to go see him even if we don't learn much above the cave. I want to see if he's still on the mend."

At the hospital Cloy appeared wide awake and rested. The twinkle in his eyes and the weak smile welcomed Jae and Mary Martha. He asked them to crank up the head of his bed to the sitting position. "Now, how come you pretty girls come to see an old geezer like me? Haint I caused you enough trouble already?" Cloy said, testing their friendship.

"Now, you listen here, Mr. Clay. We wanted to see how soon we can get you out of here and back up on the run. Okay?" Mary Martha said patting his bearded cheek.

Cloy grinned a broad, toothless response to her encouragement.

"Then there's another thing we wanted to ask you, too. Jae here was talking to Ralph and Amos and they said maybe that cave up there where you fell just might be the leadmine they say the Indians used," Mary Martha said, watching for Cloy's reaction.

"Could be, I guess," Cloy said somberly. "Yeah, I guess it's possible."

"You would know, I imagine, if anybody knows you would," Jae encouraged him.

"I kinda figured it might be. Yeah, I always kinda figured it might be," Cloy said, still holding firm to a serious, thoughtful expression. His eyes stared toward the open door and gradually a saddened expression developed and Cloy's lips began to tremble.

"Look, Mr. Clay, let's just forget about the cave. We'll just not talk about it any more now. Maybe later we can talk about it. Okay?" Mary Martha comforted him, rubbing his shoulder.

"Tell me, you do feel so much better and stronger now than you did yesterday, right?"

Cloy shook his head yes, turning his tearful eyes toward Mary Martha then to Jae.

"Now, my friend, you keep on gettin' well so you can get back up home. Stripe's a waitin' up there for you," Mary Martha said.

Cloy perked up, wiped his eyes on the sleeve of his gown and asked, "Is he doin' all right?"

"Sure he is," Mary Martha said.

"Boy, I sure do miss him," Cloy said now looking more cheerful.

"Look, you just keep it up, you gotta get well. I need you," Mary Martha said before thinking. Quickly she added, "We all want you to come on back up on the Run so we can hear all about your stay in the cave and the like."

"Mr. Clay, we'll see you again soon," Jae said, realizing she had been more reticent than usual.

"Yes, I'll try to see you tomorrow. We've got to find out how soon that doctor's gonna let you go home. I'll see Dr. Samuelson tomorrow. Okay?" Mary Martha said, squeezing Cloy's arm.

In the jeep driving toward Leadmine Jae attempted to evaluate their visit with Cloy. "You notice how affected he got talking about the leadmine?"

"Yes. I wondered about that. I wonder if he knows more than he pretends," Mary Martha pondered.

"It is strange that he never told anybody, if he did know," said Jae.

"He probably has his reasons. He's a private kind of man, I know."

"I think he wants to talk about it when the time gets right," Jae said.

"Maybe. We better not rush him."

"No, no, no, we shouldn't rush him. He'll tell us what he knows."

"May even tell us why he never told."

"It can wait."

"Sure."

Back at the house, still only a quarter till eleven, not one of the other three women was up and about. Alice had taken the day off.

Mary Martha ran back to the mailbox at the road for the Sunday *Exponent-Telegram*. She gave it to Jae. "Here take a look at a good paper," she said in jest. "I get it just to keep up on the social news. There's not much in it."

"Goodness, this must be the only paper in the country that's seven columns wide," Jae immediately observed.

"It is odd-shaped, isn't it?" Mary Martha said. "I get the *Baltimore Sun* to get a better fix on the news. It comes in the mail, too, so I'll get it tomorrow."

"My God, it's full of weddings and anniversaries and obituaries. Suppose people have to pay to have their pictures in here? I'll bet they do or they wouldn't run so many of them," Jae said as she quickly flipped through the pages before entering the house.

"Listen, how about a good brunch? Let me get you a glass of good California white wine."

THIRTY-EIGHT

Mary Martha kept Jae occupied, engaging her in light conversation through the midday Monday meal. Rena, Rachel and Alice joined them in the feast of oatmeal pancakes, pure maple syrup, boiled down to perfection by old man Cloy, and sage-spiced West Virginia sausage. But the relaxation ended with a second cup of coffee.

"Think now we can go see Dr. Roberto?" Jae asked.

"Okay, let's go find out what he knows," Mary Martha said, glad that she had slowed down her movie-making visitor long enough to learn more about her as a human being. She liked what she had learned about Jae in only one day.

Apparently it was a lazy day for the spelunkers at the field house. Even Dr. Roberto was taking the morning off with plans to spend the evening writing on the journal article.

The primary sitting area in the house was on the benches at the improvised table in the giant kitchen. Dr. Roberto welcomed them to demitasse cups of coffee, urging upon them generous portions of sugar and warm milk, Brazilian style.

Following a few minutes of chitchat Dr. Roberto inquired, "How is your project progressing?"

This opened the door for the movie-maker. She jumped in with both feet. "Dr. Roberto, in the cave up there, did you see any signs of Indians, I mean where they might have dug out lead or anything like that?"

For a moment Dr. Roberto studied what to answer. What would this lead to? "Maam, I'm not so very certain that there was such activity in the cavern. You see, we were so very busy and so very much concerned with the poor old Mr. Clay and then we had a—what do you call?—a mission of rescue with C. Baxter and Kitty."

"You know why I asked?" Jae probed. "You see I have learned that just possibly that cave or cavern, whatever, just may be the legendary leadmine. So you can see why I am so hell-bent on finding out. It makes a terrific story, that's for sure," she said loudly, watching for the Brazilians' reactions.

Jorge picked up on this, stepping to the end of the table. "You mean the village down here was given that name because of a legend?"

"Oh, yes, that's for sure," Mary Martha said. "the *History of Tucker County* has references about the Indians and the lead they got up in here."

"That's a beautiful part of my story don't you think?" Jae asked first Dr. Roberto, then looked toward Jorge.

Dr. Roberto was thinking hard how to accommodate Jae Weidimeyer-Rossi and yet preserve the precious bats in the scientific goldmine of a cavern up Thunderstruck Run. Finally he decided to try to dissuade the Hollywood lady. "I am not for very certain that the cave is of any significance. See, what I mean, maam, is that the cave is so very isolated and is not discovered," Dr. Roberto said. "If the cave was important surely many cavers would have frequented it, which is not the case."

"I realize that, sir, but since it did play such an important role in this whole dramatic plot I know for certain that I've got to go see that cave. How about it? I'd love for you all to show me. Could you do that?" Jae asked politely.

"Of no question, maam," Dr. Roberto said becoming flustered on the inside while appearing calm on the outside. "We can very much enjoy doing that," he lied.

Felecia had overheard the conversation and moved in more closely to the table. She hinted at a possible alternative. "Is it so absolutely necessary that the cave be that tiny hole in the ground? How about a larger, more convenient one right here in the area? What do you think, sweetheart?" she said, moving up behind her husband and placing her hands on his shoulders.

"Of course, that seems like a fine something to do," Dr. Roberto said, knowing that Felecia was trying to help. "If it is the cavern you wish to see here in the valley than I can show you something far better for your movie than the little place up there where the old man was lost."

"Sir, I think you don't understand. I am here, sir, to get the true story and the true story is that Mr. Cloy Clay went into that cave up there, wherever, and he fell over an embankment and he was in there for however many days and I'm not about to settle for anything less," Jae said emphatically.

"Well," Jorge interrupted, trying to avoid a heated conflict, "look, maam, we're not suggesting that you not see the other cavern. But I think what Dr. Roberto is saying is that we can possibly find much better cavern interiors for filming right here in the area so you would not have to take all that equipment so very far up the hollow over the rocks and up through the forest. Then that entrance it is so very small. Yes, I think Dr. Roberto is right. We can help you with some better place."

Both Jae and Mary Martha suspected that they were being detoured, but why?

No way was Dr. Roberto going to volunteer throwing floodlights all over that gorgeous secluded haven inhabited by the endangered big-eared bats. In fact, Dr. Roberto had begun to think rather possessively of the sanctuary and unless pushed to do so he would prevent the invasion by a movie-making crew.

"Jorge, let's show her what we have right here," Dr. Roberto said, making his first diversionary sidestep.

What they saw was exciting, the enormous room, the old Weidimeyer distillery and the potential spot for filming the Cloy Clay story.

"Oh, my good Heavens, can you believe it? Did my folks really do all of this?" Jae wondered aloud. "Not a soul ever told me about this."

"And not a soul around here has ever whimpered a word about this cave being attached to the house or anything like that," Mary Martha exclaimed, thinking about the secret that had been kept so well.

"The good Lord only knows what kind of dirty linens my folks hid from me," Jae said bewildered by it all.

"Oh, you should remember," Harry Asserman interrupted, "that what they did way back there was during Prohibition and someone was bound to make the spirits they needed for hosting parties and entertaining friends. I'll bet they took a lot of the stuff to Hollywood, too. You can just imagine that they had some good old mountain moonshiner to make it for them."

"All before my time, quite a family skeleton we've uncovered here. Instead of a skeleton in the closet this one is in the cave," Jae laughed.

"It is some good that you can now laugh about it," Dr. Roberto consoled. "Listen, this should be good for movie material, too, don't you think so, maam?"

"Oh, sure it is, sir, but the real story here is old man Clay. The actual cave where he got lost is where the story is," Jae said.

"I must tell you, Mrs. Rossi, this is the same cave. It just winds beneath the hills to the other very small entrance," Jorge confided. "So you see it is the same, don't you think? You can do your filming here and who would know the difference?"

"Sir, I see your point, but I know the difference and Mr. Clay knows the difference and the story is to be a true account, absolutely true, and it is the only way I'll have it," Jae shot back.

For a short while they stood there by the barrels and the winding coils of copper tubing. Dr. Roberto felt trapped. He began to agonize over how he could continue to protect his vitally important scientific project. All the way back up the ramp and into the house there was an awkward silence.

"Come have another cup of coffee and we can again talk about this matter," Dr. Roberto said as he cut through the confusion Jae's persistence had caused him.

"We can stay a short while but this afternoon seems the ideal time to take a hike up to the cave. Are you going to show me around up there?" Jae asked, looking directly at Dr. Roberto.

"Well, maam, it must be some obvious to you by now that I am not so much able to agree to your request."

"Yes, sir, it is and I am beginning to wonder why? Why are you so willing to show me this part of the cave and not the crucial one? What is it, sir, that you are trying to hide?" Jae asked pointedly. "See, I thought that you being spelunkers you would logically be the ones to ask to show me. But I guess I'll have to get Mary Martha here and the other girls to take me up there. They found the cave in the first place."

"Maam, I am so very much sorry but we do have our reasons. I'm sorry," Dr. Roberto said sadly. "I know it is some hard to understand but I must ask you to trust me. It is the best not to go up there."

"I think we should go now," Mary Martha said, rising from the bench. "I'm sure Dr. Roberto has good reasons for his concern. Let's just leave it at that, okay?"

"No, please sit back down. Wait just one momento. I need some time to think about this," Dr. Roberto said thoughtfully.

"We really must go," Jae said. "That's okay. I understand. Whatever the reason I understand. No hard feelings, really," she said extending her hand across the table toward the troubled scientist.

"Please, you must understand, maam," Dr. Roberto said widening his eyes and attempting to come forth with a believable explanation. "You do have your project and I have some important project, too. But before I can reveal this scientific project to you fine persons I beg to ask you to understand how very much importance is my work. For it is possible that your movie project will destroy a great discovery."

"Please, sir, I do understand and it is not necessary for you to make excuses," Jae said.

"Dr. Roberto, if you wish to share a secret with us I can assure you that we can be trusted to keep it just that, your secret," Mary Martha said wondering what on earth it could be.

"I agree," Jae followed, "However, I feel terrible that my insistence is forcing you to do it. Really all I want to do is see the cave and see where Mr. Clay fell."

"Maam, I want you to know and I know you can then see why I am trying to protect that cave," Dr. Roberto insisted.

"As my friend here agreed, your secret will be safe with us," Mary Martha reiterated.

"Then I must tell," Dr. Roberto began. Excitedly he told them of the extensive search they had made to locate colonies of the big-eared bat (*Plecotus townsendii virginianus*). The cave where Cloy was found, he said, contained the largest colony yet discovered since the bat was placed on the list of endangered species. He assured them that his secret would soon be made public when his article was published in a scientific journal. But even so, the cave itself was the important factor.

"I must take whatever measures are necessary to give protection for this appropriate habitat for them," Dr. Roberto said. "So you can now see why I am so afraid to make some more disturbance to that cave."

"I do indeed, sir. I can see, sir, that you are a true scientist. Yes, I can relate to that," Jae said.

"I believe you, maam, I can tell that you are a professional in your field, too," Dr. Roberto said.

"Sir, after hearing this, I doubt that we will be able to film in that cave but is it still possible to make a visit to the cave and maybe a quick look inside? Would that be harmful, sir?" Jae asked sincerely.

"Maam, I will be delighted to accompany you there and I am for certain we can make an exception to take you in. We will use just one light. That should be sufficient," Dr. Roberto said smiling.

THIRTY-NINE

By late Tuesday night Jae Weidimeyer-Rossi had found all but one of the major story elements for a successful motion picture. The second strongest motivation of the human character, sex, would require more research.

The visit to Cloy's cave, perhaps it was now Dr. Roberto's cave, brought Jae's creative juices to near boiling point.

How to accommodate the bat scientists' obsession with protection for the newly found big-eared colony was still unresolved.

Jae's long-into-the-night visit with Clara Bennett Baker of the Historical Society provided little more than lively conversation and several book searches including careful reading of history book references to the lead mine. She had no facts, only hearsay which found a home in legend. First, the migrants from across the Alleghenies named a creek Lead Mine Run. Later the tiny unincorporated town formed around a sawmill and a country store they named Leadmine. During the next two hundred years it was assumed that there had to be a lead mine in the vicinity even though none was ever found lending credence to the myth.

Wednesday morning Mary Martha chauffeured Jae to the airport for her flight to Dulles and on to LA International. She watched Jae's rented plane bank hard to clear the mountain and disappear into the blinding sun.

Driving back toward home she decided to make a much delayed visit with Aunt Christilina at the resthome. Again the poor old soul cried for sympathy. And as she had done so many times before, Mary Martha dug deep to spirit the aged relative away from herself and give her something more exciting to think about. She told her about Jae Weidimeyer-Rossi coming to make a movie about Cloy. The diversion worked. Christilina stopped crying. Instead of crying the sad woman stiffened and gripped the arms of the wheel chair. Her lips puckered and her eyes glassy, the affected elderly lady stared stoicly into what appeared to be a dream world. No matter how hard Mary Martha tried to coddle the poor thing into conversation, Christilina was not having any part of it. So, after a few minutes, Mary Martha credited her aunt's behavior to old age and gave up trying to talk with her. But Mary Martha was puzzled over the reaction she got just when she started telling Christilina about Jae Weidimeyer-Rossi. "Oh, well, who knows? Bet I'll be in worse shape if I ever live so long."

At the Wilshire Boulevard offices of Weidimeyer Productions Jae spilled her story to two trusted creative writers. They would construct the storyline, something she could sell to financial backers.

Saturday morning after fourteen days of gaining back a portion of his strength Cloy was discharged from the hospital with the stipulation that he get an abundance of bed rest and nutritious meals plus scheduled doses of prescribed medicine to aid his climb back to health. Fortunately the X-rays revealed no broken bones, only a hairline fracture of the pelvis.

Mary Martha volunteered to give Cloy the kind of TLC prescribed by Dr. Samuelson. This task could have been easier if she had allowed her housemate friends to participate. But caring for her real father was, as she saw it, her rightful responsibility. It took only a short time to strike a routine compatible with Cloy's needs and her security chief's job and her best friend Terry. Slowly but steadily Cloy regained strength and picked up some weight.

On Sunday following Jae's departure, Dr. Roberto and the spelunking bat-searching crew closed up the field house and returned to Washington. Jae had promised them that she would not enter the cave up Thunderstruck without having Dr. Roberto present to protect the bats. Also Dr. Roberto decided to insert a human and animal barrier in the short entrance tunnel leading into the cave. He and Carlos fashioned a frame on to which they nailed rusty fence wire. They placed it out of sight of the opening and stepped back across the creek to conclude that if you weren't looking for a hole in the ground you wouldn't find the cave. So, Dr. Roberto left feeling rather secure in the thought that it was quite possible that no one would visit "his" cave in his absence.

Clara Bennett Baker and her group moved more quickly

than even they thought possible, given that they had done so little in the three years since becoming a formal organization. Thus, the right contacts were made at the Department of Culture and History. The best information found in a search in the archives division revealed only two Tucker County history book references to the lead mine.

The letter to Mrs. Baker was just what they needed to carry forward. The archivist suggested that the group might wish to erect a plaque near the site of what they believed to be the lead mine. He even offered some appropriate wording which they could use to carefully avoid authenticating the lead mine. The plaque could refer to the legend and that it was believed that such a mine existed and was frequented by the Indians as a source for metal which they used primarily for bullets and weapons.

Mrs. Baker emphasized to the members of the society that the recognition of the legend was long overdue. Now was the time to move on it with the movie going to be made. She said it might take years to determine if the cave where they found Cloy Clay was the lead mine. Right now, she said, she had plenty of doubts but she was sure that it was better that they go ahead and put their mark on this bit of history. She proposed that as quickly as possible they should hold a dedication day in the Leadmine village vicinity.

FORTY

Clara charged ahead, as one possessed, to arrange for a big day. She drove to Leadmine and beyond to visit Cloy Clay. Mary Martha was at Cloy's, almost ready to begin the difficult task of shaving his inch-long beard. Cloy enjoyed showing her how to hone his straight razor. Never had she used such a tool but Cloy assured her that she could do it. He told her that these newfangled razors couldn't hold a candle to his old ivory-handled century-old blade. "Look, see how you hold it," he demonstrated with his trembling hand, placing the cutting edge to the hair above his wrist.

Mary Martha gritted at the sight and nearly screamed from the pain she felt shoot down her spine at the thought of the gash she was sure would result. Should she grab the razor or steady his hand or leave him alone? But what he did worked without incident. The razor steadied as it hit the skin and Cloy made sure that the blade was not drawn on the arm but instead he pulled it forward clipping hairs like a mowing machine cutter bar cutting weeds.

When Mrs. Baker arrived, the shaving project was postponed. First they talked of Cloy's ordeal and his recovery. With that out of the way, the historian gently pushed ahead toward her objective.

"Mr. Clay, you know many people believe that the Indians had a lead mine up in here. I was wondering if maybe the cave you were in bore any signs of such activity?" Clara asked.

"No, not really," Cloy said, seeming more relaxed than when Jae had approached the subject. "Oh, there were some carvings on the wall in there but I didn't see where they dug ore or anything like that. No I don't think there was anything like that in there."

"Well, what we want to do, I mean the Historical Society, is to erect a marker up here which recognizes that the lead mine possibly existed and was used by the Indians. Of course we would indicate that it was a legend and not necessarily a fact," Clara said, eyeing Cloy's reaction.

"Might be all right if you do it like that," Cloy said agreeably.

"Where you gonna put it?" Mary Martha asked.

"We haven't decided that yet. Do you have any suggestions?" Clara questioned.

"Not really," Mary Martha said. "How about you, Cloy? You know a good place?"

"Could put it up there at the forks of the road at Shaffertown," Cloy offered.

"You'd have to get permission from someone. Who owns the land there at the end of the hardtop?" Mary Martha wondered.

Cloy wasn't sure just whose land it was. Clara was concerned with protection from vandals, and said that possibly the plaque would have to be fenced.

"That is a parking place for campers and sort of a lovers lane spot," Mary Martha said. "It would be a place where they throw out a lot of trash. Always a bunch of beer cans and pop bottles and potato chip bags and tissues and the like laying around up there."

Finally Mary Martha suggested, "Why not put it here in your field, Cloy? Then you could kind of protect it?"

"Don't know why not," Cloy smiled. "Yeah, if you want it could go right out there in the field where you can see it from the road. Be all right with me."

"So it's settled," Clara said. Before she left, a date was set and Cloy told them of a big rock that lay in the fence corner that might be used as a support for the plaque. He said he had seen rocks used for such things.

Mary Martha and Clara checked it out and came back to report to Cloy that the huge three-foot oval boulder should serve the purpose well.

The first Sunday in October would be the date for the big day. A number of key people would be asked to attend and be a part of the program. Also the public would be invited to bring a picnic and share in the historical event. Mary Martha helped Clara with the VIP list. Key ones would be the governor, the commissioner of culture and history, the two U.S. Senators, the second district congressman, Jae Weidimeyer-Rossi and Dr. Roberto and his people.

Clara Bennett Baker was ecstatic. She hurried back toward Hambleton convinced that this was truly going to be a major accomplishment for the society. Such recognition was sparse for her group and for the rural mountain area. Even the newspapers and the television stations in Clarksburg and Weston might come to cover such an event. Most importantly of all was the potential for the marker and the story behind it to be included in the movie of Cloy Clay's story.

In Parsons Clara stopped by the monument shop to discuss the project. She told the owner about the rock and how she hoped to attach the metal plate to it. Clara departed the shop with a promise from the owner to move the rock and prepare a concrete base for it. He would drill holes into the stone and mount the plaque for free. She assured him that he would receive appropriate recognition at the event and in the publicity.

FORTY-ONE

The first Sunday in October opened the autumn color parade in the hills and valleys of the central Alleghenies. For Mary Martha Cosner, if she had to choose a favorite month, October definitely had an edge on all the others. She always was exhilirated by the sight of leaves dressed in yellow or red or brown falling to the forest landscape.

The big day at Cloy Clay's farm had arrived. So had Jae Weidimeyer-Rossi. She had flown in on Saturday. Also on Saturday Jae's mother had flown to Washington, stayed overnight and then early Sunday morning she set out in a chauffeured limousine on Route 50 West toward Leadmine.

Friday night Dr. Roberto and the entire crew had reopened the field house to spend a long weekend and to participate in Sunday's dedication.

Clara Bennett Baker and others of the Historical Society had planned the program for Sunday to a point then they turned the details over to C. Clement Crozier. For when it came to putting on an event such as crowning the county fair queen or steering a Chamber of Commerce awards banquet C. Clement was the only logical person anyone could think of as an emcee. C. Clement assured them that proper protocol would prevail and that every detail for a successful program would be guaranteed. Besides, he had a strong enough voice that if the P.A. system failed the hills would resound with his natural volume.

All day Saturday volunteers had set things straight at Cloy's. Sawhorses and tabletops borrowed from the Methodist church were set up to hold the food. Two hundred metal folding chairs were trucked from the high school to Cloy's yard.

The picnic was slated to begin at 1:00 p.m. to accommodate those who wished to attend church before traveling to Leadmine.

It was almost 11:00 a.m. when Mary Martha and Jae drove

to Cloy's, leaving the dinner packing to Alice, Rena and Rachel. Cloy met them at the gate looking and acting much as he had before his ordeal.

"My, oh, my, two lovely ladies comin' to see me," Cloy said, smiling broadly.

Jae ran to Cloy and wrapped him in a loving hug. "It's so very good to see you. My, but you have improved since I was here last," she said.

Cloy blushed at the affection Jae showed him and said, "A little sunshine and sassafras tea made a new man outa me."

Mary Martha smiled as she watched Cloy enjoying his celebrity status. "He is a cute old rascal," she thought.

In the house there was little to do but visit.

C. Clement, the master of ceremonies, drove in at straight up twelve noon dressed in an off-white suit, wide-striped tie and longsleeved white shirt with cuff links. He carried a manila folder of program notes.

When Mary Martha introduced Jae to C. Clement their lively conversation lasted until a steady stream of cars moved into Cloy's field.

Among the first to arrive was Clara Bennett Baker. Her husband lugged the sawed-off oak rostrum over to the speakers' table which was set in the shade of a huge white oak tree.

"What's the latest word on Congressman Workman? Is he coming?" C. Clement asked of Mrs. Baker.

"Oh, yes, yes, he called this morning assuring me that he would be here. He's speaking at Mt. Carmel Church and coming right on here," Mrs. Baker said enthusiastically.

"How about Senator Brewster? I know you said Senator Langhorn was in Nashville for a recording session but is Brewster still coming?" C. Clement said eagerly.

"Said he wouldn't miss it. I look for him any time."

"I guess we've got enough chairs here under the tree for all the special guests, don't we?" Crozier asked. "I counted all those on the list and it looks right to me."

Steadily the cars came and parked as if they were being directed into rows by parking attendants waving orange flags.

Mary Martha walked over to Mrs. Baker more to welcome her than to converse. However, she was curious about the VIP list. "Who all is coming? I mean what big wheels are going to be here?" she asked.

"You mean like Senator Brewster and Congressman Workman, they're coming and let's see, we've invited several others, of course, Mrs. Weidimeyer-Rossi and Dr. Roberto Santos and Cloy and you," Mrs. Baker said seriously.

"No, not me, for heaven's sake, I'm no celebrity. I'm Cloy's friend, that's all. Besides it's the leadmine that we're here for, not anything that I'm involved in," Mary Martha said, astounded at the thought.

"Oh, well, we'll see," Mrs. Baker said.

Mary Martha walked on back toward Cloy's porch thinking of the list of important persons when a thought came to her. She turned and hurried back to Mrs. Baker. "You didn't mention Colonel Apolla, you know, who led the search for Cloy. I'll bet no one thought to invite him."

"No, no one ever mentioned his name," Mrs. Baker admitted.

"Well, not that he had anything to do with the leadmine, but you know he did a great job up here and I just know he'd come and enjoy it. He never did get to meet Cloy, be good for him to see who they were hunting for," Mary Martha said, looking disappointed.

"That's too bad. Nobody mentioned him," Mrs. Baker said, anxious to clear this from her mind and get on with the other details needing her attention. She took a cursory look at the traffic and hurried toward the speakers' table to consult with C. Clement who was making notes with his huge silver pen.

"Clement, don't you think we ought to make an announcement that folks can bring their food on to the tables?" Clara asked.

"It is twenty till one, sure we can get that under way," C. Clement said stepping to the microphone and pushing the on switch. "Testing, testing," he tried in a normal voice. "Can you hear me out there?" he said searching for reactions. Instantly several in the crowd yelled and waved to C. Clement. He began, "Ladies and gentlemen, welcome to the home of Mr. Cloy Clay, our celebrity for the day. Now we want you all to feel right at home, so won't you bring your picnic baskets on here to the tables and spread your dinners. Then before we eat we'll have the invocation."

By now there was a mass of people gathered around and on Cloy's porch. Amos and Ralph and their wives were funnin' with Cloy. Amos had a guest with him whom he wanted Cloy to meet and Mary Martha beamed when she saw him. It was

Colonel Apolla in full dress uniform. Amos said he had called the colonel at his office in Charleston just as soon as the date was set.

Mary Martha made her way through the crowd to Amos and suggested that she would like to meet the colonel. That done she hurried and brought Jae to meet him, too. She was sure the Green Berets would be important to Jae's movie. Right away Jae saw the potential and she engaged the amiable military man in animated conversation.

Not one of the VIP guests came near the speakers' table before C. Clements digital wristwatch alarm sounded time for lunch. Taking pride in promptness he stepped to the microphone, looked out over the rows of tables spread with food and said, "Ladies and gentlemen, may I have your attention, please?"

A sudden hush enveloped the milling mass of people as the powerful voice was multiplied by the four-speaker amplifier. Feeling the great sense of satisfaction he always got when in command of a crowd, C. Clement said, "My dear friends, will you please now join me all heads bowed and all hearts in prayer." It became reverently quiet, except for the occasional cries of the infants in the crowd as they waited for the pronouncement of C. Clement's grace.

Following what seemed a minute the master of ceremonies began loudly and holy sounding, "Father God! We pray to thee on this bright October day giving thanks to thy Holy name. We beseech thee, oh, Holy One to fill each heart with thy loving kindness. Bless this grand occasion that what we might do here today will fill another page in the history of Tucker County. Oh, Father God, take each of us into thy care and protection. Feed our souls the bread of life that we may rejoice in the knowledge that you are ever with us.

"Now as we go forward in this program, inspire our speakers and divinely guide those who lead," C. Clement continued. By this time, many in the crowd had begun to fidget restlessly, thinking that the prayer would never end. It was hot standing in the sun. Many were concerned about the occasional fly that swooped down on the food and yellow jacket bees clustered about the pies and cakes. C. Clement's prayer was just too long for grace before the meal, they thought.

Finally he drew his invocation to a close with, 'Now unto him who is able to deliver us faultless before thy throne of

Grace we ask his continual blessings upon us and upon the food we are about to eat, we give thanks, Amen."

The picnic was true to the tradition of the area, plenty of food and delicious. Too many goodies in fact, for Senator Brewster and Congressman Workman to sample something from each spread, although they tried. And food was being urged upon the two popular politicians.

Mary Martha asked first, Jae, then Alice, if they had seen Dr. Roberto. Their answer was no. This bothered her enough to go into Cloy's house and call up to the field house. Sure enough they were there. Jorge answered.

"Jorge, this is Mary Martha Cosner. I was looking for you all here at the picnic?" she said.

"Maam, we have enjoyed so much our being back here that we are having our own lunch right now," Jorge told her.

"But you are coming, aren't you?" she pleaded. "Listen, we really want you here for the program. And listen, we have so much food. I know you would like my made-from-scratch mayonnaise chocolate fudge cake or my homemade egg custard pie."

"Mary, it does sound so very good, but please understand we are coming in time for the program. Maybe sometime we can share your good food too, okay?"

"Okay, the important thing is that you all are coming. See you in just a little while."

Mary Martha walked out of Cloy's living room onto the porch and spotted the large forest green limousine entering the lane. It proceeded on past the entrance to Cloy's field and moved slowly toward the house to where it stopped at the gate. It was a real puzzle for Mary Martha as to who it was until Jae pointed out that her mother had arrived. Sheena Weidimeyer had come even though she had some misgivings about what might crop up after so many years.

FORTY-TWO

The brown four-door Pinto with Maryland plates entered Cloy's lane moments after C. Clement called the crowd to attention and began his introductory oratory setting the stage for the momentous day. The woman driver proceeded toward Cloy's yard fence and parked beside the much larger Cadillac bearing District of Columbia license.

Mary Martha was so caught up among the hundreds of friendly people that she failed to see this car.

Jae was excitedly talking to the aging but vibrant Senator Brewster. Well, more appropriately, she was mostly listening but she was thrilled at the politician's knowledge of the history of the area. It seemed that he knew every book and author, and Jae loved it.

Right now her mother was seated on the porch in a lawn chair beside Cloy. Their conversation reminisced of better times, the heyday at Foredsa, the Weidimeyer estate just up the road.

The driver of the brown Pinto and her passenger, who was seated in the back seat, remained in the car. Even though they were parked beneath a huge sugar maple tree the aged heavyset woman had to fan her face with a Sunday school quarterly to dry the sweat. Beside her lay a collapsible aluminum walker.

"Now, ladies and gentlemen, it is my distinct pleasure to introduce the driving force behind this special history-making day, the president of the Tucker County Historical Society, Clara Bennett Baker," C. Clement bellowed into the microphone.

Mrs. Baker read her prepared statement in one minute or less. She stressed the significance of what they were doing in erecting a marker. She then thanked all those who helped her to this point.

The crowd fervently applauded Mrs. Baker. They recognized the valuable asset they had in this native who, after a career elsewhere, returned to revive and revere the colorful history of the Fairfax corner of the state.

C. Clement continued his scheduled program by introducing the only person in full dress military uniform. "Ladies and gentlemen, here is a man to whom we owe our unbridled gratitude. Please make welcome the honorable adjutant general of the great state of West Virginia. Col. H. M. Apolla." C. Clement led in the applause, lifting his arms dramatically upward and exposing the gold cuff links.

The colonel made a striking appearance in the brass, braids and stripes. His comments were brief. "Ladies and gentlemen, I sincerely appreciate being invited to this fine occasion. Would you please recognize my good friends, Amos Sell and Ralph Clay. We had several days together here when we searched these hills for one tough soldier, Mr. Cloy Clay. Cloy, we tried, believe me, we tried," the colonel joked. "But you must have had too good a hiding place," he laughed turning and looking directly at Cloy. "Well, we're just delighted, sir, that you were found and that you are here with us today. Oh, by the way, please don't tell anyone that I almost forgot, but the governor asked me to tell you that he had to be out of the state today and could not be here. He sends his regrets. Again I thank you for inviting me and I thank all the fine Tucker County people who helped us in our search here. Thanks."

Jae was convinced. Colonel Apolla and his Green Berets must be in her movie. "What a handsome man," she thought.

Back at the microphone C. Clement made a quick switch in the order of VIP introductions, feeling that it was appropriate following the colonel's talk. "Ladies and gentlemen, now let me introduce to you the real heroine of the Cloy Clay story. She's the one that found him, you know. Well, she's one fine lady who also went away to seek her fortune and has now returned to us. Security chief at Canaan Valley Resorts, Ms. Mary Martha Cosner."

Mary Martha knew she would not, nor did she want to, make a speech. But she did want to say something. "Thank you, Mr. Crozier. I feel so good about this day. I sure do hope everybody is having a good time. That fine food helped, don't you think?" she said feeling herself warming up to her brief comments. "Listen, what I want to say is this. I have three fine friends who were just as responsible for finding Mr. Clay as I was. Stand up girls, Alice, and Rachel and Rena. You know of course I'm glad we found him but what I am more proud of is that I have had a chance to get to know this fine man. He's a real old teddy-bear, that Cloy Clay is. I love him. I think he's just wonderful. Now about the leadmine. I am so delighted that Mrs. Baker and her Historical Society decided to place a marker here for the leadmine. Thank you very much for everything you all did for Mr. Cloy. Thank you."

When Mary Martha stepped away from the microphone Amos motioned for her to come over to where he was by the yard gate near the brown Pinto.

"Yes?" Mary Martha inquired.

"You know that your aunt Christilina is out here in the car?" Amos asked.

"My goodness no. Really?" Mary Martha gasped.

"Yeah, I tried to get her to come in but she said she could hear everything out here." Amos said.

"Well, I swear, I never thought she'd even want to come, it's so hot and all. She never gets out of that wheelchair anymore," Mary Martha reasoned. "Thanks, Amos, I'll go see about her."

At the car Mary Martha tried to be cheerful. She hugged and kissed her dear old aunt and encouraged her cousin, Ora, to come out of the car to the yard where the meeting was under way.

"Come on now, Aunt Chris, it's just too hot in the car and besides I'll take you over there to Cloy's porch where you'll be in the shade," Mary Martha said maternally.

The feeble woman insisted that she could use the walker but she proposed they get the fold-up wheelchair out from the trunk for her to sit in.

Mary Martha helped her aunt who today seemed more motivated and stronger than when she last saw her. In fact, she did not require any assistance to transfer from the walker to the wheelchair.

"Can I get you something to drink? How about some iced tea?" Mary Martha asked and hurried into the house to bring the cold drink.

C. Clement next introduced Cloy, pointing out that he really had become a legend in his time and that the dedication ceremony they were about to perform might not have happened, even in this century, had it not been for Cloy's misfortune. "Come on up here, Mr. Clay, and let everybody see our hero."

Cloy jumped up and walked briskly the ten steps to where C. Clement stood. But Cloy wasn't about to make a speech. C. Clement lifted the mike from the stand and began to question Cloy, eliciting one-word answers.

"Mr. Clay, did you think you were going to die in that cave?"

"Yes," Cloy answered.

"Was that the first time you ever went in the cave?"

"No."

"Do you expect to go back in the cave anymore?"

"Yes."

"Did you see where Indians might have got lead in that cave?"

"No."

Finally it seemed that C. Clement asked a question demanding more than a one-word answer.

"Cloy, how do you feel about this dedication?"

"Fine," Cloy said.

"But what do you think?" C. Clement impatiently asked.

"I think it's about time somebody did something like this. Everybody knows there had to be a leadmine up here somewhere."

"Thank you, Cloy, for allowing us to take over your place here today. Folks, let's give Cloy a great big hand for all he has done to inspire us. He's one fine gentleman that's for sure," C. Clement concluded.

Carefully the afternoon program production was building toward the climax, the unveiling of the distinctive bronze marker mounted upon the huge boulder. Right now it was hidden at the spot out near the road shrouded in a large piece of rich red satin cloth anchored to the ground to prevent viewing before the appropriated moment.

It was time to introduce the last VIP before the real dedication would begin. The emcee pushed her introduction with every bit of his professional prowess. "Ladies and gentlemen, now it is with the utmost pleasure that I bring you another one of our very own who also has made her mark in the world as a leader in the motion picture business. This great lady has built upon the great pioneering work of her grandfather, who at the turn of the century established the highly successful Weidimeyer Productions. Won't you please make welcome this distinguished lady, Jae Weidimeyer-Rossi."

The applause was loud and long. Jae urged them to stop so

she could get on with her brief comments. She recognized her mother, complimented Mary Martha, Amos and Ralph, Mrs. Baker and Cloy Clay, looking toward each as she did. Then she looked about, puzzled that she could not locate him. "Another fine person I wish to recognize for his tremendous assistance is Dr. Roberto Santos. Is he here?" she inquired.

Dr. Roberto stepped forward from the crowd standing behind the carefully arranged folding chairs.

"Here I am!" Dr. Roberto yelled.

"Oh, there he is. Yes, Dr. Roberto, won't you please come here? I want these good people to meet you."

The handsome scientist walked down the aisle through the mass of seated people. As he came forward Jae said, "Come on up here by me a moment. Folks, this man is a really fine scientist. He and a number of others have been occupying our old homeplace up the road which my granddaddy named Foredsa. Some of you will recall that. In fact some of you knew him. Dr. Roberto is a Brazilian who works in Washington but he has a fondness for this lovely area, possibly for the same reasons that my folks came here to build a home, a place where they could escape from Hollywood and New York. You know Dr. Roberto and his people helped to rescue Mr. Clay."

Dr. Roberto stood for a moment until Jae finished. She concluded by saying "Folks, I have become fascinated with the Cloy Clay story and right now we are working on plans to produce a motion picture built around him and the legendary leadmine. This special dedication of the leadmine is indeed a major step in giving our story a historical foundation. Now, please let me thank each of you for your cooperation and support as we proceed to make the movie. And if all goes well next autumn by this time we should be well on our way to completing the filming. I think it will be one fine movie, one you'll be proud of, too. Thank you very much for inviting me here and for all the kindness so many have shown me. Thank you."

When Jae finished she and Dr. Roberto stepped over to the porch where she introduced the Brazilian to Cloy and her mother.

FORTY-THREE

Mary Martha's aunt Christilina squirmed restlessly all during Jae's talk. The old lady glared back and forth between Jae and Cloy. Cloy and Jae's mother continued to sit just an arm's length apart on the porch.

Now that Christilina was there in her ailing condition, Mary Martha felt almost total responsibility for her welfare. She leaned forward from her seat in the VIP section so she could see Christilina and was astonished to see the glowering expression on her pale wrinkled face.

"Oh, my God, the poor old thing's gonna faint," Mary Martha thought. She started to go to her when suddenly Christilina began waving her arms and screaming. "Give me that speaker!" she cried to C. Clement, who had just stepped back to the microphone to launch the dedication ceremony which would be pronounced by the United States senator and congressman.

"Just one moment," C. Clement told the crowd.

Quickly Mary Martha ran over to try to calm the poor old lady, fearing that a heart attack or stroke might fell her sickly relative.

Rather than be calmed, however, the enraged Christilina yelled, "You leave me alone, you hear. Everybody's had their say, now it's my turn." Again she motioned to C. Clement, "Bring me that speaker thing. Bring it here," she demanded.

C. Clement hesitated. He looked for Mrs. Baker for advice on what to do. "Mrs. Baker, would you please come up here?"

The crowd was startled. They began to talk among themselves about the disturbance up there by the porch. Christilina was hidden from the view of those in the seats.

Mrs. Baker told C. Clement to hold up for a moment while she checked out the problem.

Mary Martha, more concerned than embarrassed by her aunt, tried in vain to soothe her.

Again Christilina screamed, "Leave me alone. I know what I'm doin' and I want to talk."

Jae could see what was happening but she too felt helpless. She knew that if Mary Martha couldn't handle the situation, no one could.

Cloy could see the whole episode. Although he was not sure why she was acting that way, he knew that Christilina had a temper. Always seemed to have a chip on her shoulder, he thought.

"Aunt Chris, please, you're gonna hurt yourself. Please, dear, calm down. You can tell me," Mary Martha pleaded, wiping the old lady's forehead with a handkerchief.

"You get outa my way. I'm gonna go up there and tell these people somethin'," Christilina yelled, tearing away from Mary Martha.

The distraught old soul surged up, grabbed her walker and charged toward C. Clement. "Here, give me that thing," she said, reaching up and seizing the microphone.

C. Clement, somewhat baffled, lifted the mike from its cradle and let Christilina hold it.

For a moment the incensed soul stood there, leaning on the walker and holding the microphone in her trembling right hand. Then she began in a calm voice. "I know all you people here think Cloy Clay is some kind of saint. Well, when that nice lady Jae told all those good things about Cloy I couldn't take it anymore. See, all my life I've kept my mouth shut. I've had to live a lie, as they say. Well, if I die today, and I think I just might die after this, I've gotta tell the truth."

Christilina continued, sounding rational and believable. "See, I knew about Cloy and my sister. Oh, yeah, Cloy always did love her. Fact is, he even fathered her child. That's right, Mary Martha was Cloy's baby. I know that."

The crowd was hushed. "My God, is she for real?" Jae said, moving over near her mother.

"Now listen to me," Christilina said. "That's not all I've got to tell. You know that pretty lady from Hollywood that was just up here. Well, Cloy Clay is her father, too. That's right, believe it or not, I know what I'm talkin' about. Cloy is her daddy all right because I am that girl's mother."

"Oh, my God, Mother, what is she saying?" Jae gasped.

"She's telling the truth, dear," Mrs. Weidimeyer said very slowly, appearing to be relieved that Jae now knew.

That was it. Christilina let the mike fall down across the walker. C. Clement grabbed it before it hit the ground.

Mary Martha rushed to assist the old lady as she collapsed backwards onto the grass. Colonel Apolla and Ralph and Amos carried Christilina into Cloy's living room to the couch.

In Cloy's kitchen Mary Martha grabbed the hand towel from the nail on the wall and tilted the water bucket over the sink to saturate it. She hurried back to the living room and tried to revive her aunt by wiping her face, then she applied a thick fold of the dripping towel to the back of the woman's neck.

Christilina did not stir.

"Check her pulse," C. Clement suggested.

Mary Martha pressed her fingers into the side of Christilina's flacid neck and searched for the heartbeat. Colonel Apolla pressed his fingers into the old lady's inner wrist, feeling for the regular surges of blood in the veins. He looked into Mary Martha's eyes as they both listened.

Urgently Mary Martha pushed forward and lay her head on Christilina's chest and listened. Moments later she said, "I can't hear a thing."

"Maam, there is no pulse in her wrist," Colonel Apolla said. "I think, maam, the excitement was too much for her."

Mary Martha rose, looked at the old lady a moment, and urged C. Clement to return to his duties with the ceremony to dedicate the plaque. "Colonel, you should return to the program. I'll handle this," she said.

"You are sure?" the colonel said.

"Yes, yes, I'm fine. You go ahead." Then she cleared the concerned and curious from the door and asked her cousin Ora to come in and close the door. "The poor old soul has passed away," Mary Martha said, drawing a deep breath.

Next Mary Martha called the hospital for Dr. Samuelson. He was there, the nurse said, but she would have to locate him.

The doctor suggested that he would send the ambulance and have the body brought to the hospital for examination as the county coroner.

"No big hurry, doctor. I don't want them rushing down here with the sirens wailing while this program is going on. Please tell them that, will you?" Mary Martha said before hanging up. "You stay here while I go see about Cloy and Jae," she told Ora.

On the porch she leaned over Cloy's chair and told him that Christilina was dead. She patted him on the shoulder and then noticed that Mrs. Weidimeyer and Jae were gone. "Where's Jae?" she asked Cloy. "Where'd she go? Did you see where she went?"

"Jae took off out through the gate there and her mother took after her. That's all I know," Cloy said, sounding distressed.

Mary Martha calmly stepped off the porch, walked by the several persons standing near the gate and moved quickly between the limousine and the Pinto. She spotted the limousine driver sitting on a log beneath the towering walnut tree down the bank toward the long bottom field. "Where'd they go?" she asked him.

"A woman went runnin' down the road there and Mrs. Weidimeyer was right behind her. Last I saw 'em, they went through the field down there," he pointed, scratching his head. "That Mrs. Weidimeyer shouldn't be runnin' like that at her age."

"I know, poor thing," Mary Martha agreed and hurried on, a bit wobbly in two-inch heels, belted sky blue cotton dress and seamless nylons. She ran down the rocky farm-wagon road past the sugaring shed and through the grove of towering sugar maple trees now at their peak of red and yellow leaf color. At the loose-boarded bridge across the twelve-foot slough, which bordered the twenty-acre long narrow meadow, Mary Martha stopped. For certain they would not have gone all the way to the far end which curved along the creek out of sight. Straight ahead she looked toward the Horseshoe Run just beyond the trees and barbed wire fence border of the far side of the field—the same field where Colonel Apolla's Green Berets camped during the five-day search for Cloy Clay. It was now more obvious why Dr. Roberto's party had not seen the lights of the Green Beret camp that Saturday night and become aware of the search when they had driven by on their way to the field house. No wonder they didn't know there was a search underway. The field was nestled in the valley hidden by hemlocks and hardwoods.

They must have gone across this narrow end of the field and into the woods by the creek, Mary Martha guessed. And she was right. As she approached she could hear them. Jae was crying. "Mother, how could you? You were cruel," she pleaded.

"For God's sake, mother. All these years. Me, a grown woman. Have to find out this way. My father not my real father. No, no, that's not enough. You my own mother. You're not even my real mother. Oh, God, I trusted you. You. Oh, how could you? A really awful thing," Jae trailed off, crying as the broken-hearted daughter of Sheena Weidimeyer.

"Please, baby, please don't be so hurt," Mrs. Weidimeyer pleaded breathlessly, following the long run trying to keep up with Jae. "Please, just listen to me."

"Mother!" Jae screamed and jumped up from the beach of creek rocks. She looked straight at Sheena Weidimeyer who sat on the bank, her legs resting in a patch of yellow blossomed touch-me-nots, common along the shaded banks of Horseshoe Run. "I am so ashamed. Really ashamed. I'm hurt and ashamed. Think of you of all people. You let me live a lie. A complete lie. A life of a lie."

Mary Martha sensed when it was time to step in. She hoped she wouldn't have to but now it looked like she was needed. She climbed through the chestnut pole bars serving as Cloy's gate to the creek. Quickly she spoke in an attempt to stop Jae's rage. "Jae, honey, listen to me. Listen." Mary Martha scaled down the short four-foot bank to where Jae stood and wrapped the distraught lady in her arms. "Please, my wonderful sister, let me help you. You are my baby sister, you know," Mary Martha teased, whispering into Jae's hair.

The sisters stood there for several minutes while Mary Martha comforted Jae. Jae's crying moderated to short jerks in her chest. Tears issued in a steady stream on to Mary Martha's shoulder, wetting her dress. Slowly Jae's anger subsided.

"Come on, let's go up here on the bank and sit down and think about this a little, okay?" They climbed up to where Mrs. Weidimeyer sat. Mary Martha eased down on the right of Jae's mother, motioning to Jae to sit on her own right.

This way she was between the mother and daughter, hoping it would be a better position from which to mediate the strained relationship. "Listen, you two, I just learned that you, Jae, honey, are my half sister. Not that that makes any difference about how I feel about you. For I have to tell you, honey, I already had begun to love you like a sister before I knew all this." Then Mary Martha turned to Jae's mother. "Mrs. Weidimeyer, I only met you today, so I haven't had any time to get to know you. But I feel I already know you and I have to say you must be a pretty special person."

"Oh, yeah, she's something special, the way she's treated me," Jae said, almost resuming her crying.

Mary Martha reached for Jae and placed her right arm around her shoulders and pulled her close. "What I was saying is that, as your mother, Mrs. Weidimeyer must have loved you just like she would have her very own, to have turned out someone special like you. Am I right, Mrs. Weidimeyer?"

"Believe me, I've never, ever once questioned did I love my daughter. She's always been the most precious thing in my life. And the reason we quit coming here, really, was to keep from ever hurting Jae. Since the day we brought Chris back here after the baby was born, I never came back. I just didn't want to stir up anything. We even gave up Foredsa for Jae. Don't you see," Mrs. Weidimeyer said, beginning to cry herself, "I didn't want to tempt that girl to want her baby back and I didn't want to lose my lovely daughter. All this time we sent Jae's mother a check. Every month even now I send her a check."

Mary Martha reached her left arm to Sheena Weidimeyer pulling the two, mother and daughter, tightly to her. Each lay their heads against their consoling friend. For a long quiet period of several minutes the two weeping women acceded to the compassion shown by Mary Martha.

Slowly they became aware of the peaceful quietness and the fragrance—pungent sycamore trees, the sparkling water of Horseshoe Run, the calendar picture landscape of rhododendron, hemlock, shaggy birches, the green moss-covered rocks bordering the creek which today was a perfect mirror and the soft melodic sounds of the birds, the insects and the serene water slipping past after escaping the miles of tunnels inside the legendary leadmine. They watched the foot-deep creek swirl around the smooth worn rocks protruding bare-backed and cleanly polished beneath the afternoon sun.

The solace of the setting, the friendship they felt and the kinship they shared set the stage for a future free of anxiety about the past.

FORTY-FOUR

A crown of thorns or a bouquet of roses, which was it, dumped upon this October's first Sunday at Cloy Clay's farm. Mary Martha's aunt Christilina dead, Jae a sister she didn't know she had, Cloy described as an adulterer in front of all his friends and few relatives. All this had to hit old Cloy hard as a thunderbolt since he was accustomed to thinking the seeds he had sown never germinated. Never in a million years did he expect Christilina to tell about those times up there in the vineyard.

Cloy's elder daughter knew what she had to do—get back to the house before the funeral home ambulance came to get the body. What about Cloy? Had it hit him yet? Was he embarrassed by it all? Or, was he bursting inside with fatherly pride?

"Come on, you two, let's go on back up there. The guys from the funeral home will be there and won't know what to do," Mary Martha said grabbing Jae and Sheena by the shoulders in a caring embrace.

"You mean?" Jae questioned, "really is she?"

"She did. Yes, the poor old soul died right there where she fell," Mary Martha stated. "You didn't know? Right, she is gone. Best thing, really."

An eternity of seconds ticked away. Nothing stopped except the talking. The water in the creek rippled below their feet, slithering downstream around the rocks, hurrying to plunge into the ribbon of rivers stretching to the harbor at New Orleans. The pungent fragrance of hemlocks and sycamores oozed off the valley floor like fog on an April morning. Upstream two bullfrogs burped out sounds that had it been springtime surely would be mating calls. Across the creek, some thirty yards, lifelong mates of mourning doves cooed their eerie lonely correspondence from the top branches of two huge shaggy water birch trees.

Jae heard none of it. Her eyes were fixed upon the silver

skeleton of a chestnut tree that died more than fifty years ago. She pulled free from Mary Martha's embrace. "I guess it's best," taking care to say what she really meant. "I'm sure it's best, has to be, to have only one mother."

Sheena sat up straight. "Please don't say that, dear. After all, she was your natural mother, you know."

"Oh, momma, I'm so confused, but you know what I mean. You're my mother, really, and I want it to go on that way."

"Of course, I'm delighted you feel as you do, for that's the way I want it, too, but I am responsible for this. I wouldn't want me or anything to stand in the way, ever again. I mean that," Sheena said leaning around Mary Martha to gain eye contact with Jae.

Jae had to go to her mother. She drew up onto her knees and walked that way, crushing weeds as she went, and fell upon Sheena's shoulders. "Momma, I love you so very much. Please forgive me for acting a fool. I'm sorry, momma, I'm sorry," she cried as a child begging forgiveness for spilling blueberry pie on the shag carpet.

"Come on, now, let's go. We have things to do," Mary Martha said, scrambling to her feet and reaching to assist Sheena up from the creek bank.

How the three nicely dressed women managed to run as they did, in high heels, among the rocks and weeds, under different circumstances, would have been cause for hilarious laughter. Now they walked back toward Cloy's yard, selectively stepping to miss the rocks, lady-like and more friendly than before. Mary Martha eagerly stepped out a dozen paces in the lead. At the limousine she waited for Jae and Sheena to climb the hill out of Cloy's bottom field.

Pickup trucks and cars moved slowly end to end, leaving the dedication. Small clusters of people talked among the chairs and out by the plaque. Mrs. Weidimeyer said she would wait in the limousine. Mary Martha and Jae pushed through the yard gate toward C. Clement and Mrs. Baker.

"Where'd he go?" Mary Martha asked. "Where'd Cloy go?"

They didn't know, hadn't noticed, they said.

"Don't leave, we'll be back in a minute," Mary Martha told them turning toward the porch.

Inside the house Mary Martha asked Ora, "Where's Cloy? He out in the kitchen?" she asked before looking.

"I don't know where he went. He came in here about an hour

ago and I heard him fussin' around out there in the kitchen then I heard the screen door slam when he went out back."

"Didn't say where he was goin'?" Mary Martha questioned.

"No. Never said a thing to me, he didn't, just seemed to be in a hurry," Ora said.

"What do you suppose? Maybe he's out back," Jae suggested.

Mary Martha bounced into the kitchen and out the back door. She called, "Cloy! Hey, Cloy! You out here?"

There wasn't any answer. Back inside she reported not finding him.

"Where's the dog?" Jae questioned. "Wonder if the dog's gone too?"

A quick look for Stripe found him missing.

"Jae, you sit down and wait here with Ora, fix you some iced tea or something. I'll go see Mrs. Baker," Mary Martha said, continuing to take charge. "Be back in a minute, then we'll think about what to do about Cloy."

The few steps from Cloy's porch to the speaker's rostrum fixed a thought in her mind and a smile on her face.

The ever-diligent Mary Martha discharged her obligation to thank the Historical Society for the honor they had brought to Cloy by erecting the marker on his place. Right now she was through with history, though, and wanted only to live in the present, not looking back. That looking back let a lot of the past catch up with you. It was reason, she believed, she had never been a collector of antiques. Too much of the past can drag you down, and like today, nearly trample you into the ground. No, the heck with the past, what does it get you but hell and heartache. Might have been better had she never known about Cloy and her mother or for that matter, Cloy and Christilina. What good is it knowing Jae is her sister, anyway. Her mind just wasn't on socializing with C. Clement and Mrs. Baker. Hope soon they'll get going.

"Oh, my dear, I know you have so much to think about right now, but you must join us at our next meeting of the Society," Clara Bennett Baker urged upon Mary Martha, eagerly waiting for her response.

Here we go, a continual diet of history. Yet, Mary Martha was a polite person, never wanting to offend, always aware that some folks dearly love sauerkraut while others can't stand the smell of it. She could smell sauerkraut cooking with the

Historical Society and she hated that odor lingering through the house and tainting her best clothes in the wardrobe. "Mrs. Baker, let me think about that. I appreciate your invitation, I really do, but I need a little time to catch my breath," she said and turned to leave, again thanking the two before going back inside.

The black funeral home panel truck came. The two young men loaded the body and moved on, informed by Mary Martha that she would come along later in the evening to make the arrangements.

Ora agreed that she would notify the few known relatives, so Mary Martha should call her as soon as the visiting hours and funeral time were set. She departed for home, across the mountain at Cumberland, Maryland.

Sheena listened to what they were saying, thought for a moment, then advised that she would forego the invitation to stay at Mary Martha's until the funeral. "No, now listen to me, I think it best I go. Jae, dear, you and Mary Martha are the important ones to be there," Sheena told them from the back seat of the big car. "You two need to spend some time together without me. Oh, how's Cloy?"

"He's gone, momma. We don't know where he is," Jae said, emphasizing the mystery of her father's exit while so many of his friends were present.

"Well, I don't think we'll have to call on Colonel Apolla and his Green Berets to hunt for him this time." Mary Martha smiled and reached to unlatch the limousine door. The hour down by Horseshoe Run gave her an appreciation of the woman and her love for Jae. "Mrs. Weidimeyer, you know you're welcome to come on to my house and make yourself at home. We'd love to have you, but you're right, Jae and I will be fine if you feel it best you go."

"I think it best I go."

"Whatever you say," Mary Martha said agreeably.

"But listen, you have to promise me, though, that you will come to see me, you and Jae. I must insist on that," Sheena said, smiling for the first time in the past hour.

Jae and Mary Martha entered the limousine to sit, one on each side of Sheena. In turn they hugged the older woman and promised to come to Connecticut at Thanksgiving. The driver sat in his seat ready to roll.

The sisters watched the limousine enter the county road

then they huddled to talk about Cloy. Mary Martha was convinced that he was affected far more than he showed when she left him sitting on the porch. "Look, sis, let's go down to my house and check in with Rena, Rachel and Alice and get on a change of clothes before we undertake that hike."

Quickly they closed up Cloy's house and drove out the lane, meeting Amos. Said he was going over to visit a while with Cloy now that the crowd was nearly gone. He, too, was a bit amused when they told him that Cloy had run off. He said Ralph had gone, was having company and needed to get home. "I'm glad the colonel got away not knowing about it. He'd want to get up a search party," Amos said laughing. "No, this time he shouldn't be too hard to find."

Just in case Cloy was in the cave again Mary Martha took along flashlights. If it weren't for the need to console the old fellow, their motivation to make the rock-rattling trip up Thunderstruck would have been weak as a third cup of tea from a single tea bag. Then, too, Cloy just may not be able to make the climb up the Run like he did before his tragic fall.

There was ample time to think and talk as they walked, took long rests, then walked on up Thunderstruck Run toward Cloy's cave. Or was it Dr. Roberto's cave?

Before they reached the side creek, up which they'd go a hundred yards to the cave, Jae thought of one conversation she'd had with Dr. Roberto and Jorge and the others at the field house. "You know, I like to think of the cave as neither Cloy's nor Dr. Roberto's. Jorge used a Brazilian word to describe the people in the Leadmine valley. He called them capabaxias, said that meant the natives of the area. I believe it would be more appropriate to call it capabaxia's leadmine. That way it could even be yours, too."

"Why not, sounds good to me," Mary Martha agreed. "Yeah, how do you say that?"

"Cap-a-shee-a," Jae spelled phonetically.

"Cap-a-shee-a, cap-a-shee-a," Mary Martha repeated. "That's pretty. Cap-a-shee-a."

They were right, just as Mary Martha had predicted. The hidden woven wire gate Dr. Roberto and Carlos had put in the mouth of the cave lay down by the creek. Inside they found Cloy sitting on the floor propped against a calcite stump. Stripe lay between Cloy's outstretched legs.

"Cloy, do you mind? May we join you?" Mary Martha asked as they approached.

Cloy did not answer, just stared straight ahead at the light shining on the high waterfalls. Mary Martha moved up behind her father, eased down on her knees and put a hand on his shoulder. "We care about you, you know," she said softly into his right ear.

Jae moved in close beside him placing a hand on his left shoulder. "We came for you, sir. We came because we love you," she said bending down and kissing Cloy on the left cheek.

Cloy's arm fell, dropping the light beam onto the lake, his hand resting on Stripe's head. Mary Martha reached down, picked up the light and switched it off. Instantly total darkness filled the great cathedral within the cavern. It was eerie to have only the rushing water sounds and the occasional gusts of misty wet wind hit their faces. Even though their eyes remained wide open there were round colored dots dancing in their heads, all the colors of the rainbow.

"How about those colorful dots in your eyes, you see them?" Jae asked.

"You, too, I thought maybe it was only me," Mary Martha said marveling at how pretty they were and how long they lasted.

Presently they settled down beside Cloy, sitting on the gritty floor. Long minutes passed, one on top of the other, until three were gone and the seconds ticked into a fourth.

What if we stayed here forever, just the three of us, Mary Martha thought. What a crazy thing to even consider, for heaven's sake. The durned darkness does strange things to you.

The two nice friendly women, his two pretty daughters, cuddled up to Cloy. Their caring closeness melted the old man's thin shell and produced a flood of tears that streamed down along the age lines of his troubled face and dripped off each side of his quivering chin. Surely they would have abandoned him. Yes, he had learned, only today, that the two lovely women beside him were his daughters. He knew there was a chance that they could be but not once in all these years had he thought of the possibility. God knows he never felt like a criminal-type father who abandoned his children. He never knew he had any. Now this, it was more than he could stand, their kindness to him after the embarrassment inflicted by that Christilina. Truth is, he wouldn't have given that girl a second look, never liked her, the smart ass she was. Yet, she kept throwing herself at him up there at the Weidimeyers, came on to him the first time when he was working in the grapes in the field beyond the house next to the woods.

She would climb up the ladder over him so he could see everything she had. When she came down she would act mighty friendly, keep picking at him until they were at it right there in the grass. Oh, she must have come back out there a half-dozen times while he was picking grapes. One time a yellow jacket stung her on the hip as they were right in the middle of the act, didn't know what made her holler so till they finished and she showed him the puffy welt. But he could never like her, nothing like he did her sister, Mary Martha's mother, now she was a lady. Marry Christilina, or even her sister, if she had been free to marry, never entered his mind. Betty was his love, and he still talked to her, about as often as he talked to Stripe. Her love and his love made a match to last.

Cloy stirred, moved Stripe's head, bent forward onto his knees and boosted himself up. "Come on, daughters, let's go home."